Shattered Innocence 2 *Edition 2020*

Dedication

This work is dedicated to all those who supported and encouraged me to continue writing when I thought that this field might no longer be an option for me.

Also by Author Denise Coleman

Drama with a Capital D

The Shattered Innocence Trilogy

This is a work of fiction. It is not intended to depict, portray or represent any particular persons. All of the characters, incidents and dialogue are the products of the author's imagination. Any resemblance to actual events or persons living or dead is purely coincidental .

CHAPTER 1

"Teek and Angel, it's time for you two to come inside." Leigh said to her daughters.

"Awe mom." The twins spoke in unison, as they usually did.

"Awe nothing. Tomorrow's the first day of school and you two need to get your things ready" she stated.

"Aunt Leigh, can't they stay out for just a few more minutes, I haven't finished telling them about everything they need to know about being freshmen" Troi said.

"Girl, I don't care about that. They'll learn what they need to learn when they get there. It's getting late and as a matter of fact, you and Keisha need to get your asses around that corner. Both your moms just called looking for you. Now get over here and give me my hugs so you two can get your behinds home." Leigh said with a smile as her nieces stood to leave.

"Alright Auntie, we're going" Keisha said. The twins exchanged "good night and see you tomorrow" with their cousins as they headed into the house. Leigh stood on the stoop watching until Keisha and Troi turned the corner. She smiled again as she thought about who her children, nieces and nephews could all become. Doctors, Lawyers, Indian Chiefs…the sky's the limit.

Leigh and her siblings, of which, there were many, ten in all, had been raised with a tremendous amount of love and support from their parents and they all raised their own children with just as much of the same.

When Leigh entered the house, her husband Gary asked, "What are you grinning so hard about?"

"I just can't help it." Leigh responded as she sat down next to Gary. "I'm so proud of all of the children in this family. How did we get so blessed?" She questioned. "Think about it. We've managed to raise four really good kids and my brothers and sisters have as well. They're well behaved, smart young people who have such bright futures ahead of them."

"Leigh honey, you're gushing again."

"I know, right? Leigh said with a big smile on her face. "But, seriously Gary, our first-born babies are starting high school in the morning and from there, they'll go on to college! I'm excited babe. I can't wait to see who they'll become."

"That's just the schoolteacher in you talking" Gary laughed. "I've never heard either of those girls talk about going to college" he said.

"That's because you don't ask them about things like that. You spend most of your time with them trying to scare them away from boys" Leigh laughed.

"This is true…Just the thought of some tack head little boy trying to mess with one of my girls, pisses me off." Gary placed his girls on pedestals from which he felt they'd never fall.

"Well, since we're on the subject of our girls and those tack head boys as you call them, there's something that's been bothering me a little" Leigh said. Gary became serious as he noted the expression on his wife's face. "What is it" he asked.

"Well, to tell the truth, I'm not completely sure but, I think that Teek has no interest in boys." Leigh said with a bit of hesitancy.

"Well, they just turned fourteen and there's no need for either of them to rush into all of that nonsense." At Gary's comments Leigh became slightly frustrated that he wasn't grasping what she was trying to say. Leigh took Gary's hands in hers and said, "No, that's not what I'm trying to say. I think Teek may not be interested in boys at all, she stressed. Leigh squeezed Gary's hands a little tighter, not really sure at all of why she was having these thoughts about her daughter but, Leigh saw things in Teek that weren't usual for girls her age.

"I can't really explain it but there's something very different in the way that Teek reacts to boys as compared to the other girls. You know how much these girls sit around talking about the boys they like. Well, Teek, who always has something to say about everything, gets very quiet when that subject comes up, and she's never mentioned a boy she likes…*ever*."

"Maybe she's just shy about that stuff Leigh" Gary exerted. Leigh knew better. Teek wasn't shy in the least. There was definitely something going on in her daughter.

"I think it's more than that honey" Leigh said.

"Whatever it is, I wish you would just say it because I'm not following."

Whether or not her suspicions about her daughter were true or not, Gary was not prepared to deal with any of it. How could she tell her husband, who saw nothing wrong in either of his twins, what she suspected? Gary may have seen it as shy, but Leigh's take on it was that her precious daughter hid her true thoughts and desires very well.

For more than a year, Leigh had noticed the changes in Teek's demeanor. Her walk became a little more seductive, as did the look in her eyes. The sway of her hips… the bright glint in her eyes that appeared to put the world on notice. There was always something playing in Teek's mind just beyond the surface, and as far as Leigh was concerned, it wasn't good. The problem was that Teek's change in demeanor and behavior only surfaced when she thought no one was around to notice. Her mother noticed.

Leigh's only desire for her children was for the four of them to be happy. Some intuition told her that Teek would be the one to go down the most difficult road before she got to happy.

"OK honey" she said. Maybe you're right. I could be looking at this all wrong. Let's just forget about it. I really should go check on the little ones anyway. *Je'Teime*." Leigh said as she kissed Gary on the cheek.

"I love you too." Gary responded, and she left him sitting with his thoughts and went up to check on their two younger children, Kya and Quentin.

Denise Coleman

CHAPTER 2

Bright and early, Teek woke up full of excitement about her first day of high school. She was up and dancing around the bedroom like she was at a party. Angel on the other hand was not feeling it at all.

"Teek, for real, would you please turn that damn radio down? It's too early in the morning for that shit" Angel said.

"Are you kidding? This is my jam! Anyway, you need to get up before mommy comes in here. You know how she is about school" Teek laughed.

"Yeah, yeah, I know, it's the biggest deal in the world to her." Angel laughed as well. "You know mommy don't care nothing about blasting the music, but she'll have a fit if we sleep one minute past that darn alarm clock" Angel continued laughing.

"Yup." Teek agreed

Angel got up and headed to the bathroom as Teek continued to dance around their bedroom.

Destiny and Teek Kyle, AKA Angel and Tiki respectively, were identical, mirror image twins. While Teek had a small mole on her right cheek, Angel had one on her left. Angel was right-handed but, Teek used her left. Their tiny pear-shaped birthmarks were also located on opposite feet. When standing face to face they were mirror image reflections of one another.

The twins were considered beautiful by all standards of American culture. They had both grown an inch over the summer, catching up with their cousins and, at fourteen years old, they each stood at five feet, eight inches tall. The two had big, bright hazel-colored eyes that seemed to sparkle continuously. Their café au lait colored skin tone coupled with the often called "good hair" that flowed to the middle of their backs (compliments of their French great grandfather) made them the desire of teen boys and the envy of teen girls. However, the twins as well as all of the other kids in the huge Marchon clan seemed to be oblivious to their outward beauty.

Their mother Leigh came from a large family of six girls and four boys. Her grandfather, the Frenchman, married a beautiful Creole woman from New Orleans. The two made a striking couple who's "good looks" genes were passed down to future generations.

Nevertheless, Leigh and her siblings would not allow their children to focus on their looks in any way that would instill vanity or conceit. In fact, the children were never allowed to participate in any activities which focused on beauty. Pageants and fashion shows and such were an automatic, no. The Marchons, the grandparent's sir name, believed in developing their children's intellect, compassion for others and appreciation for the arts, music in particular.

There were always some lessons the children were going to. The twins played several instruments as did most of their cousins. At any given time of day, music would fill the homes of Leigh and her brothers and sisters. They all loved to party and, the majority of the kids inherited that same passion for music, singing and dancing.

Although Angel and Teek were hard to tell apart, the two possessed very different personalities. Teek was ten minutes older and much more outgoing, or at least louder. She was always willing to dive into new things headfirst. Angel tended to be more cautious and thoughtful about the moves she made. Although she was the younger of the two, Angel was the nurturing, more protective twin. Always looking out for, and taking care of her brother, sisters and cousins.

The adults in the family who loved to party would throw all of the kids into one house together whenever they had plans to go out. Therefore, the older cousins were always responsible for the younger ones. None of them seemed to mind however, because they were taught very well and loved one another deeply.

CHAPTER 3

By the time Angel returned from the bathroom, Teek had finished dancing and was finished dressing.

"Come on Angel, you really need to get moving" Teek said.

"Oh please. We have time, so stop rushing me." Angel responded as she began getting dressed.

Teek being so caught up in the excitement of her first day of high school, failed to notice Angel's less than enthusiastic approach to that particular milestone in their young lives.

"Tiki, let me ask you something" Angel said.

"Sure, what is it?"

"Aren't you even a little nervous about going to high school" Angel questioned.

"No why, are you?"

"Yes I am." Angel said as she bent down to tie her laces.

"Ok but, why? I think you should be happy. Twin, it's like this is getting us one step closer to being grown and gone."

Angel rolled her eyes and said, "Is that all you care about? Getting out of the house?"

Teek finished brushing her hair and sat down next to her sister.

"Look Angel, it seems like all we do is what mommy and daddy want us to do. Not to mention all of the aunties and uncles. Don't get me wrong... I love being in this family and I know how much love and support we get from all sides, but sometimes I get tired of living *their* dreams. Don't you?"

Angel looked at her twin with a curious expression before she spoke. "What do you mean, living *their* dreams?"

"I'm talking about this music stuff. OK, we're very good singers and dancers, but it's not my dream to have a career in the music business. That's what *they* want for us. Is it your dream?" Teek questioned.

"No Tiki but, it makes them happy to see us performing in talent shows and stuff."

Teek sucked her teeth. That may be true, but what about what we want?"

"I don't know Tiki." Angel sighed heavily. "I'm not thinking too much about the future right now. I'm more worried about what we'll have to deal with at this new school."

Teek got up to gather her backpack then turned back to her sister and asked, "What's the matter with you Angel? It's just school, what's there to be worried about?"

"I'm not sure Tiki, something just doesn't feel right."

It was now Teek's turn to give her sister a curious glance. Angel continued speaking. "I'm supposed to be excited about all of the new things we'll get to do like, pep rallies, football games and dances, but I'm not. I just get the feeling that high school is not going to be as great as we want it to be." Angel's nerves tingled and pulsated with every breath she took in anticipation of the changes she could feel barreling in their direction.

Teek didn't know how to respond to Angel's comments, but what she did know was that Angel's feelings about certain situations were usually dead on.

Teek grabbed Angel's hands and pulled her to her feet. "Alright Angel, I'm going to be *you* for a minute."

"What?" Angel asked with a chuckle.

"Yes, I'm going to be you…the supportive, encouraging twin. Now don't you worry about a thing. You'll have me, Keisha and Troi with you every step of way. You'll never be alone in this and we'll make sure that school is the best thing ever! OK?"

Angel laughed full out at Teek's imitation of her motherly ways.

"You're right, I do sound like that. Damn, just like the parents do."

"Yup, you're an old lady at fourteen" Teek laughed.

Angel plucked Teek in the forehead and said, "Oh yeah? Would an old lady fuck you up Teek?"

"Oooh, I'm telling, you in her cursing!" Teek yelled as Angel grabbed her backpack and ran out of their bedroom.

Angel, Teek, Keisha and Troi stood in front of what would be their Senior High School surrounded by hundreds of new and returning students.

"Damn, how many kids go here?" Teek asked in awe, to no one in particular. Nevertheless, Troi responded. "A couple thousand I guess."

"Yeah well, it's going to take forever just to get through the front doors." Keisha said to her cousins. Only Angel remained silent as the girls began chatting incessantly about anything.

Although Angel had never been afraid of anything, her sense of foreboding about what lie ahead had not lessened in the least. The girls stood for another thirty minutes before they were let into the auditorium.

After freshman orientation, during which time, class schedules, school rules and home-room assignments were given out, Teek, Keisha and Angel found themselves in the same homeroom. As it turned out, their home-room teacher was one of only two who taught advanced English, which each of the girls qualified for. The knowledge that Angel would have her family with her for part of the day helped to ease her mind a little, but not for long.

Just before orientation, Troi agreed to meet her cousins in the cafeteria so she could give them the scoop on some of their teachers. The moment fourth period English ended, Angel, Teek and Keisha made a bee line for the cafeteria, relieved that they were due for a break from classes.

Troi was already seated at a table when her cousins arrived. She waved them over as soon as she spotted them. As was the norm in their family, Troi greeted each of them with a hug and a kiss on the cheek.

They were fortunate enough to come from a very loving family which exhibited affection openly. None of the cousins noticed the strange looks they were getting from the four girls sitting at the next table.

"So how was your first morning" Troi asked. "What teachers do y'all have?"
Teek and Keisha started talking at once. Angel, however, took note of the girls from the next table, openly staring at them.

"I know we're in high school now but damn, our English teacher gave us homework already. It's the first damn day" Teek said. Troi laughed as she asked, "Who do you have?"

"Ms. Little, she's our home-room teacher too" Teek responded.

"Ours, who" Troi asked.

"All three of us."

"Get out of here! How did that shit happen?"

"Beats me but, it's OK with us." Keisha chimed in.

"Y'all are so lucky. I wish I had some of my female family here with me last year. Anyway, I had Ms. Little last year and she ain't no joke. Damn, that's advanced English and she will work you." Troi told her cousins.

"I don't care nothing about that" Keisha said. "I just want to know when basketball tryouts start." While dribbling an invisible basketball

"Dag Keisha, football season ain't even started yet and you already worrying about that stupid basketball" Teek teased.

"Shut up Teek, you know that's my game and I have definite plans for a future in the WNBA." Keisha said passionately. Basketball was her life and she couldn't wait to play on the high school level.

While the cousins were going back and forth, none of them paid attention to the fact that Angel was not participating in their discussions. She was focused on the girls who seemed to be overly curious about the four of them. They were talking and giggling while watching the cousins. Angel could tell by their demeanor that they were talking shit or making fun of them.

Teek brought her twin's focus back to their table. "Angel, we're about to get in line, are you eating or what" she asked.

"Uh, yeah I am" Angel answered.

"Well then, let's go" Troi said.

The girls got up to go get in the lunch line, but they had to walk past the table of the starrers and as soon as they got close enough, one of the girls stuck her foot out and tripped Teek. She stumbled into the back of Keisha who was just ahead of her, as the table of troublemakers burst out laughing.

"Yo bitch!" Teek said, "I don't know what your problem is but I am not the one to fuck with." Jackie, the ringleader jumped up in Teek's face, ready to do battle. The other three immediately pulled Teek away from the confrontation.

"Come on Tiki, let's just go get our lunch" Troi said.

"What? Are you serious? I'm supposed to just walk away like it's nothing?"

"Hell yeah. It's the first day of school and we don't need to be getting into it with those girls. They're trouble in a big way" Troi cautioned. Although she wasn't the least bit afraid of any of the girls, she knew that it was best to keep her cousins away from the bullshit.

"So the fuck what? I'm not here to be taking shit off of anybody" Teek yelled.

Angel spoke up, understanding her sister's outrage.

"Teek, Troi's right. It's the first day and fighting isn't the way to get started. Besides, Mommy would have a fit if she found out. You know how our parents feel about us getting into trouble at school." Teek looked into her twin's eyes and understood Angel's strong need to let this incident slide. As identical twins, Teek and

Angel read one another pretty well and rarely would either do anything to upset the other.

"Alright y'all, I'll let it go this time, but believe me when I say, I'm not going to be dealing with a bunch of shit with these silly ass girls." Teek said emphatically. She was the least patient of the four and couldn't deal with silly bitches on any level.

The cousins had a few minor incidents in Junior High with girls who thought that because of the way they looked, they would be punks. Not so. Regardless of their looks, the cousins were raised in the hood. It quickly got around that they would not be taking any shit off of anyone. But they were never really able to make friends no matter how hard they tried. The cousins found out the hard way that people would judge them before they got to know them and that friendships were not something that they would soon experience. This only served to make them closer to one another.

Wanting to avoid any more drama, Troi suggested the cousins have their meals outside in the courtyard. Fortunately, the troublemakers didn't follow. As soon as the girls were seated, Keisha asked, "Troi, who are those ridiculous girls anyway?"
Troi took a bite out of her sandwich before she answered. She considered how much she should reveal about her history with Jackie, the leader of the other four girls.

As close as she was to her cousins, there were things about herself and her life that Troi played close to her vest.

"That was Jackie Mason and her friends. They spend most of their time harassing people and starting shit. Those girls spent most of freshman year fighting. They fucked with one girl so bad that, she had to transfer to another school."

"You're kidding right" Teek asked.

"I wish I was. Those fools don't know how to act and I hate to say it, but it looks like we might be their new target." Troi chose not to further explain that she might be the reason for it.

"But why" Angel implored. We don't even know those girls. What could they have against us already?"

"It doesn't have to make sense Angel. They are who they are and they're going to do whatever they want." Troi told her cousin.

"All I know is, if they keep it up, they will be sorry." Keisha chimed in.

"Look, the bottom line is, we'll deal with whatever we have to, however we have to. As much as I can't stand the thought of having to go through a bunch of nonsense, it's going to be whatever it's going to be. We just can't tell any of our parents about it" Angel said. She may not have liked the drama but, she damn sure wasn't going to take it.

"She's right. If they find out we're having any kind of trouble at all, they'll be running up here and showing out every five damn minutes" Keisha said.

"True that. I can just hear mommy now, "Who's fucking with my babies" Teek laughed.

"Ok? Teek's right. The last thing we need is our moms up here embarrassing us. Besides, this was nothing. Maybe we'll be lucky enough not to have to even deal with anything else from Jackie and them" Troi added, but she knew better.

Although Angel wanted to believe that Troi was correct, her intuition told her that they hadn't heard the last from Jackie and her friends.

Denise Coleman

CHAPTER 4

The first half of the school year went by pretty quickly for the girls. Keisha spent every waking moment preparing herself for basketball tryouts. She ate, slept and breathed basketball. Without it she didn't exist. Without being a basketball player, there was not one other thing she knew about her own self to be true.

Troi spent her time doing cheerleading activities and trying to convince Angel, who focused on her studies, to join. Eventually Angel gave in and tried out for the squad. Teek on the other hand, didn't seem to be interested in anything at all, in or outside of school. She just went through the motions, trying to rush the time.

Jackie and her cohorts seemed to pull back after that first incident. They reduced their drama to minor bumping in the halls, name calling and eye rolling whenever they ran into one or more of the cousins.

This all changed during home coming week however. Although the girls weren't allowed to run for home coming queen or her court, they were allowed to take part in the talent show.

The aunties had the girls rehearsing for weeks for the show. That was their thing! As their Aunt Hillie would say, *"These girls can blow!"* As much as the girls didn't like working as hard as their mothers made them, they did enjoy performing, and they each knew how happy it made their parents to see them shine.

The night of the talent show, the school's auditorium was packed. The girls had to sit through an hour of other kids singing, dancing, reciting poetry and playing violins and such, before it would be their turn.

They used their grand parents' sir name – Marchon- as their stage name. When announced, they stepped out onto the stage ready to tear the house down. The girls looked like seasoned professionals. Their Aunt Hillie had designed their dresses; Two gold and two silver sequined halters which stopped at mid-thigh.

The dresses were paired with matching stilettos, and they wore their hair flowing straight down their backs. The look was completed with faux diamond jewelry and their makeup, while subtle, enhanced the cousin's young beauty.

The DJ cued the music and when the first cords of Teena Marie's Square Biz filled the auditorium, the cousins broke out singing and dancing like stars. Angel sang the lead and together with her family, they sang the hell out of that song. By the time they'd gotten to the rap portion of the song, the crowd was going wild. When they were done, the audience erupted in thunderous applause. Hands down, the girls were the best in the bunch. They received the only standing ovation of the evening.

While the cousins were winning over the crowd, Jackie and her cronies were sitting in the front row, shooting daggers with their eyes. The girls had no idea that the next few months would completely change the course of their futures.

On the very first day back from Christmas vacation, the drama began. Teek had left right after school ended but, Keisha stayed for basketball practice and Troi and Angel stayed for cheer-leading practice.

The cheer leaders held their practices in the smaller, second gym. The squad had just finished stretching when Jackie and her girls came strutting in. Although practices were closed, the captain of the squad was so afraid of Jackie, she didn't have the guts to ask them to leave. Knowing that no one else would stand up to them, the girls went and sat down on the bleachers.

After stretching, the girls had to move on to tumbling. Angel was the second in line to do her tumbling pass, and as soon as she had completed her round off, back handspring, Jackie yelled out, "Ill, I smell fish!" Her girls fell out laughing.
Angel looked at them, then at Troi. Before she could say or do anything, Troi was at her side. "Don't even pay

them any mind. They're just a bunch of miserable bitches who ain't got nothing better to do."

"Maybe not but, I don't understand why they have to start stuff with me" Angel said.

"Don't worry about it. Let's just get back to practice." Troi said as she put her arm around Angel's shoulders and guided her back to the group.
Angel was usually the one who mothered the others when things bothered them, but she needed Troi's support in that moment, because Angel couldn't stand being picked on or bullied. She knew she had a temper and being pissed off was not a feeling she wanted to deal with too often. Angel preferred peace in her young life.

Coming from such a large family and living with the different levels of drama that comes from constantly being around so many people, she couldn't stand to have to go through any outside drama on top of all that.

Jackie and her girls quickly realized that Angel and Troi were not going to feed into their bullshit, so they decided to leave it alone, for the time being. The next day however, the bullshit reached a whole new level.

Just after third period, Teek was headed to her locker when Jackie and her sidekick Nina walked up behind her. "Hey bitch, you better watch your back" Jackie said. Teek barely turned around, knowing full well who was talking shit.

"All I'm going to say is, you better back the fuck up before I show you some shit" Teek responded.

"Ain't nobody scared of you or your cousins' stuck-up asses" Nina added. Teek slammed her locker door and turned around. "Stuck up? Are you for real with that dumb shit?"

"Yeah bitch. You and your cousins walk around here with your snooty ass heads in the air like y'all own this school" Nina said.
Teek was shocked by Nina's statement to the point where she couldn't even respond. Never in their lives had Teek or any of her family thought or acted as if they

were better than anyone else. Such an attitude would never occur to any of them. Teek just rolled her eyes and walked away. All the while, Jackie and Nina were yelling behind her, calling her all kinds of bitches and whores. Teek heard every insult and although she was pissed off, she knew it would not be wise to get into a fight at school, especially while she was by herself.

Teek was relieved to reach her English class because she knew Angel and Keisha would be there. She was still dumbfounded by that "Stuck up" comment. She spotted Angel the moment she stepped into the room and made a mad dash to the seat next to her. Angel immediately noticed her sister's agitation. "What's wrong Tiki?"

"That bitch Jackie and one of her bitch friends started some shit with me when I was at my locker."

"What did they do?"

"They called us all stuck up and snooty. Can you believe that?"

"What? Stuck up, are you for real?" Angel asked, just as shocked by that characterization of her family.

"Yeah, they called me a bunch of other names as I was walking away from them but, I didn't pay that any mind. I was too busy trying to keep from kicking somebody's ass."

"I know how you feel but, whatever you do, don't do it in the building. If we get into trouble, we'll never here the end of it" Angel expressed.

"I know, I know. Mommy will have a cow if we're not being ladies at all times" Teek said. Angel laughed and said, "Mommy would drop dead if she heard how dirty your mouth is."

"I don't know why, since I learned to curse listening to her and her sisters." Teek said, laughing and feeling a little better since her confrontation.

Keisha walked in just as the late bell was ringing. She found a seat next to Teek and asked,

"What's up with you and Jackie? Some guy said she punked you in the hall."

"What? Ain't nobody punk me. I just didn't want to get into it in school."

"Well, I hate to tell you this but, we may not be able to avoid getting into it in school. After that dumb stuff they said to Angel and whatever happened with you, it looks like they won't be letting up and something's going to happen" Keisha said.

"That's what I'm afraid of. Even though it hasn't been a big deal, I get the feeling that Jackie and them are about to go overboard" Teek said.
Keisha nodded in agreement with her cousin, knowing that she was probably right in her assessment of the situation. Angel listened to their exchange knowing full well that it was about to be on.

The cousins may have wanted to stay away from trouble but, there was not one in the bunch who wouldn't protect themselves in any way they needed to. Unfortunately, they didn't have to wait long to see what Jackie would do next.

During the lunch break, Jackie, Nina and the rest of their little terror squad started immediately. As soon as they walked in and saw the cousins sitting at a table, they approached them. This time their target was Keisha. Jackie spoke first, of course.

"What's up Keisha Dyke? Yeah, that's your new last name, Dyke. Hey Terri, I heard that only lesbian, dyke girls play basketball." Jackie and her girls laughed like that was the funniest thing ever said. Keisha and the cousins however, jumped up from the table ready to do battle at that insult. Before the girls were even finished laughing, Keisha punched Jackie dead in her face. They sure as hell stopped laughing then. The entire cafeteria got quiet for one split second before Keisha commenced to beating the shit out of Jackie.

As soon as her girls realized that she was on the losing end, they tried to jump in but, the cousins were on it right away, holding back Nina and the others. By the time security had pulled Keisha off of her, Jackie's nose was bleeding all over the place and her left eye was already starting to swell.

"Let me go!" Keisha was yelling. Teek was yelling at the other girls, "That's what happens when you start shit with the wrong people! Y'all didn't know who you were fucking with!"

Security dragged all eight girls off to the principal's office. Principal Carter, addressing no one in particular asked the girls how the fight had gotten started, and they all began yelling at once. "Everybody be quiet" he yelled.

"One at a time. Jackie what happened?"

"Are you kidding?! Why does she get to talk first? She was the one who started it" Teek questioned.

"Because I said so. You'll get your turn, now, go on Jackie. What happened?"
Teek sat back in her seat with her arms folded across her chest, fuming.

"Me and my girls were in the lunchroom minding our own business when Keisha jumped in my face, talking mess" she lied.

"That's a lie!" Keisha jumped up and yelled.

"Sit down and shut up" Mr. Carter said.

"Why?! She's in here lying and you're telling *me* to sit down and shut up?!" Keisha was livid.

"As of this moment, you're only looking at three days suspension Ms. Kyle, but if you say another word, it'll be ten."

None of the cousins could believe what they were hearing. Mr. Carter was treating them as if they had been the instigators of the fight.

Jackie continued telling her story. "When I asked Keisha what her problem was, she hit me!" All four cousins gasped loudly at the blatant lie Jackie had just told.

"That's not true!" Keisha and the rest yelled at once.

"So, you didn't hit her first?" Mr. Carter asked.

"Well, yes but, she started it! Keisha said in her own defense. "She called me a dyke!"
Jackie yelled, "That's a lie!" The cousins yelled, "No it's not!" And all eight girls started going off. Mr. Carter promptly suspended Jackie and Keisha for three days each and sent the rest of them back to class with a warning that if he had to see any of them in his office again, they'd all be expelled.

As soon as the girls left his office, Jackie said, "This ain't over. Y'all bitches think y'all cute. When I get back to school, I'm going to take care of that."

"Whatever, bitch" Teek said.

"Who you calling a bitch?" Nina jumped to Jackie's defense.

"Whoever heard me." Teek responded and the girls all started pushing and shoving again. Fortunately, a nearby security guard stopped them before they started an all-out brawl.

Troi, fed up with the entire scene spoke up. "What the hell is your problem? You just got your ass kicked, can barely see out of one eye and you still talking shit." Troi pointed out as they all stood in the hall facing off.

"Ain't nobody get their ass kicked." Jackie said, totally pissed by the truth of Troi's statement.

"Uh, yeah, you did, but that's beside the point. We never did anything to any of you but, since the first day, you've been picking at us. Why" Angel asked.

"Because ever since the talent show, y'all bitches all think you're too cute; Walking around with your heads in the air like you own the world. So, what if y'all got some long hair and these stupid boys be chasing after you. That don't make y'all better than us" Jackie yelled.

"That's right" Nina added.

"Yeah" said the other two, nodding their heads in agreement.

Three of the cousins didn't give a damn about Jackie's little speech, especially Troi. They had a history of their own. Jackie's ex-boyfriend Aaron was the one guy Troi had set her sights on freshman year. She played every little game she could think of to get him away from Jackie and it worked. From that point on, Jackie was out for revenge.

Angel, however, did care about what was going on in that moment. Being the most compassionate, she could see the sadness just under the surface of Jackie's anger.

"Listen Jackie, we don't act like that. The truth is we don't care anything about hair or looks. Those things aren't important to us. We just got what our parents gave us. We don't have any control over that stuff and as far as these boys go, we don't have time for them." Angel expressed with great sincerity.

"Bullshit!" Jackie yelled and stormed off with her crew following behind.

Teek immediately noticed the sadness in Angel's eyes. She knew her sister couldn't stand to see another person hurting. "It's OK Angel, you tried, but some people are just more comfortable acting a fool."

"Yeah but, I don't get it, why us?"

"Angel, they're a bunch of haters" Troi said.

"Yes, haters with a capital H" Keisha added.

"Why hate on us though" Angel asked.

"The way we look compared to them. I know you might not want to hear it, but in this world, most especially with our people, the color of a person's skin – the lighter the better- and the texture of their hair is how beauty is measured" Troi explained.

"But that's ridiculous" Angel said.

"I know it and you know it, but that's how people are sometimes." Troi continued to explain.

"Jackie and them all have short hair and well, Jackie hardly has any. Her skin is really dark and she's a little chubby."

"So what? I think she has beautiful dark skin" Angel said.

"Yes but, *she* doesn't think so and, neither do a lot of people... that's the problem" Teek interjected.

"We have all different shades of blackness in our family, so we don't even pay that sort of thing any mind, but for some people it really bothers them to be dark skinned. If I were Jackie, I'd be mean too. Haven't you ever heard how some of the boys tease her about the way she looks?" Troi asked, knowing full well that she had stolen the only boy who had given Jackie any positive attention.

"No, I haven't. I stay as far away from that girl as I can." Angel told her cousin.

"I have." Keisha spoke up. "Darnell Jenkins called her a black, bald headed skank last week."

"That's a damn shame" Teek said.

"Yeah, that was a really mean thing to say" Angel added.

"OK, who gives a damn about Jackie and her issues?! I just got suspended for three days. My mom is going to kill me" Keisha snapped.

Keisha's outburst got her cousins off the topic of Jackie and back to handling her dilemma. Troi taking the lead as she usually did, being the eldest said, "Don't trip Keisha. It's only three days and once you tell Auntie what happened, she'll probably let you slide with this one."

"Are you out of your mind Troi? She'll probably pop a damn blood vessel. Oh shit! I'm going to miss three days of basketball practice! That bitch! I could just fuck her up again!" Keisha said with rage at the reality of how much trouble Jackie's crap had caused her.

"Keisha, you need to bring it down some. It's not that serious." Teek said as the girls headed towards the front door.

"That's easy for you to say. You're not the one who got suspended. Don't you get that I'm going to be grounded, *and* I may even lose my starting position on the team" Keisha implored.

"Calm down girl. We'll figure something out. How about if you go talk to your coach and explain what happened? I'm sure she'll cut you a break, and as far as telling your mom goes, I don't think you should" Angel said.

"What? How am I supposed to get away with that?"

"Angel's right" Troi said. "Think about it...Your mom leaves for work before we leave for school, and she gets in way after we get home. Uncle Mercer never checks the mail, so all you have to do is make sure you get it before she sees the suspension notice. She'll never have to know" Troi finished.

"That's true." Keisha said, feeling more relieved by the moment as Troi's plan seemed so easy to pull off.

"Good, then it's settled. We won't tell. Now let's get out of here" Troi said.

Denise Coleman

CHAPTER 5

Although the girls hated that Keisha wasn't at school with them for the next three days, getting a break from the drama with the others was welcomed. Without their ringleader Jackie, Nina and the others were less inclined to get into the bullshit.

The following Monday, however, was a different story. Jackie's jealousy and rage had boiled over by the time she and Keisha were allowed to return to school. Jackie convinced her girls to lay low for the day but as soon as the final bell sounded, they went looking for the cousins.

They found Troi alone on her way to cheer practice. Without any warning whatsoever, Nina and Terri grabbed Troi from behind, and Jackie grabbed a chunk of her hair and cut it off with a pair of scissors.

Troi was screaming bloody murder, trying to get out of the vice grip Nina and Terri had on her. The fourth demon, Rena, was standing guard in case any school officials happened by. When Jackie was finished with her viscous assault, she said to Troi, "I bet your ass ain't so cute now. Next time you'll think twice about fuckin' with other bitch's men. If you or your cousins even think about trying something, I'll cut more than your hair." Then the four ran off laughing.

Troi was sitting on the floor, leaning up against her locker, with her head in her hands, crying when Angel came looking for her.

"Troi, what's wrong?" Angel asked as she kneeled down in front of her cousin. Only when she was eye level with her cousin did she notice how upset she was.

"Jackie cut off my hair" Troi cried.

"What?!" Angel asked, then noticed Troi was holding the hair she had gathered up after the attack.

"Oh my God! What is wrong with that girl?!" Angel questioned as she immediately started pulling Troi to her feet.

"Come on Troi, we have to go tell someone."

Troi was visibly shaken when she and Angel entered the office. "I need to speak to Mr. Carter, right now." Angel said to the secretary.

"What happened to her?" The woman asked once she noticed how distraught Troi was.

"That bitch, Jackie Mason cut off her hair! Can we please see the principal?!"

Hearing all of the commotion, Mr. Carter came out of his office before the secretary could pick up the phone. "What's going on out here?"

"Look at my cousin's hair!" Angel said as she took Troi by the shoulders and turned her around for Mr. Carter to see. Troi continued to sob the entire time.

"Oh, my goodness, who did this to her?" Mr. Carter asked.

"Jackie did it, and all I want to know is what you're going to do about it."

Mr. Carter turned to his secretary and told her to get him the home number for Jackie. Troi spoke up then. "That's all you're going to do, have a conference with her parents?! She attacked me with scissors. Who knows what she'll come at me with next?" Troi said as she began wiping her tears, her rage building. "You can waste time calling her parents if you want to, but I won't be waiting around for that. I'm going to handle this shit myself!" Troi said and she and Angel stormed out of the office on the war path.

There was no way in hell the cousins were going to let this incident slide. It was on.

"Aren't you going to go after them?" The secretary asked.

"No, I'm not. There's no need to. I'm sure that Jackie's long gone by now. We'll deal with it in the morning."

A few minutes later, Troi and Angel were in the gym looking for Keisha and Teek, who'd decided to stay and keep an eye on her cousin her first day back.

They spotted Teek sitting on the bleachers and ran toward her.

"What are y'all doing here? Why aren't you at cheer practice" Teek asked. However, before either could answer her, she noticed Troi's hair. "Jackie!" She jumped up and yelled out to Keisha, who came running over.

"What is it" Keisha asked.

"Look at what Jackie and them did to Troi" Angel said.

"Oh, hell no! Enough is enough. Let's go get those bitches" Keisha responded.

The cousins knew exactly where to find the girls. Those fools didn't have enough sense to lay low. Everyone knew they hung out at the corner store after school every day; where they would torture and harass anyone they didn't like.

The store had several tables and a counter where food could be ordered. The girls were sitting at the counter, laughing about the damage they had done to Troi when the cousins entered.

"Hey Jackie, get your punk ass outside right now" Teek yelled.
Jackie immediately jumped bad.

"I know you snooty bitches ain't come up in here like y'all going to do something" Jackie questioned. Without skipping a beat or wasting time responding, Troi snatched Jackie off the stool she was sitting on, and the cousins followed her lead. Each grabbed one of the other girls and dragged their asses out of the store.

There were at least ten to fifteen other students in the store when the cousins came in and they immediately ran out to see the fight. Within seconds all eight girls were going toe to toe with one another. There was punching, kicking and scratching going on. Before long, Jackie and Terri were both knocked to the ground by the force of the blows they were receiving.

Troi wasted no time jumping on top of Jackie, and began banging her head on the sidewalk, she was so enraged. Keisha was holding her own with Nina, matching her blow for blow. Every time Keisha punched Nina in the face, her head would snap back like a bobble head doll. Nina quickly got tired of Keisha whooping that ass, so she reached in her pocket and pulled out a razor blade.

Before Keisha even knew what had happened, Nina had cut her across her upper arm. Keisha never felt the razor cut her, but she noticed the blood pouring from her arm almost immediately.

When Teek and Angel heard Keisha's screams, they released the two girls they were pummeling and ran to Keisha's side. As soon as they'd realized what Nina had done, they began fucking her up. Teek and Angel were kicking and stomping Nina while Keisha was still screaming. The mêlée was in full force by the time a few of the boys who'd noticed the blood, decided it was time to break it up.

When the boys who'd stopped them finally got the cousins to calm down, somewhat, Terri and Rena were doubled over in pain, Nina was lying on the ground, curled up in the fetal position, and Jackie was unconscious.

One of the kids who'd come out to watch the fight said, "Damn, is she dead?" Another said, "I think she is. She's not moving anything!" A third said, "We better get the hell out of here." And the crowed scattered like roaches. The cousins didn't stick around either. They high tailed their ass's home. They chose to go to Keisha's house because they knew her parents were the last to get home.

"What are we going to do?" Troi asked as soon as they'd closed the front door. "What if she's really dead?" Troi continued to ask. Angel grabbed Troi's arms and looked in her eyes. "She's not dead Troi. You didn't kill anyone."
Troi began to cry. "But I don't think she was breathing."

"She was breathing, now go upstairs and wash your face and change your clothes" Angel directed.

31

"OK, OK, OK." Troi said while shaking her head up and down and sniffling. Keisha, who was trying to staunch the blood with a towel she'd gotten from the kitchen, ran upstairs behind Troi.

As soon as the two were out of sight, Teek turned to Angel and asked, "What the hell are we going to do?"

Angel, who was always calm when the others were freaking out said, "I don't know. I think we should just tell the truth about what happened."

Teek grabbed Angel's arms and began shaking her like she was trying to shake some sense into her.

"Are you crazy Angel? How is telling the truth going to get us out of this mess?"

"I didn't say it would get us out of it, but what other choice do we have? There were too many people there to witness what happened. Do you really think all of those people would cover for us? Be for real."

"Maybe they would, you don't know." The wheels began turning in Teek's head as she continued speaking. "I mean think about it. Nobody can stand those girls, and after all the stuff they've done to us for no good reason, maybe those kids will keep quiet."

"Fool! Use your brain. What stuff have they really done to us? A smart remark here, an insult there… none of that will get us out of what we did today."

"But what about what they did to Troi? You saw her hair" Teek reiterated.

"That's exactly my point Tiki, we can't run from this. Everyone knows about their hatred towards us and after what they did to Troi, we went straight to Principal Carter's office and told him. Listen, the truth is all we have, and we'll have to deal with whatever comes next."

Keisha and Troi came back downstairs just in time to catch the tail end of what Angel had said. Neither of them wanted to agree with her point considering they had both gotten physically harmed in the fight, but neither could dismiss the reality of the situation. There would be no covering up the day's events as they had Keisha's suspension.

"Angel, do you think we're going to go to jail" Keisha asked.

"No, of course not. It was just a street fight" Angel answered.

"Good, because I can't go to jail right now. I think I need to go to the hospital instead." Keisha said just before she passed out.

Denise Coleman

CHAPTER 6

By the time the ambulance arrived, so had the girls' parents and the police. Keisha was still lying on the floor bleeding from her arm, and her cousins were all hysterical, thinking she was going to bleed to death.

"What the hell happened today?!" Leigh yelled as she entered her sister's house. Teek and Angel both ran into their mother's arms. Troi remained seated on the floor with Keisha's head in her lap. When Hillie came in and saw her daughter lying on the floor, she too became hysterical. "Oh my God!" She yelled as she fell to her knees.

"What happened to my baby?" She continued to cry. Troi wiped her eyes with the back of her sleeve and said, "This girl named Nina cut her while we were fighting."

"What? Who is Nina and what the hell happened to your hair?" Hillie asked as the paramedics bent down to check out Keisha.
Troi began crying again as the paramedic asked her to give him room. He checked Keisha's wound, which had actually stopped bleeding. His partner put smelling salts under Keisha's nose, and she immediately began to cough and sputter as she opened her eyes.

"Oh, thank goodness! *Tout bagay anfom?*"
Hillie asked the paramedic as she crouched behind him.

"Pardon me" he said.

"You'll have to excuse my sister. She tends to speak in our parent's native language when she's upset" Leigh explained. "She asked is everything OK."

"Oh, yes ma'am. The cut isn't as deep as the blood made it seem. It was probably just the combination of the adrenaline from the fight they mentioned and the blood loss. She'll need a few stitches, but I think she should be fine" he explained.

Fifteen minutes later, the cousins and their parents, as well as the police were at the hospital with

Keisha. While her cut was being stitched up, the police used that time to question the others about the fight.

Everyone had calmed down by then and was ready to clear things up. Leigh and Gary, however, did not understand that the police were not there for them to press charges on the other girls.

Gary snapped at the first officer. "What do you mean you need to question them about what happened? You see what happened. My niece is in there getting stitches in her arm, and my other niece is missing half of her hair!"

"I understand that Mr. Kyle, but the other families have already pressed charges against your daughters and nieces. That's what I came to your home about."

Gary jumped up from his seat. "What?! What the hell do they have to press charges about?!"

Leigh grabbed Gary's arm and coaxed him back down to his chair.

"I understand you're upset Mr. Kyle, but the injuries that the other girls have, are more serious. A Miss Jacqueline Mason was brought to the emergency room, unconscious, and as of a few minutes ago, she still hasn't woken up. Then there's a Miss Nina Kramer who has several cracked ribs. Injuries allegedly inflicted by your girls." The officer further explained.

Gary could not believe his ears. He and Leigh sat there stunned by what they'd heard.

Angel immediately began to cry. "We didn't mean to hurt anyone. We just wanted them to leave us alone. They just kept picking and picking and, today they cut off Troi's hair! What were we supposed to do? Principal Carter wouldn't even help us. Nobody would make them stop!" Angel said through snot and tears.

Gary wrapped his daughter in his arms and told the officer that there would be no more questions answered that night. He would gladly bring the girls to the station in the morning. Seeing the condition the girls were in, and given they were all minors, the officer agreed with Gary that everything could be taken care of in the morning.

Shortly after the officer left, Troi's mom, Tess arrived. When she saw Troi, she began ranting in Creole about the attack on her daughter. It took Leigh ten minutes to calm her sister down. When it came to Troi, there was nothing she could or would do wrong in her mother's eyes.

Once Tess had sat down and agreed to stay calm, the girls then told their parents about the events leading up to the fight, including the minor incident on the first day of school.

Although their parents did not condone the violence, they all understood their daughters' need to stand up for themselves. After all, that's what they'd been taught.

The next day the cousins and their parents presented themselves at the police station. During this time, the girls gave their statements and were informed that they would be receiving a court date in the mail very soon.

They had all been charged with assault. As had the other girls, because Tess and Hillie wasted no time going to the station the night before and pressing charges as well. Fortunately for the cousins, they hadn't used any weapons. However, that didn't help them much when their court date finally rolled around.

It was about a month later when the cousins were due in court. Needless to say, the girls were all very nervous, not knowing what their fate would be. The juvenile courtroom was small and almost empty when they arrived. There were few people in attendance at the hearing. Jackie and her friends were there with their parents, as were the cousins.

Unfortunately for the family, they could not afford an attorney. If they had, maybe things would have turned out differently.

Because both sides had filed complaints against the other, the prosecutor did no more than present the complaints and witness statements from a few of the students who were at the fight, to the Judge.

Judge Matthews struck an imposing figure at six feet tall, two hundred fifty pounds. No doubt the entire group was intimidated by his demeanor. What they didn't know was that this particular judge had no use for teenagers, male or female.

He secretly believed that they were all useless criminals and never bothered to give any of them a break.

The Judge reviewed the information he had read over previously and had already made a decision about what to do with the girls. Although he understood that Jackie and her friends were indeed a little terror squad; with the severity of the injuries inflicted upon them, he was left no choice other than to punish *all* of the girls. Not that he cared either way. He addressed all eight girls at one time.

"I must say that I am appalled by your behavior. Miss Mason and friends, the Judge began sarcastically, your fighting and terrorizing of other students is unacceptable, and this court will not be taking your behavior lightly. Now, as far as you other four, your actions won't be taken lightly either. Today our public schools are filled with children who have no regard for the rules, and that simply won't be tolerated by this court." He took a breath before he continued.

"Fortunately for you all, I won't be sending anyone to a juvenile facility. However, none of you will be allowed to attend public school in this city for the remainder of your high school careers."

The cousins and their parents were confused by what they'd heard, and not sure at all if they'd heard him correctly. Jackie's mom jumped up and yelled, "What the hell does that mean? Where is my daughter supposed to go to school?"

The Judge banged his gavel and advised Ms. Mason that she had better sit down and be quiet. He continued with his sentencing. "They will have to attend either a parochial school or any school outside of the city school district. Now, before you even think about saying another word Ms. Mason, this sentence is final." The Judge stated emphatically and banged his gavel again, done with the case.

"What, just like that, it's over?" Leigh said to Gary. The entire family sat there stunned by what had just occurred. The bailiff informed everyone that copies of the Judge's order would be available to them shortly, and that they should wait.

"Mommy, what does this mean" Troi asked.

"I'm not quite sure, but it sounds like you girls can't go to school here anymore." Tess tried to explain to her daughter, even though, she didn't really understand it herself. The shock of the abruptness of it all hadn't quite worn off.

The family decided to go into the hall outside of the court room while they waited for the court order to be given to them. As soon as they'd stepped out, the other families followed. Tess wasted no time speaking up. "Which one of you little demon children cut my daughter's hair?"

"Who the fuck are you calling a demon child?" Jackie's mother yelled.

"Which ever one of those little bitches that did it! What are you going to do about it?" Tess continued.

"Bitches?!" Nina's mom yelled.

"Yeah, bitches!" Tess responded just as Gary, Leigh and Mercer (Keisha's dad) jumped in between them.

"This is not the time or place for this Tess." Leigh said to her sister. "Let's just go to the snack bar and wait."

"No. We're staying right here until it's time for us to leave." Tess told Leigh.

"OK, but only if you can sit here and keep your mouth shut."

"Yeah, whatever. I can't make any promises."

Both families took seats on either side of the hall. They sat and stared daggers at one another for the remainder of their wait. Twenty minutes passed before the bailiff came out and handed copies of the order to the cousins' parents. He informed the others that theirs' would be a few more minutes.

No doubt the court officers knew it would not be wise to have these families leaving the building at the same time.

Denise Coleman

CHAPTER 7

Shortly after the clan arrived home, they sat down to read the court order thoroughly. The girls sat anxiously waiting to find out what would be their high school fate.

"Girls, could you leave us alone for a few minutes. We have some things we need to discuss" Gary said.

"But what are we going to do about school daddy? We've already missed a month as it is" Angel said.

"Just give us a few minutes and we'll talk to you when we're done."

"OK." The girls all went out onto the front stoop to wait while their parents discussed their futures.

"OK, the bottom line is that we're stuck between a rock and a hard place with this. No matter how we try to spin this court order, there's no way our girls can go to school in this city. None of us can afford to send them to private school, nor can we send them to another district. The closest public school outside of the city is simply too far away. They'd have to be out the door by five a.m., and they'll have to catch two buses and a damn train. That's entirely too much for them to have to do to get to school" Gary expressed.

"What can we do?" Leigh asked, clearly distraught over the bind they were in.

"I don't know. I hate to say it, but it looks like we're stuck" Gary answered.

"What are you talking about" Mercer asked.

"Well, since we can't send the girls to school here and they certainly can't drop out, I think we should call Tim."

"Call Tim for what?" Mercer asked, clearly perplexed.

"Look, he's the only relative we have outside of this city. Maybe he will let the girls live with him and his family until they finish school."

"Are you serious Gary? Tim lives in New Jersey! How can we possible send out children that far away, for that long" Hillie asked.

"I know it seems harsh, and even a little far-fetched, but what choice do we really have? Our children have to go to school, *and* we have no other alternatives at this point." Mercer expressed to his wife. He held on to her, hoping that she wouldn't lose it. She was *the* most dramatic of the sisters.

The others were sitting around mulling over Gary's idea. Unfortunately, none of them had a better plan, and no matter how painful that reality was, they had to make a decision.

"Hillie, I don't like this anymore than you do. I don't want to lose my baby either" Tess said. She then turned to her brothers-in-law and asked, "Do you think Tim would actually go for this? Really guys, this isn't a small favor we'd be asking. He'd be taking in four teenaged girls. That's a lot to ask of anyone."

"This is true, but you have to remember, our family is just as close as yours, and I'm sure that once we explain the situation to him, our brother will gladly help us out" Gary said. Mercer nodded his head in agreement.

The women were all in tears by now. Certainly, they wanted to keep their daughters at home, but it didn't look like that was going to happen. Leigh, usually the leader of the pack when it came to her siblings said, "Make the call Gary. We have to know either way before we call the girls back in."

Gary picked up the phone and dialed his brother's number.

"Hey little brother!" Gary said as soon as Tim answered the phone.

"How the hell are you" Tim asked.

"Not too good right now. Merc and I need your help."

"What's going on? What can I do for you?"

Gary went on to explain the situation to his brother, hoping that he could help them out. It took Tim less than thirty seconds to agree to take the girls in. Tim told his brothers that he did not need time to think about it, and that there was nothing he would not do to help his family. He also told them that his wife, Karen would not have a problem with it at all. She'd love to have the girls around to dote on.

With that out of the way, Leigh called the girls back into the house.

"Please girls, sit down" Gary said. The girls all sat, staring at their parents expectantly, waiting for someone to speak. For the parents this was not easy. How do you explain to your children that they'll have to be sent away from their home? Leigh had to be the one to speak up, because although they had made the call, Mercer and Gary were beginning to fall apart, as had Tess and Hillie. Leigh cleared her throat before she could speak.

"Girls, I hate to have to tell you this but, the only solution we could come up with for this situation, is to send you all to live with your Uncle Tim in New Jersey."

"What?!" Troi screamed out.

"Nooooo!" Was Keisha's response. While Angel sat there in shock and, Teek began to sob uncontrollably. The sight of their daughters in so much pain ripped at the hearts of their parents.

They could do no more than hold on to each of the girls. No doubt this truly was the saddest day in their lives.

It took the family several weeks to come to terms with the new development in their lives. Although no one was happy about what had to be done, they were gradually becoming more accepting. At least Angel was a little better at accepting that she couldn't change what had happened, or what would be.

The cousins were at home for the three months before they had to leave. They were due to go to Jersey at the end of July so that they would have time to acclimate themselves to their new home before school started.

When that day came, saying goodbye was more difficult than any of them could have imagined. The scene at the airport was like that of a funeral service. There were non-stop tears the entire morning. For four teen girls being forced to leave home, it *was* a death.

Denise Coleman

CHAPTER 8

T.J. Kyle and his friends, Kelly and Andre`
Taylor, were sitting on his front porch, waiting for his
cousins to arrive. T.J. was an only child, and although
his cousins were girls, he looked forward to having other
teens in the house.

"So, T, what are these girls like" Kelly asked.

"I don't know man. I told you I only met them a
few times when we were little. My dad moved here for
work way before I was born. I ain't seen 'em in about
five years."

Dre` laughed, "Who the hell moves to Camden, New
Jersey on purpose?" Kelly and T.J. laughed as well.

"Yeah man, it's not like Camden is the land of
hopes and dreams" Kelly said.

"Yo, our mom is always talking about how
beautiful and prosperous this city was back in the day,
and how Campbell Soup was the shit. Half the people in
the city worked in that factory" Kelly continued.

"Yeah well, those days are over. Folks are just
scraping by these days" Dre` added.

"So anyway, back to these cousins. Tell us what
you do know about them" Kelly pressed.

"Alright, damn! All of their moms are sisters,
but the twins' mom and Keisha's mom married my dad's
two brothers" T.J. explained.

"What" Dre` asked.

"Pay attention dumb-ass. My Uncle Gary went
with the twins' mom, Aunt Leigh, and my Uncle Mercer
went with Keisha's mom, Aunt Hillie, all through high
school, so they married sisters. OK?"

"Yeah nigga, I got it. Now what about the other
one?"

Her mom is a sister too, but technically, Troi's not my
cousin." T.J. told the brothers.

"OK, wait, what?" Dre` asked again, not
following.

"Yo man, you really are slow" T.J. laughed.

"Fuck you nigga. Now, tell me how she's not your cousin" Dre` said.

"I'm related to the twins and Keisha on our dad's side, and they're *all* related on their mom's side as well. Got it now?"

"Yeah man" Dre` lied.

"No, you don't." Kelly said and he and T.J. fell out laughing at the confused expression on Dre`'s face.

Just as Kelly got up to move to the step, the boys got quiet as Tim's car pulled up in front of the house. All three boys' mouths fell open when one by one, the girls got out of the car. Dre` said, "Wow."
Kelly gulped loudly but didn't say a word. T.J. just shook his head and said, "Damn, I'm going to be fighting dudes left and right, trying to keep them off of my cousins."

The boys were stunned by the beauty of the new arrivals. Not one of them moved towards the car to help Tim with the bags until he spoke up.

"Boys, close your mouths and get down here and help" Tim said.
This snapped the boys back to the moment. In a flash Dre` and Kelly went running. T.J. shook his head again, *"I'm going to have to kick my boy's asses first."* He laughed to himself.

T.J. quickly ran down to the car and stepped in front of his boys. "Excuse me." He said to the brothers as he pulled Teek into a hug. "Which one are you" he asked. Teek smiled at her cousin and said, "I'm Teek but everybody calls me Tiki."

"Oh, like a tiki torch thing, huh?"

"I don't know about all that, but it's nice to meet you again cousin."
Angel stepped forward and reintroduced herself to her cousin, and Troi and Keisha followed her lead.

"I know y'all aren't happy to be here, but I'm glad you came." T.J. said to the girls.

"Does being an only child get lonely" Angel asked.

"Yeah sometimes, but I have my boys to hang with most of the time, so it's cool. Anyway, these are my best friends, Kelly and Dre` Taylor." T.J. said, as Kelly and Dre` stood on either side of him, openly staring at the girls in awe.

"Hi!" The brothers said in unison. Teek, Keisha and Troi said hi with disinterest, still overwhelmed by sadness. Angel on the other hand tried to be nice. She offered her hand first to Dre`, then to Kelly and at the very moment Angel and Kelly's hands made contact, an electric like charge passed between them.

Her entire body seemed to explode from the inside out. Her legs began to wobble, and she momentarily felt faint. Angel had never felt anything like that in her life and found herself unable to remove her hand from his.

"It's very nice to meet you, Kelly." She said with a smile. Kelly's eyes were locked on their hands, unsure himself of what had just happened between them.

"It's nice to meet you too" he whispered.

"I might believe that if you'd actually look at me when you speak to me" Angel teased.

"I'm sorry about that." Kelly said as his eyes reached hers. He quickly gathered his senses and leaned in close and said, "I'm going to marry you one day." Angel smiled, held eye contact for a moment and said, "I know."

The others had gotten busy carrying the bags into the house during Angel and Kelly's exchange.

"What's that?" Kelly asked of the item he spotted T.J. carrying.

"Oh, that's just my guitar."

"What, you play the guitar?" Kelly asked, truly impressed.

"Yes, I do, and so does my twin. We all play a few different instruments. It's always been important to our parents" she shrugged.

"That's cool. I sing." Kelly said with a huge grin.

"Oh yeah, we do too."

"Get out of here! For real, are y'all any good?"

"Maybe."

Kelly, never letting go of Angel's hand, guided her back to the house to sit on the porch swing.

"Angel, can I ask you a question?"

"Sure, what is it?"

"How come the other girls ain't as friendly as you are?"

"It's not that they aren't friendly. It's just that they're unhappy. Well, sad is more like it" she explained.

"Are you sad too?"

"Yes, but I'm starting to feel better already" she smiled.

"Yeah?"

"Yeah. Anyway, I have to go in now."

"Why?" Kelly asked with a disappointed expression on his face.

"Because my sister's coming." Just then, Teek came to the front door and told Angel that their uncle wanted her inside.

"How did you know she was coming?" Kelly asked with surprise in his voice.

"She's my twin, I could feel her getting closer. Anyway, don't leave. I'll be back." With a smile and good feeling in her spirit, Angel got up and went into the house.

"Angel, come say hello to your Auntie, then you can go up and unpack your things" Tim said.

"Hi Angel, welcome to our home." Her Aunt Karen pulled her into a hug.

"Hello Auntie. It's good to see you again. My mom wanted me to thank you for taking us in" Angel smiled.

"There's no thanks necessary sweetie. You're family, and this is your home too" Karen smiled in return. Karen's comments brought up the sadness that Kelly had helped to lesson for a brief moment.

Angel could not forget the reality that she and her sisters were living in a strange house in a strange city. No matter how much her aunt and uncle cared for them, they were not their parents. It wasn't the same.

Angel excused herself and went up to get unpacked. When she entered the bedroom, she was surprised to find that all four of them would be sharing one room.

Teek noticed the look on her face and said, "Can you believe this? Bunk beds! We're supposed to sleep in this one room together?" Teek asked, not at all happy about their new living space.

"Right, and I'm damn near six feet tall, how am I supposed to sleep in a bunk bed? As a matter of fact, we're all a little too tall for bunk beds" Keisha added.

"Damn y'all, it's only a three-bedroom house. There's nowhere else for us to sleep, so just get over it." Troi said, her anger bubbling just beneath the surface.

"Besides, you and Angel shared a room back home Tiki."

"So, it was only two of us, not four" Teek continued.

Angel walked over to her sister and cousin and took their hands.

"It's OK y'all. We'll be alright here. We still have each other."

"OK little Miss Mary Sunshine, I'm not in the mood for a pep talk right now" Teek said.

"Oh no, smart ass? Just for that, you're sleeping up top." Angel said as she hurried to claim the bottom bunk. Teek tried to stop her, but Angel was one step ahead of her.

"It's a good thing I like you, otherwise I'd have to kick your ass." Teek said, laughing at her twin.

"Oh really, I'd like to see that." Angel replied. But, just before Teek could pound her with the pillow she had picked up, T.J. walked in.

"Hey, my mom wants to know if you finished unpacking. We have food on the grill for dinner.

"I don't want any," Keisha said, not trying to hide her resentment at having to be there at all.

"Yes, she does. Just ignore her. We'll be down in a minute. And by the way, for future reference, this is a girls' room, you should knock before entering" Angel said.

T.J., not put off at all by Angel's remarks said OK and left the girls.

"Angel, don't be speaking for me" Keisha admonished.

"Whatever Keisha."

"I don't belong here, *and* I'm not a Kyle." Troi spoke up with a harsh tone.

"Troi, I get that you're upset about this, we all are…but the bottom line is that we can't take it out on these people. They're our own blood and the way we've been raised, we're all one, so stop tripping" Angel said.

"She's right." Both Keisha and Teek said.

"Shoot, Uncle Tim wouldn't even know how to treat you any differently from the rest of us, if he's anything like our dads" Keisha said. "I promise right here and now that I'll try to be nicer. We're family and I'd better act like it."

"That's right. Now let's hurry up with this so we can go eat. I'm starving" Teek exclaimed.

"Fuck that! I'm not one of them, and I don't want to be." Troi stated, not at all comforted by the others' statements.

"Well stay up here and act funky by yourself. We're going to eat.' Teek said as the others exited the bedroom.

Everyone, including Dre` and Kelly were in the backyard when the girls finally made it down. The smell coming from the grill had their mouths watering. They hadn't eaten since early that morning.

"The food will be ready soon" Tim said.

"Come sit over here with us." T.J. said to the girls. Angel wasted mere seconds making a bee line for

Kelly. She sat in the chair next to him, wondering why she was so drawn to him after just one introduction. Whatever it was, she wanted to know more.

"What's that about?" Keisha whispered in Teek's ear.

"Who knows?"

"What are y'all talking about?" Troi asked as she walked up next to them.

"Oh, so you decided to join us, huh?" Troi rolled her eyes. "Whatever. Like I said, what are y'all talking about?"

"Angel. What the hell is up with her and that guy? She just met his ass like five seconds ago" Keisha answered.

"It doesn't matter. If she likes him, she likes him" Troi said.

"Yeah, whatever." Teek said with attitude before she walked away and sat at the table away from everybody else.

"What the hell is her problem" Keisha asked.

"I don't know, and damn it, you need to stop cursing so much" Troi chastised.

"Imagine that." Keisha said sarcastically as she and Troi walked to the corner of the yard where the boys were and sat with them.

"What's wrong with Tiki" T.J. asked.

"We don't know. She has an attitude about something, all of a sudden. Don't pay her no mind, she'll be fine." Keisha told him.

Dre` was sitting there staring at Keisha the entire time. The first thing he noticed about her after he'd noticed her period, was the basketball in her hands. That alone had him curious about her.

"Yo, what's your name again" he asked.

"I'm Keisha, and who are you, yo?" She asked sarcastically.

"I'm Andre Taylor. I told you that when I was helping you carry your heavy ass bags in." He said, not phased one bit by her standoffishness.

"OK Dre`, what's up?"

"I see you must like basketball a lot since you're carrying it around with you. Are you any good?"

"I got mad skills, if I may say so myself." Keisha said with pride.

"Oh yeah?" He laughed. "I might have to take you up to the courts and show you something." Keisha feeling a little more comfortable with a fellow ball player said, "Really? Anytime you're ready, it's on." From that moment on, she and Dre` hit it off. Except for the time they took to eat, the two spent the rest of the evening talking about the sport.

After a while, T.J. noticed that Teek still hadn't warmed up any. He had been looking forward to having the opportunity to get to know his relatives from his dad's side, although they were girls, but things didn't seem to be going the way he'd imagined.

"Troi, do you think Tiki will curse me out if I go over there and try to talk to her?"

"I don't really know. She's not being herself right now. This is hard on all of us."

"Maybe I'll just stay over here then" he laughed.

"No. Go ahead over there. She's more likely to curse one of us out. She doesn't know you like that to be cursing you." She said with disinterest.

"OK, here goes." T.J. said and headed in Teek's direction. He sat down on the bench next to Teek and said, "What's up cuz? Why are you sitting over here by yourself?" Teek looked at T.J., and for a brief moment thought about snapping at him, but her cooler head prevailed.

After all, Teek knew that her feelings had nothing to do with the people around her. She was feeling like shit because of the people who *weren't* around her...the family she actually knew.

"I'm sorry. I'm not usually this rude, but I really miss my parents and my little brother and sister" Teek explained.

"I guess that must really hurt, huh?"

"Yes, it does." Teek tried to smile at her cousin.

"So maybe if you come over and try to get to know my boys, you might feel a little better. Look over there, even Keisha is laughing, and I think she's hard" T.J. laughed.

Teek laughed with him. "I'll let you in on a little secret. Keisha's not so hard at all. I mean, she don't take any crap for sure, but she's not hard. Don't let that ball fool you. When we were in the sixth grade, she was already the tallest girl in junior high, so the gym teacher asked her to try out for the team. She did and she fell in love with the game. Except for that, she's a girly girl just like me." Teek laughed. "Don't tell her I told you that either, she might try to hurt me. She actually likes it better if people think she's tough."

T.J. laughed along with Teek, and that moment with her stranger cousin helped her loosen up a bit. She then turned to see what the others were doing. "T.J., my sisters do look like they're having a good time."

"Sisters?" T.J. looked confused.

"Oh well, it's so many of us, always saying my sister and cousins gets on my nerves, so I just call them all my sisters. It's easier, and we were raised like sisters anyway" Teek explained.

"Oh, then I guess I'm your new brother" T.J. chuckled.

"Whatever blows your hair back, brother." Teek said, while cracking up at her own corny joke.

"So you got jokes, huh?" T.J. said as he elbowed her in the arm.

"Yup, and don't you forget it. Now let's go over there and see what's up with Angel. She's stuck up under that stupid boy and she don't even know him." Teek said and got up from her spot on the bench.

Although she didn't realize it then, T.J. would soon become more than a cousin to her. He would become her friend and confidante. There would come a time when Teek would go to him before she would one of the girls, in the near future.

Troi, Teek and T.J. spent the rest of the evening getting better acquainted. While Keisha continued to talk sports with Dre`, Angel and Kelly spent the evening staring at one another, not really saying much of anything.

During dinner, Troi began to shut down and tune everyone else's chatter out. She was sitting across from Tim, and for the first time, since they'd arrived, she noticed just how handsome he was. Her mind began to work overtime. She thought that if she had to stay with those people, she might as well make it interesting.

Her mother's "user" genes were kicking in with a vengeance. Tim was the head of the household; he had a good job and could make her stay there easier if she played her cards right.

After everyone had eaten, Tim took the time to get his wife's attention. "Babe, do you think there's anything to worry about with them?" He asked as he nodded towards Angel and Kelly.

"No, not at all. They're just smitten with one another, and in case you haven't noticed, your nieces are pretty good girls. You can see it in the way that they carry themselves. Don't fret honey, Kelly is a decent boy anyway."

"Smitten, fret? How old are you again?" Tim laughed with little humor. The truth was, although he attempted to present a normal family to the outside world, his wife wasn't one of his favorite people anymore.

True, the girls were good but the events of the past several months had already begun to cause changes in them which might not have otherwise occurred. Being ripped from their home and security and dropped off elsewhere would take a toll on them all.

CHAPTER 9

The girls' first week in Camden was awkward for them all. Becoming familiar with their new surroundings, and their new family had them all a little on edge. Troi harbored the most resentment about having to defer to strangers for everything. More than anything, she resented Karen for trying to fill the role of mother.

Karen seemed to be hovering at every turn, and while the others clung just a little, Troi couldn't stand it. She needed some space. Her relationship with her own mom was as close as any mother and daughter could be, and every time Karen tried to give comfort or motherly support, Troi missed Tess even more.
As far as she was concerned, the sun rose and set with Tess.

Tess was the only sister who had never married. She didn't have time to lay down roots with a man. Her only desire was to get what she could out of them and keep it moving. Her own young beauty was at once a curse and a blessing. She used what she had to get what she wanted and believed that this was the most important lesson to teach her daughter.

Tess was sixteen years old when she had Troi, so instead of being a mother she and daughter built a best friend bond. Her mother's self- absorbed all about me ways, were definitely passed on to her daughter/best friend.

No matter how much Troi had tried to maintain the loving nature instilled in her by the rest of her family, she was becoming more like her mother with each passing day. The older she got, the more she took on the worse parts of Tess' personality.

By day three, she simply could not stand Karen. Troi stormed into the bedroom, pissed off.

"She makes me sick!" Troi said as she slammed herself on her bed.

"What's wrong with you" Angel asked.

"I can't stand that bitch!"

"Who?"

"Karen."

"You mean *Aunt* Karen?"

"Whatever Angel, she's not my aunt. I hate her!"

"Why Troi? What has she done to you?"

"That bitch had the nerve to leave a chore list for us. She wants me to do her dishes. I'm not her damn maid!"

Angel looked at Troi like she had lost her mind. While she may have understood Troi's anger, it was still a little over the top for the situation.

"How dare her! Aunt Karen should be shot for asking you to do something like that." Angel said jokingly.

"Not funny Angel."

"Damn Troi, it's just the dishes. We all have to pull our weight around here."

"Fuck that! I'm not here to be her housekeeper. Besides, our parents are sending money for our expenses. It's not like we're living here for free."

"I think you're going overboard, but I'm just going to leave you alone right about now."

"Yeah, you do that."

Angel left Troi to stew in her anger by herself. Troi continued to sit until she began to cry. She missed her mom more than she could handle. Just the thought of having to spend the next two years, *at least*, in a strange place pissed her off even more.

Troi always had a difficult time keeping a lid on her temper and being thrown into her current situation didn't help. She sat until she could no longer contain the rage that was boiling inside. Her skin felt like it was on fire. She needed to take it out on someone or something. Troi got up, grabbed a pair of scissors she'd spotted sitting on the dresser and headed for Tim and Karen's bedroom.

She went directly to the closet and found some of Karen's clothes, which still had the tags on them. She quickly commenced to cutting up Karen's shit without a second thought. When she was done, Troi surveyed the pile of scraps lying on the closet floor. She smiled, "That bitch better not fuck with me." She closed the door and left the house.

A few hours later when Karen returned from work, the girls were all sitting around, having just finished their chores. Karen greeted everyone with a smile and went upstairs to change out of her work attire.

After a couple of minutes, they heard a loud scream just before Karen came running down the stairs with the scraps of fabric in her hands.

"Who did this" she shrieked.
Keisha and Teek looked shocked. Angel took less than two seconds to figure it out, and Troi didn't even bother to look in Karen's direction.

"What is that" Keisha asked.

"It used to be a brand-new blouse! Now, which one of you cut up my clothes?!"
Teek immediately became offended and jumped to the defense of her family.

"Why would you automatically think one of us did something like that?"
Karen swung around to face Teek, enraged.

"Who the hell else would do this?! Certainly not my husband or my son!"

"Says you" Teek said indignantly. "We don't know what kind of people y'all are, or what kind of stuff goes on around here."
Karen's head snapped back as if Teek had slapped her, in disbelief at her implying that her family was in some way nuts, and that such things happened on the regular in her home. She screamed in frustration and ran back upstairs.

"Can you believe she accused us" Keisha asked.

"I know...that's fucked up" Teek said.

Angel stared at Troi until she finally glanced back and made eye contact.

"What?"

"You know what. Why did you do that to her?"

"Because I felt like it."

"Damn, it was you" Teek asked.

"Yup, and if I want to, I'll do it again."

"That's messed up Troi" Keisha added.

"Look, I don't care what y'all say. I don't want to be here, and I don't like that woman. Now, drop it before I get pissed again."

Although the others weren't afraid of Troi, they knew when to leave her alone. When she got angry, Troi could be vicious, and no one wanted to deal with that.

A few minutes later Tim came in looking worn down from his day.

"Hey girls, how's it going?"

"Ok uncle how was your day" Angel asked.

"Long. Where's your aunt?"

"Upstairs" They all replied.

Tim continued up the steps to say hello to his wife. He found her lying on the bed, sobbing. He sighed heavily, not in the mood for Karen's hysterics, as he called it. Although he still had love for his wife, things between the two were not good at all, and hadn't been for years.

Tim had been extremely attracted to Karen when he'd met her. She was so sweet, kind and full of laughter, that he'd fallen for her quickly. However, once they'd married, another side of Karen began to surface. She was weak, easy to cry at the most minimal of life's inconveniences.

She would cry over something as simple as a flat tire. There wasn't much she could actually handle. As for their sex life...it wasn't all that great to begin with, and over the years it had become virtually nonexistent. Because of this, Tim got it elsewhere, whenever the mood struck him.

"Babe, what's the matter?" He asked as he slowly approached the bed.

"Look at this" she cried. "One of those girls cut up my clothes!"

"What?" Tim blinked several times. He was shocked into silence.

"Say something Tim!"

"I, I, I don't know what to say" he stammered. "Why would any one of them do such a thing? It doesn't' make any sense."

"Oh, no? How do you know that for sure? Those girls may be family, but they're strangers to us. We don't know who they are or what they'll do."
As much as Tim wanted to argue the point and defend his nieces, Karen was right. They didn't really know the personalities they had invited into their home. However, his heart didn't want to blame his brother's children. After all, they were his blood too.

Nevertheless, determined to get to the bottom of the destruction of his wife's property, Tim ran back down to question the girls. He took a seat in his favorite recliner and turned off the television. Each girl faced Tim knowingly. He gathered his thoughts before he spoke.

He understood how volatile their emotions were, and that if he didn't handle the situation diplomatically, he could possibly cause a chasm between his family and the girls that might not ever be repaired.

"I'm not here to accuse anyone of anything, but it's obvious that at least one of you is acting out."
No one responded. They each stared at him waiting to see what he'd say or do next. When no one spoke up, he continued.

"OK, let's do it this way…Who cut up my wife's clothing?"
Still no response… just blank stares. If Tim believed for one second that any one of his nieces would rat out another, he was mistaken. Shit was not going down like that with those girls.

Fed up instantly with the non-cooperation, Tim stated, "Since no one can be honest, you're all grounded."

"Oh no, we don't do grounded Uncle Tim. That's not happening" Teek stated.

"Oh really? Well young lady, this is my house, and in my house, you get grounded when you do childish shit like cutting up someone's clothes."
The girls all looked at one another, silently communicating. They shared one collective thought...being stuck up in that house for who knows how long wouldn't work for any of them. They all spoke at once, "I did it!"
Tim gawked at them. *"Are they serious?"* He thought.

"Honestly, I see what you're trying to do, and I know full well it did not take all four of you to do this. One last time, who did it, or you're all grounded, period."

"Alright, I did it" Troi spoke up. She couldn't have everyone else in trouble because of her.

"*Why* did you do it?"

"Well damn, you didn't say this was going to be an on-going interrogation. I confessed already; do we really have to keep going with this" Troi questioned.
Tim could not believe his ears. Was this girl really challenging him?

"I know you must be losing your mind, talking to me like that."
When she heard the bass in his voice, and saw the expression on his face, Troi decided to change tactics. On a dime she began to cry- something she'd perfected when trying to get out of trouble with her mom. She cried the blues about how much she missed her mom, which was true, and went on to explain how left out she felt because she was the only one in the house without any biological ties to his family.

She also cried that she just didn't know what to do with the feelings she was having. Some of her little speech was bullshit of course. She no longer cared about not being related, but Tim fell for all of it.

He felt so bad about having any negative thoughts about the girls, considering their situation, that he let Troi off the hook far too easily. He simply made her apologize to Karen, which didn't go over well with her at all. Karen wanted her tarred and feathered and strung up by her fingernails. However, because of Tim's passionate plea on behalf of Troi and her struggles with her new surroundings, Karen let it go for the moment.

Tim had noticed almost immediately that Troi had a different vibe from the others. Theirs was an innocence which wasn't very common anymore. It was refreshing to see that his nieces were not among the fast asses. Troi on the other hand was a different story all together.

She projected her experience. Unusually sensual for a seventeen-year-old, Troi's sexuality bounced off her skin and surrounded her in the most undeniable way. *It,* just like *her,* was a force to be reckoned with.

Tim realized when he'd picked them up from the airport a week earlier, that she stirred things in him that no grown, married man should feel. He also realized when she was crying that those feelings hadn't dissipated.

The girl walked with a natural sway. Her hips moved from side to side like that of a dancer. Inherited from her mother, her seductive movements were something she couldn't turn off. Just that walk alone, drove men and boys out of their minds.

Later that evening, Troi went out to join Tim in the yard where he was raking up some leaves. She figured this would be a good time to get on his good side, hopefully. Troi saw the way Tim looked at her when he thought he was being discreet, so she looked at him as a potential opportunity to at least make her stay in Camden as comfortable *and* profitable as possible. He *had* defended her to his wife, maybe the door was open a little.

"Hi Tim, can I talk to you for a minute?"

"Sure. What's on your mind, Troi?"

Troi slid up to Tim in her most seductive way, not realizing that she didn't have to make any extra effort with that. Although she knew it worked on teen boys, she wasn't sure how a grown man would respond. All she had was knowledge of how her mother handled men and the responses she would get from them.

She turned on her young girl charm and stood as close to Tim as she could without actually touching him.

"I just wanted to say thank you for taking up for me today and understanding how I feel." She smiled sweetly with just a hint of knowing in her eyes.

Tim immediately felt a vibe from her that he wasn't comfortable with. However, he couldn't turn away from it. The slight breeze in the yard carried the gentle, womanly scent of Troi's favorite fragrance, and lingered just under his nose. Tim's mind was raging with inappropriate thoughts of her that'd hit him so hard, with barely any effort from her.

"Uh, it's Ok Troi," He stammered, and took a step back.

"I really just want to make sure you know how sorry I am for what I did, and how much I appreciated what you did for me." She stated, as she took a step closer to him.

"Can I have a hug?" She asked innocently.

Tim was stuck. He couldn't be sure if this child was coming on to him, or if she really was the innocent, she was presenting to him. She sensed his hesitation and said, "In our family, we are openly affectionate, and a hug is one of the small ways we say thank you."

Tim silently chastised himself for having had such thoughts of this girl. Of course, she wasn't making a pass at him. She was seventeen years old and living with strangers… that's all. Tim was more concerned with the fact that something in him continued to respond to her at all.

"Sure, you can have a hug." He said as Troi stepped into him. She wrapped her arms around his waist and squeezed a little too tightly. Tim tried to step out of the embrace but, Troi held on.

"Thank you so much Tim." She whispered then, kissed him lightly on the neck using just a bit of tongue. Tim's penis swelled just enough for her to feel, and she quickly released herself from him, satisfied that she'd had an effect on him.

Troi turned and headed back into the house with a smile on her face.

"Damn, this might be easier than I thought." She said under her breath once she was out of ear shot.

Tim's mind was reeling. He felt both embarrassed and scared by his physical reaction to the teen. "What the hell was that?" He breathed deeply, trying to calm the heat that had risen in him so quickly. Tim decided right then and there that he did not want to know the answer to that question. He intended to stay far away from Troi, as much as he could.

Denise Coleman

CHAPTER 10

By the end of the first week, the girls were somewhat familiar with their new surroundings. Adjusting to the rules of the house was pretty easy. Their Uncle Tim didn't put any more on them than they had already being doing at home.

Troi still resisted as far as she could, but at the urging of the others, she tried to make the best of things in order to keep the peace. At least until she could get what she wanted out of Tim.

However, by the end of that week, Karen could not stand Troi anymore than Troi could stand her. She noticed the dirty looks Troi would give her when no one else was looking. Troi also took every opportunity she got to make some rude or snide remark when the others weren't around to hear them. She definitely was the sneaky one.

Saturday mornings were the same in that house as they were at home. As long as they got their chores done, everyone was allowed a free day to do as they wanted. The only difference was that at home, there was always music blasting during cleaning time.

The girls' mothers believed that you could get your best cleaning done if you had good music to move you. Even Troi tried to help out that day, although she didn't intend to make this a regular habit. She simply wanted out of that house as quickly as possible.

Around noon, Kelly came knocking on the door.

"Hey man, what's up?" T.J. asked as he opened the front door.

"Ain't nothing. Where's Angel?"

"Damn man, you don't even pretend to be looking for me no more" T.J. laughed.

"Whatever fool, where she at?"

"Upstairs getting dressed. We about to go up to the park" T.J. informed.

"Cool, I'm going too."

"Did I invite you?"

"Man, get out of my way so I can come in." Kelly laughed and pushed T.J. out of the doorway. As soon as Kelly got into the house, Angel came walking down the stairs.

"Hi Kelly" she smiled.

"Hi Angel. You look good." He smiled in return.

"It's just jean shorts and a tank, but thanks anyway." Angel blushed. "We're going to the park soon… you should come with us." Angel suggested as she stepped closer to him.

"OK" was all he could say. Kelly couldn't keep his eyes off of her. He was totally mesmerized by that young girl. He'd said to T.J. a few days earlier.

"Where did those girls come from? Don't no girls in Camden look like that."

"What are you talking about fool? There's plenty of pretty girls at our school."

"I know, but it's like they're rough around the edges or something. You know, kind of hard or some shit like that. Your cousins seem a little more classy or something. They even walk and talk different too" Kelly expressed.

"Oh right, it's called English, dumb ass" T.J. had laughed.

"Damn Angel, what are they doing up there?" T.J. asked after her little exchange with Kelly.

"They're still getting dressed." Angel then took Kelly by the hand and said, "Come outside with me." He gladly followed her out onto the front porch. They sat on the swing goofily smiling at one another like they had been doing all week long.

"Kelly, what's your middle name?"

"It's Ronald, why?"

"Ronald, so why'd your mom give you a girl's name?"

"It's my mom's maiden name" he explained.

"Oh, OK. Anyway, I like it. It doesn't matter to me that you have a girl's name. Troi has a boy's name except that it's spelled with an "I" instead of a "Y". I think it's kind of cool."

"Are you sure? Would you rather call me Ronnie?"

"No. I don't like that name." Angel stated seriously.

"What? Why not?" Kelly asked with amusement in his voice.

"Because there was this boy in third grade named Ronnie Reed, and every day he would pull my hair. I hated that snotty nosed little bastard."

"You're funny Angel."

She raised her left eyebrow at that assessment and said, "Not really, but if you say so." Kelly just laughed at her some more.

"I'll just call you Kelly like everybody else does. We have a lot of nicknames in my family, but I really like that name" Angel continued.

Kelly could not believe he was having such a ridiculous conversation with that girl, but more than anything, he didn't care. He would talk about anything she wanted. Besides, he was fully aware of her innocence and the fact that she probably didn't know what to talk to a guy about.

"You can call me anything you want."

"OK then, Kelly" she smiled.

"Angel, I really like you a lot" he confessed.

"I like you too, but don't you think this is a little weird?"

"No, why do you think you and I liking each other is weird" he wanted to know.

"Because we just met a week ago and even though I've seen you every day, we haven't talked much. We really don't know anything about one another."

Kelly considered her point before he responded. He would tell her anything she wanted to know.

"You're right. So, what would you like to know?"

"How old are you?"

"I'm sixteen, and my birthday is in January. How old are you?"

"Well, for future reference, never ask a woman her age, but since this is the "get to know" portion of our program, I just turned fifteen a month ago."
Kelly just laughed some more, while Angel raised that left eyebrow again. Angel never thought she was funny, especially when she was being serious.

"OK Angel, what else do you want to know you little nut?"

"Do you have any brothers and sisters besides Dre` and stop laughing at me." She said as she plucked him in the forehead.

"Owwwe, yes, I have an older brother Marcus and a little sister named Rachel. That shit didn't tickle." He said as he rubbed his forehead. "Now what about you and your twin, is that it?"

"No. We have a little brother Quentin and a sister Kya. I miss them so much already." Angel said as her eyes began to well up with tears at the thought of her family.

Kelly noticed the tears in her eyes but didn't know what to do. Usually when a girl cried in his presence, it was because of some asshole thing he had done to them.

"Angel, are you going to cry?" He asked and squeezed her hand.

"No. Like I said, I just miss my family, that's all."

"I know you must be sad. If I had to leave my family, it would mess me up, especially since they depend on me."

"What do you mean, they depend on you?"

"I'm the oldest in the house. Marcus went to prison two years ago and won't be getting out anytime soon. Our dad left before Rachel was even born, and my mom works all the time, mostly at night. That leaves me to make sure Dre`'s simple ass, Rachel and the house are all in order. I guess I'm the man of the house" Kelly explained.

Angel slid a little closer to him. "I sure do understand that. My sister and I had to be responsible for Quentin and Kya a lot of the time. As a matter of fact, in our family, the parents love to party, so they would always stick us older kids in one house with the younger kids, and we'd have to look after them. Feed them, bathe them, keep them safe…everything a parent would do. They taught us well though."

"Oh yeah, what was that like?"

"It wasn't so bad really. I mean, sometimes they got on my nerves, but mostly it was a lot of fun. I guess that was because I wasn't doing it all by myself, I had my cousins to help. The only thing about it was that we had to kind of be parents."

"Well, did that part bother you?"

"Sometimes it did. It can be hard coming from such a large family. There would be times when I just wanted two minutes to be by myself, but there was always someone around. Even when I was home in my room, I couldn't have *that* to myself for too long because it was Teek's room too."

"Damn, it sounds like you didn't get a chance to breath."

"I didn't, but if I could be back there right now, I'd never complain again." Angel said with sadness creeping back in.

"Forget that!" Kelly said as he jumped up from the swing. "No more of this sad shit today, OK? We're going to the park, and you're going to have a good time!"

Before Angel could respond, he dragged her up out of her seat and into the house.

"Are y'all finally ready?!" Kelly asked when he saw the girls coming down the stairs.

"Yes, we are, and why the heck are you yelling?" Troi asked.

"Because we're ready to go have a good time damn it, now come on" Kelly answered.

"That's right!" T.J. chimed in. "You girls are too damned slow!"

"Whatever boy. Let's go." Keisha said as they all headed out the door.

"Kelly, where's Dre`" Keisha asked as they exited the house.

"He's already at the park." This made Keisha smile inside. She didn't understand it, but Dre` had been taking up a lot her thoughts that week.

****

Saturday at the park was a big deal in Camden, no matter which area of the city you were in. It seemed as if every teenager in East Camden was there that day. The girls were in awe when they walked up and saw all of the activities that were going on.

Dudley Grange Park was set up like a fair ground without the rides. There were arcade games lined up like the boardwalk in Atlantic City. There were vendors everywhere, with a huge assortment of food, beverages and anything else a teen would want to win or buy. The DJ was working up a sweat while several couples were actually dancing in that heat. There was a softball game in progress when the girls, Kelly and T.J. arrived, and a basketball tournament was scheduled to begin shortly.

"Wow, this is what you call a day in the park in this city" Troi questioned.

"Yeah, ain't this shit something?"

"It sure is. What's the occasion?" Troi wanted to know.

"No special occasion. Our mayor had this big idea that if there was something for us to do that we enjoyed, then maybe kids would stop acting a fool in the summer. Every park in every section of the city does this."

"So, how's that working out?" Angel wanted to know.

"It's not. The ones that were getting into trouble are hard asses that wouldn't be at something like this anyway" T.J. said.

"Unless they wanted to come up here to start some shit" Kelly added.

"Oh."

"Come on Angel, let's go play one of those games" Kelly suggested.

"OK, how about the ring toss?" Angel asked, as she and Kelly wasted no time going off by themselves.

"So, what would y'all like to do?" T.J. asked his cousins.

"Let's go do the basketball game." Keisha said, and T.J., Troi and Teek agreed to go with her.

Over at the ring toss game, Kelly was trying his best to impress Angel.

"OK Angel, which one of those stuffed animal things do you want? I'm going to win it for you" he boasted.

"That one!" Angel pointed to the biggest bear there.

"OK, the big ass bear it is."

When all was said and done, Kelly had to spend ten dollars to win that bear for her. She squealed like a little girl when he had finally won the toy. She took the bear from his hands, then kissed him on the cheek.

"Thank you, Kelly."
He laughed, thrilled that he could put such a huge smile on her face.

"For a minute, I thought you were going to blow it" she laughed.

"So did I, but my manhood wouldn't allow that."

"Well good for your manhood."

"OK girl, let's go find your peoples."

Keisha and the others were over at the basketball hoops games, kicking ass when Kelly and Angel walked over to join them.

"Look what Kelly won for me" Angel cheesed.

"Who the hell cares" Teek said.

"I do, smart ass."

"You're nuts anyway, getting all excited over a stuffed animal." Teek said and walked away. The others just laughed, "Yeah Angel, you are nuts."
Kelly laughed too, "Y'all leave her alone. It took some work to get that bear."

"I ain't thinking about my stupid family. It looks like the tournament is about to start, lets' go watch" Angle said.

"Oh yeah, Dre` is playing" Kelly said. Keisha's ears perked up at that news.

"Dre`'s playing? Cool, let's go!" Keisha said and ran off.

"Awe damn don't tell me she got a crush on that fool" T.J. said.

"If she does, she'd be wasting her time" Troi said.

"Why do you say that?"

"Because I can tell just by looking at him, that Dre` wouldn't be interested in someone as innocent as Keisha. He needs someone a little more experienced."

Kelly nodded knowingly. "I guess you could say that my brother isn't really the kind of guy you want to get serious about." He told the girls.

"If that means what I think it means, I'm telling you right now… you'd better keep your brother away from my cousin" Angel stated.

"Back off Angel. He don't have any control over what his brother does; just like we can't stop Keisha from doing whatever she wants to do" Troi said.

CHAPTER 11

The basketball tournament was the highlight of the da,y and the girls were excited to be there. For a while they forgot about the sadness that permeated their spirits. Angel had clung to Kelly almost instantly. Troi being the eldest, naturally tried to hold it together for the sake of the others, but she was failing with that, and Keisha found herself gravitating towards Dre`.

Teek however, didn't seem to be fitting in or loosening up at all. She spent the first week keeping to herself. Even Angel couldn't snap her out of the funk she was in.

Once they'd made their way over to the courts, Angel noticed Teek sitting at the top of the bleachers alone. She made her way up to the top, sat down beside Teek and took hold of her hand.

"What's up Tiki, why are you sitting up here by yourself?"

"I just don't feel like being bothered with all of this."

"Tiki, are you so sad about being here that you feel like you can't try at all?"

"No Angel, it's not that. I really don't know what it is. I just don't feel like me, and I don't know how to shake that feeling." Teek tried to explain.

"I wish I could say I understand, but I don't. Mostly I wish I could make you feel better, but I'm not sure if I can." Angel told her sister as she rubbed Tiki's back.

"I know you would, other mommy." Teek laughed a little. As much as she was feeling out of sorts, she tried a little humor because, she didn't want to bring her twin down, and Teek knew without a doubt, that if she was feeling bad, Angel would too.

"Was that an actual smile?"

"Maybe."

"OK, then glue that damn smile to your face until it feels like the real thing, and let's go down here and watch these boys ball" Angel encouraged.

As soon as Teek was seated with the others, Troi asked, *"Ou Byen?"*

"Wi, mwen oke" Teek murmured.

Kelly's mouth fell open when he heard the strange exchange.

"What the hell language was that pig Latin or some shit" he asked. Teek and Troi just rolled their eyes, Keisha told him to shut up and Angel said, "It's Creole. That's our family's native language, I guess you would say. Anyway, I'll tell you about it later."

"Cool, so what did she say?"

"Basically, Troi asked if she was OK, and Tiki said yes, more or less. Now can we watch the game? It looks like Dre` got some skills" Angel noted.

"Yeah, he does." Kelly said proudly.

Angel wasn't the only one to take notice of Dre`'s skills on the court. Keisha was grinning from ear to ear at the sight of him, but Troi however, had taken notice of Dre` in a completely different way. For the first time, she looked at him with interest. Dre`'s strong young body glistened with sweat as his muscles flexed and contracted with every stride.

Troi broke out into a sweat of her own. Her mind took her to places she couldn't control. Her mouth began to water, as her thoughts drifted to licking the sweat off of his body. *"Damn! I bet that guy can put it down!"* She thought and decided in that moment that she was going to find out for sure, very soon.

As far as she was concerned, Tim wasn't yet a done deal. Besides, she still only looked at him as her personal Bank of Camden New Jersey…Just someone she could charm to get the extras she wanted. She also knew that she wanted to have things her way, get what she wanted, and not have to answer to Karen. As for Dre`, he'd satisfy her physical needs.

It was almost eight o'clock when the teens returned home from the park. Dre`'s team had won two of their three games and would be playing for the championship the following week. Everyone was still hyped over the victory when they entered the house.

"Hey guys, how was your day" Tim asked.

"We had a good time! Dre`'s team is playing for the championship next week" Keisha exclaimed.

"That's great! Maybe your Auntie and I will go out there."

"I'd like that. I think we should go and support the boy. After all, he spends as much time here as he does at his own house" Karen said.

"Then I guess it's settled, we're going."

"Alright mom and dad but could you do me a favor and not sit with us" T.J. laughed.

"Boy, go on with that. I thought only girls were embarrassed to hang out with their folks."

"Sorry pops, don't nooo body want to hang out with their parents." T.J. laughed some more.

"Let me enlighten you about something son, your mom and I are a little too hip to hang out with you. How you like that" Tim said playfully.
Everyone fell out laughing when Tim said that.

"Uncle Tim, no you didn't just say "hip" Keisha laughed.

"I sure did. Now, you all take your behinds upstairs and wash up for dinner."
Everyone except Angel ran up to get cleaned up.

"Uncle, can you sit down with me for a minute" she asked.

"Sure honey, come sit over here with me." Tim said as he led Angel to the sofa.

"What's wrong?"

"Oh, nothing's wrong uncle. I just want to ask you if I can go to Kelly's house for a little while."

"Oh Angel, I'm not sure if that's such a good idea, it'll be dark soon." Angel gave her uncle a curious glance.

"Uncle Tim, I'm fifteen years old. I'm allowed to be out after dark. Besides, it's just up the street. Please, uncle."

Tim wasn't sure of what to say. His brothers had entrusted him with the welfare of their children, but Tim had no idea of what to do with teenaged girls. Karen decided to speak up when she sensed her husband's hesitation.

"Angel, why is it so important for you to go see this boy tonight? You were just with him all day." Karen pointed out.

"I know Auntie, but it's Saturday night and his mom has to work, so he has to babysit for his sister. He asked me to keep him company for a little while." Angel quickly explained.

"That's not what I mean sweetie. You've only been here for a week, and you've spent every free moment you've had with him. Why is that? You hardly know him."

"I' don't know Auntie. I like him, and when I'm with him, I forget that I'm here and not at home." The sincerity with which Angel expressed herself and the little bit of sadness that Karen saw creep into her eyes as she spoke, pulled at her heart strings. She and Tim understood how difficult it was for the girls to be there, and they wanted to do as much as possible to make things less painful for them.

"Alright sweetie, you can go, but you have to be back here by ten, and I want you to stay out on the front porch where I can see you. I'll be checking, and I'd better be able to see you when I do" Karen advised.

"OK Auntie, I promise" Angel said. She jumped up, kissed her aunt and uncle and ran out the front door.

Angel ran halfway up the block then decided it would be in her best interest to slow down. She didn't want Kelly to see her, because then he would know how anxious she was to see him. Her mother always told her, *"Never let them see you sweat. Play it cool and they'll do the chasing."*

When she reached Kelly's porch, he was standing in the doorway watching her. *'Damn, I'm glad I stopped that stupid ass running.'* Angel thought as she walked up to the front door.

"Hey Angel, I didn't think your peoples were going to let you come over here."

"Me either really."

"Come on in." He said as he held the screen door open for her.

"I can't. My Aunt only let me come on the condition that I stay out on the porch, and trust me, she will be checking up on me."

"That's OK, you can sit down, and I'll go check to make sure my sister finished her bath."

"OK, where's Dre`, he can come out here with me."

"He didn't get here yet. He's probably still with his teammates."

"Oh, OK."

"Angel, I know you're not afraid to sit out here by yourself, are you?"

"No, boy! Go ahead in the house."
After about ten minutes, Kelly came out to sit with her.

"Is your sister alright?"

"Yeah, she's watching TV now."

"How old is she anyway?"

"Rachel is ten." Kelly said with a smile. He too was very protective of his siblings.

"Oh, I don't know why, but I thought she was younger."

"Yeah, she's grown as hell too" he laughed. "Anyway, did you have a good time today?"

"I sure did. It's been a while since I had any real fun."

"Really, why?"

"Well, before we left to come here, life wasn't so great. We spent most of the last few months dreading the day we'd have to leave home."

"Oh, that makes sense. What happened with y'all anyway? I mean, how did you get into so much trouble in the first place?"

Angel spent the next fifteen minutes telling Kelly about the trouble with Jackie and her girls, and the subsequent fight that led up to all eight girls being kicked out of school.

"Damn, y'all must've done some serious ass kickin'," Kelly exclaimed.

"You say that like you can't believe it. We know how to handle ourselves." Angel said with amusement.

"Obviously! Seriously though, anybody who looked at y'all wouldn't think that you could go hard like that. That bitch Jackie was really in a coma?!" Kelly asked, still a little shocked by that particular piece of the story.

"Yes, but for only like two days. Personally, I think she was just afraid to wake up and get beat down again." Angel said, and Kelly burst out laughing.

"Girl, you are too funny!"

"Yeah, yeah, that's what you keep telling me."

"Now, tell me about that Creole thing."

"Short version, my family is Creole. French Creole, and most of the grown- ups prefer to speak the language before they use English. So of course, we speak it too, just not nearly as much as they do."

"So where are they from?"

"Louisiana. And our great grandfather was French. Our great grandmother was Creole and actually, the languages are kind of similar."

"That's cool. So, teach me how to say something."

"Something like what?"

"Teach me how to say, I love you." Angle looked at him oddly but did as he asked.

"Je'tieme" she said.

"Je'tieme." Did I say that right?" He asked.

"Perfectly" she smiled.

"Angel?"

"Yes, Kelly."

He hesitated for a brief moment but chose to follow his young heart. *"Je'tieme,* Angel." Kelly said in all seriousness.

"What?!" Angel's heart, stomach, and brain did flip flops all at once.

"Are you serious, we just met?"

"Hell yeah, I'm serious."

As much as Angel wanted to believe that this boy was telling her the truth, she couldn't trust his words. She wasn't old enough or experienced enough at fifteen to handle such an admission.

"Oh please, you can't possibly love me already. Are you one of those guys who tells a girl that, so she'll have sex with you? My dad warned me about boys like you, and if that's where you're coming from, you're wasting your time" Angel stated.

Kelly's face fell and his entire demeanor changed. He let go of her hand and stood up.

"I think you should go home Angel."

"What, why?"

"Just go home Angel." Kelly didn't even waste another second. He went in the house and closed the door with finality. Angel was shocked at Kelly's reaction to her statement. Her young mind could not understand why he had reacted in the way he had. She knew without a doubt that she had angered him, and that knowledge upset her.

Angel slowly got up and made her way back down the street. By the time she'd reached home, she was in tears. She was glad that her aunt and uncle were nowhere in sight when she entered the house. Angel did not want to have to explain why she was crying. She didn't know anyway.

Angel went to the bedroom that she shared with damn near everybody in the house and found Teek laying on her bed.

"Hey Angel, what's wrong?" Teek asked before she'd even noticed the tears streaming down her sister's face.

Angel sat on the bunk across from her. "Kelly got mad at me and sent me home, and I don't even know why" she cried.

"What do you mean, he sent you home... he's not your father." Teek was indignant.

"He got mad at me then he told me to leave, and he went in and closed the door in my face."

"So, what did you do to piss him off?"

"That's just it, I don't know. He told me he loved me, and I told him, he didn't. Then I told him, if he was just saying that to get sex, then he was wasting his time."

Teek laughed a little at Angel. "Girl, it sounds like you insulted that boy."

"What? How?" Angel asked, truly perplexed.

"Well twin, I think that Kelly really likes you. I mean, *really* likes you, and even though he's a sixteen-year- old walking hormone, I get the feeling that he wouldn't lie to you just to get you. Oh, and you better not even think about having sex with that boy!"

"I won't, but I still don't understand why he's mad and I really don't understand why I'm crying!"

Troi and T.J. came in at that moment and asked what was going on. Angel told them what happened with Kelly. Troi sat down on the bed next to Angel and rubbed her back. "First of all, stop trippin' over that boy, and second of all, Kelly's a little more mature than most guys his age usually are-just a little- and I think that if that's where he was coming from, he would just come straight out and tell you sex is what he wants" Troi expressed.

"How the hell do either one of you know what you're talking about? It's only been a week, so you don't know him any better than I do. It's not like you've developed some great damn insight in a week" Angel said.

Tori and Teek looked at one another, then at Angel, then back at one another. "Teek, did this girl just call us stupid?"

"I think that's exactly what she did" Teek giggled.

"I see your hands moving Tiki, don't even think about hitting me with that pillow." Angel warned with a slight smile.

"OK so, you ain't crying no more" T.J. asked.

"No, I'm fine except, now I think I owe Kelly an apology. I misunderstood."

"You don't owe that boy no apology. He may not be after you like that, but don't you dare go telling him you're sorry!" Teek yelled and marched out of the room.

"What the hell was that about? Was that one of those PMS girly things y'all do?"

"Boy, shut up! Who knows what's going on with that girl? She's been up and down like that all week" Troi said.

"Maybe I should go check on her" Angel said.

"No, leave her be. Whatever it is, if she needs us, she'll say so when she's ready."

"Damn, do all of y'all change moods on a dime like that?" T.J. asked seriously.

"Sometimes, and you'd better get used to it." Angel told him.

"Awe shit, I might have to hurt one of y'all up in here" he laughed. "Anyway Angel, I'm going to tell you something and this will be the only time I put my boy on blast like this. Blood or no blood, I can't be selling him out, but I'm going to let you in on something.

You got that boy's nose wide open. I swear I ain't never seen him like this with a girl before. He spends every damn minute he can with you...I never saw him do that. And when he's not up in your face, all he talks about is you. For real cuz, Kelly can be a dog. Hell, he *has* been, but with you it's different. It's like he's all calm and shit now. That nigga is clearly into you."

Angel didn't know what to make of everything T.J. had just told her. T.J.'s cell phone rang, "Got to go!" He said and ran off.

"I bet it's some silly girl calling him" Troi laughed.

"Maybe it is. T.J had all kinds of girls in his face today."

"Or maybe, if what T.J. just said is true, Kelly done calmed down by now, and he's calling him asking, what's up with you."

"Yeah, whatever."

"Angel, don't start getting sad again."

"I'm not, but what am I supposed to do with a boy who's a dog? I'm a virgin for goodness sakes!" Angel threw her arms up in the air. Troi fell out laughing at her.

"What are you laughing at?" Angel asked, exasperated.
"You should see yourself! Girl, you're getting a little hysterical right about now. Stop it. Listen, no matter what happened, you shouldn't worry about it. You only have to be true to yourself. As long as you do that, not Kelly or anybody else can talk you into something you're not ready for."

"How did you know when you were ready with that guy Aaron?"

"I knew when I started imagining all the sexual things, I wanted to do to him." Troi smiled at the memory.

"What? You were a virgin before him, how could you be imagining anything?"

"I don't know, but I did, so I went for it." Troi said, knowing full well that Aaron hadn't been the first guy she'd been with. The others simply didn't need to know that much of her business.

"You're such a whore" Angel laughed.

"Sometimes." Troi laughed as well. "Anyway, seriously, you'll know when you're ready."

"You know what, you're right. Anyway, how is he going to get mad at me for thinking that about him when apparently, he *is* a horny ass boy?"

"Beats me. Now go wash your face, you look like crap."

"Oh, are you my mom now Troi?"

"Hell no! I just want you to come out front with us. It's still early, and it's hot as hell. Let's just sit out and have a good time. You never know, Kelly might find his way down here" Troi teased.

"Whatever!"

Troi sat there thinking that if Angel or the others knew who she really was, they might not like her so much anymore. They certainly wouldn't continue to look up to her as their leader.

Denise Coleman

CHAPTER 12

Troi was correct about Kelly calling T.J. about Angel. However, she was incorrect about him having calmed down. Not only had he not calmed down at all, he stayed away from the Kyle house for the entire week.

Angel's fifteen-year-old heart was broken. With every day that passed without a word from Kelly, her suffering deepened. Nothing her family tried to do to pull her out of her funk helped.

Teek became increasingly angry as she watched her sister hurting and by Friday, she couldn't stand another minute of her sister's blues over *'that stupid boy'* as Teek referred to him.

That morning the girls were scheduled to meet the guidance counselor at Woodrow Wilson High School where they would be attending in the fall. Due to the circumstances of their transfer there, by having missed the last two months of the previous school year, the school agreed to test them to gauge whether or not they could be placed in their proper grades.

Their transcripts and the results of the testing allowed the girls to be placed where they should be.

They returned home just before dinner time, and Teek, fed up with her sister moping around, marched right up to Kelly's house. Dre` was sitting on the porch with Rachel.

"Hey Teek, what're you doing here?"

"I'm looking for your brother, where is he?"

"He's in the house, go 'head in."

Kelly was watching the Phillies game when Teek entered. Although he'd heard her out on the porch with Dre`, he didn't bother to take his eyes off the television screen when she came in. Looking at Teek would be like looking at Angel and he couldn't handle that.

"Hey Kelly, we need to talk." Teek stated with both hands on her hips.

"I don't know what you're trying to prove but whatever it is, you need to give it up!" She said with much attitude.

"I don't know what you're talking about."

"Look boy, stop playing stupid. You've got my sister down there all sad and shit over you. Whatever she said to hurt your feelings, she didn't mean it, however you took it."

"Ain't nobody's feelings hurt!" Kelly stated with anger. Teek had hit a nerve.

"Fine! Then whatever it is, snap out of it and go talk to that girl." Teek couldn't be bothered to wait for a response. She had said what she wanted to say, and promptly left Kelly sitting there with his thoughts.

Kelly could no longer concentrate on the ball game after Teek's little visit. He was completely frustrated by Angel, or better still…the feelings he was experiencing over her. At sixteen he had never really felt such a connection with any girl.

He was usually the one affecting them. Already six feet two inches tall, Kelly had a swagger about him that kept the girls chasing after him. He was a handsome, brown skinned young man with eye lashes that women would kill to have.

Behind those lashes were dark brown eyes that seemed to bore into a person's soul. Although Kelly was kind by nature, the reaction of girls to him, coupled with living in perpetual teenaged horniness, kindness usually didn't enter into the equation.

There was a short time when Kelly would pretty much tell girls what they wanted to hear, get what he wanted and then get bored with them. With Angel it was a different story. He liked to hear her laugh. He liked the way she spoke softly to him. He liked the way she smelled. He liked the way she looked into his intense eyes without being intimidated by his stare. But mostly, he liked the way she had let him know in no uncertain terms, would he be fucking. She had balls and secretly,

Angel not being easy was what he really wanted deep down.

Ultimately, sex was always Kelly's objective, yet he had the audacity to get offended when she'd questioned his intentions. However, more than anything, Kelly was upset because for the first time in his short life, he actually loved a girl; one he hardly knew, and to confess that to her only to have her reject him, had in fact hurt his feelings.

He did, however, have a glimmer of hope. No doubt he wanted to see Angel again. It had not been as easy as he made it seem to stay away from her, but there was no way he was going to let that girl know she had him twisted over her. Since she hadn't made a move either, he thought she didn't care. However, after Teek's visit, he knew that Angel had been just as upset as he was for the past few days. Maybe he *could* get her back.

Kelly turned down the volume on the game and picked up the phone to call T.J. over to his house. As soon as T.J. walked in the door, Kelly said, "Teek just came over here and snapped out at me about Angel. She said that she's sad or upset. Is that true?"

"Yeah man, she is. What went down between y'all anyway?"
Kelly sat and gave T.J. the blow by blow of what had happened.

"Yeah, that's basically what Angel told us. So, do you really love my cousin after only a week?" T.J. asked seriously.

"Honestly, I think I do, and I swear, if you repeat that to anybody, I'm going to fuck you up T."
T.J. just laughed. "Look man, I ain't going to tell nobody, but seriously, if that's how you feel, you need to go talk to that girl. She's miserable, you're miserable, so what's the point? Grow some balls and go fix it."

"I don't know man. I mean I told a girl I *love* her! Can you believe that shit?! And even worse, she shot me down!" Kelly said in disbelief.

"Oh so, your ego got bruised? Get over it. Besides, she didn't shut you down. I think you scared her, *that's* what she reacted to."

"Scared her how?"

"Yo man, you've got to understand that my cousins have more or less been sheltered 'til now. Angel just turned fifteen, she don't know nothing about guys. All she knows is that she likes you more than she can handle, and from what I know, she's never even had a crush on anybody. Think about the stuff she's gone through lately, and then you throw something that heavy on her, how do you think she should've reacted?"

"Damn T, that was deep. I didn't know you had it in you" Kelly smirked.

"Whatever nigga, I've got to go. I told Shelly that I'd take her to a movie" T.J. announced.

"Shelly huh? That girl is feelin' your yellow ass" Kelly laughed.

"Don't hate, nigga. Anyway, seriously though, you're my boy, and that will never change but, if you fuck my cousin over, *I'll* be fucking *you* up." T.J. said and left.

Denise Coleman

CHAPTER 13

While doing their Saturday chores, Angel informed the others that she would not be joining them at the park.

"Angel, don't tell me you're not going with us because of that stupid boy" Teek said.

"Maybe."

"Are you kidding?! You let that guy make you miserable all week long and now you're going to let him keep you from having a good time today too?! You can't let him have that much control over you."

"Tiki, please shut up and finish washing those dishes so I can get them dried."

"Teek is right" Troi added. "I know you think you care for that guy, but you hardly know him, and think about this…how much does he really care for you? He's T.J.'s best friend, but not once all week has he come down here to see him. And for what, just to avoid seeing you? That doesn't seem like he cares much for you at all."

"That's right Angel, and maybe you haven't thought about it, but you may have been right when you thought he was trying to get sex. If he actually loved you, how could he stay away from you" Keisha asked.

"OK damn, would all of you shut up for a second?" Angel said as she threw the dish towel down. "I agree with everything you've said. I'm not going to let Kelly make me sad for another minute. I spoke to mommy last night and I woke up this morning thinking…I don't know anything about loving someone, well a guy anyway, and if romantic love hurts this much, then I don't want no parts of it. One thing's for sure, no guy is going to take me through any changes. Do y'all realize I've never seen my dad make my mom cry? Not once have I seen that, and there's no way that I'm going to let him do that to me." Angel stated, meaning every word she said.

"That's great Angel, so what's the real reason you're not going to the park with us?" Keisha asked as she finished sweeping up the kitchen floor.

"I'm not going because I'll get to have the house to myself finally! No offense, but I could stand to have a day alone. I've never been completely alone in this big ass family, so today I'm going to be an only child."

"Well, I think I'm offended" Teek teased.

"That's OK, you'll get over it" Angel giggled.

Just as the girls were finishing up their chores, Karen entered the kitchen to survey their progress. "Good job ladies. Now I need a favor; could one of you run down to the store and get a couple of loaves of bread?" Keisha chose to volunteer. Troi rolled her eyes and walked out.

Karen sat at the table rummaging through her purse with a look of confusion on her face.

"What's up Auntie? Give me the money so I can go."

"Uh, just a minute. I could have sworn I had a fifty wrapped up with this ten." Karen shook her head, wondering what she could have done with the missing money.

"Anyway, hurry up Keisha. I want to make sandwiches to take to the park today."

"OK Auntie."

Tim came down the stairs just as Keisha was leaving for the store.

"Hi Uncle Tim."

"Hi Keisha."

"By Uncle Tim."

"By Keisha" he laughed.

"Hi Tim." Troi said in her most seductive voice from her spot on the sofa.

"Uh, hi Troi." Tim responded. Troi smiled a wicked smile at him as if to say I've got something you want, and it worked perfectly. Tim was not mistaken in what he saw in her eyes. Troi projected a wantonness that few girls her age possessed, and Tim recognized it. He just stared at her, unsure of what to say to a girl so bold.

As he turned to walk away, he bumped into Karen.

"Oh, hey honey."

"Hey honey my ass. Why is that child calling you Tim, instead of mister or uncle?"

"It's no big deal, Karen. I'm not her uncle and she's nearly eighteen. Don't make something dramatic out of it."

"Yeah Karen, don't make a big deal out of it." Troi smirked and left the house.

Karen was stunned and furious at once.

******

Having the house to herself gave Angel a chance to breath and she enjoyed every minute of it. She spent the day writing in her journal and listening to her music. Angel would much rather write songs than sing them. Writing and playing music was what made her happiest.

Although she was young, Angel already possessed a strength and fortitude that would serve her well in the future. Once she'd made up her mind that Kelly would not be given another thought, he didn't cross her mind more than once, and even then, she shook it off immediately. As far as Angel was concerned, she was completely over Kelly. Not!

****

When everyone returned home, Angel was knocked out. Keisha immediately woke her up. "Angel, Angel, get up. I've got something to tell you "she said.

"What is it?" Angel asked, trying to shake the sleep off.

"Guess what?"

"What, damn it?! You woke me up to play guessing games?"

"Damn, you're a grouchy bitch when you wake up" Keisha laughed.

"Would you just tell me what you want to tell me Keisha!"

"Alright, alright! We saw Kelly at the park right, and when I asked him what was up, he said, nothing. So, I straight up asked him if he was missing you, and he said, no, but that was a big ass lie."

"Oh really, and how do you know that?"

"Because, as soon as I mentioned your name, his eyes changed." Keisha said while bouncing on the bed with excitement.

"His eyes changed? What does that mean? And would you stop that damn bouncing?"

"Alright, his eyes got real sad. They even got a shade darker. I swear it was weird. You know how guys always try to play shit off like don't nothing bother them, but for real you can see it written all over them? Well, that's what Kelly was doing!"

Angel didn't understand why, but she was a little excited about what Keisha had just told her. Her stomach fluttered at the thought of Kelly actually missing her. *'Awe damn, here I go again. What is this?'* She thought.

"OK Keisha, even if you're right, what am I supposed to do with that information? I'm not about to give that boy another chance to act stupid with me."

"That's just it, I don't think he will."

"Oh no, and why not?"

"Because if he's that sad about not being around you, I think that if you gave him another chance, he'll try hard to hold on to you." Keisha said, nodding her head like she had figured out something amazing.

"Well, first of all, he never had me, and second, that's ridiculous, and why do you care so much about any of this?"

"Look girl, I didn't believe any of that crap you said this morning in the kitchen. Remember, I sleep in the same room with you, and I don't know about the rest of them, but I've heard you crying yourself to sleep. I also know how quickly and deeply you fell for that guy. From what I saw today, he feels the same way about you. So, the way I see it, you might as well try to see where it goes."

"I don't think so."

"Angel, didn't you say that the first thing he told you was that he was going to marry you? Maybe that crazy shit could actually happen. If anybody's made for that marriage crap, it's you. You were born to take care of others." Keisha said as she stood to leave.

"Oh yeah, get up and get dressed. Uncle Tim is going to drop us off at the skating rink."

As Keisha exited the bedroom, Troi entered. She stuck her hand up under her shirt and pulled out a Forever 21 bag.

"What's that?" Angel asked as she got up to grab something to wear.

"It's a skirt."

"So, where'd you get money to buy a skirt?"

"Out of that bitch's pocketbook."

"You stole from Aunt Karen? What the hell is wrong with you Troi?"

"Shut up Angel. The way I see it, she owes me."

"Owes you for what?"

"For doing her damn chores, that's what."

"You don't make no sense Troi. Whatever's gotten into you, you need to stop trippin'."

"Ain't nobody trippin'."

"Sure, you are. First you cut up her clothes, now you're stealing from her. That's messed up, childish, whack ass shit…take your pick."

"Whatever. You just better not say anything."

"Of course, I won't, but for real, you need to get a grip. These people didn't do you wrong and punishing Aunt Karen won't change or help anything."

Troi ignored Angel's last statement. She placed her bag in her bottom drawer and left without another word. She knew there wasn't really anything she could say to rationalize why she focused all of her anger towards Karen. The only thing she was sure of was that, making Karen miserable made her feel better.

Angel wasn't sure of what to make of the news Keisha had just brought her. All she knew was that she more than likely was not done with Kelly. If the flutters she felt at the mention of his name were any indication, they still had a way to go with one another. The only thing she was sure of was that she would not be making a move towards him. Intuition told her that this was the best course. She was right.

When they arrived at the skating rink, Kelly was the first person she spotted on the floor, and as if he could feel her presence, his eyes caught hers. Angel quickly turned away and went to the booth to rent her skates.

The cousins found a table to claim for when they wanted a break. They all sat and put their skates on quickly. They loved to skate.

"Alright now, can y'all skate for real or do you do that too cute to sweat girl thing" T.J. asked.

"Boy, why is everything a "girl thing" with you" Troi asked.

"You know, I don't know." He answered with his finger on his chin like he was thinking hard about it.

"T.J. you're a clown, and yes, we can skate. Our moms would make all of us go skating with them every Sunday night when we were younger" Troi explained.

"They sure would…they were fiends. It was like you couldn't be in the family if you didn't skate" Keisha laughed.

"I know, right? That's the same way they act over the music thing" Teek added.

"OK T, you want to see how girls do it" Angel asked. "Let's roll man!" She said as she raced out onto the floor with the girls following and laughing all the way. They were gone before T.J. could blink. He was impressed and proud to say they were his cousins. He liked that they were athletic and out-going. He was finding out more each day that he couldn't have guessed about who they were based on outward appearance. These girls were full of life and laughter.

Angel skated by Kelly several times without giving him a glance. She found that seeing him again after their fallout didn't unnerve her like she thought it would. She also learned that night that, she was cool under pressure. In fact, she was so busy having a good time with her family, that she didn't have time to feel anything about Kelly.

Kelly on the other hand, was totally discombobulated over her presence. He stumbled so many times that he finally gave up and went and sat down. However, two seconds after he sat, there was a swarm of girls at his table. Kelly quickly decided that he could use the situation to his advantage.

He definitely noticed that Angel was ignoring him, and this was eating him up so, he figured he could do the same by giving his admirers his attention.

He made it a point to sit at the table closest to where the cousins had placed their belongings. When they took a break, Angel would have no choice but to see him with other girls. The problem with that was he had underestimated her.

When Angel rolled by, she arched her left eyebrow with that little smile that drove him nuts, and he lost his damned mind. That kid got to sweating and breathing hard, all from one simple look from that girl.

Angel, however, didn't think twice about Kelly or his little groupies. One thing he would learn about her was not to waste time trying to make her jealous. Not only would she not feed into it, Angel didn't possess a jealous bone in her body. She couldn't even comprehend that particular emotion. Whether it was because of being raised to have confidence and self- assurance and to believe that she was worthy and good, or a blessing of birth, Angel never felt the emotion of jealousy. It truly went over her head.

The girls went to get drinks from the concession stand to take back to their table and Dre` rolled up behind them and bumped into Keisha.

"Boy, what's wrong with you?! You almost made me spill my soda. When did you get here anyway?" Keisha asked.

"I've been here for a while. You just didn't notice me because you were busy skating like a maniac" Dre` laughed.

"Like a maniac? Don't hate Dre`, you wish you had skills like me" Keisha laughed.

"I don't think so girl. So, Keisha, you got mad skills on the court, and you can skate your ass off, how did you become such a tomboy?"

"You're a jerk! Keisha said and punched Dre` in the arm and skated away.

"Dre`, you really are stupid. Just because a girl is good at things that are supposedly *male* things, it doesn't make her a tomboy. And, if you insult my cousin again, I'll kick your ass myself." Angel said and skated away from him as well. Teek just sucked her teeth and rolled her eyes before she skated away.
Dre` looked at Troi and asked, "What did I say?"

"Listen you nut, you don't call girls names, most especially Keisha. She gets her feelings hurt easily and she'll kick your ass for real" Troi answered. Dre` laughed at that statement.

"I'm not joking, she'll hurt you Dre`" Troi warned.

"Come on Troi, that girl can't kick my ass."

"Keep thinking that if you want to, but you'd better not keep teasing her." Troi said and sipped her drink to relieve the sudden dryness in her mouth. She quickly became painfully aware of how close she and Dre` were standing. She licked her lips, unaware of how sensual the act was. Dre` on the other hand, noticed the gesture along with the glint in Troi's eyes and his dick jumped.

"Damn Troi" was all he could say. Troi smiled, totally aware of what that meant. However, before she could respond, or he could say anything else, a friend of Dre`'s skated up and ended the moment.

Back at the table, the cousins were laughing, talking and getting better acquainted still with T.J.

"So, T.J. what do you like to do other than skating and hanging out with those Taylor boys" Teek asked.

"Didn't I tell y'all I play football?"

"Really, I can't believe you didn't mention it before now" Teek said.

"Are you any good" Angel asked.

"I think so. I play wide receiver and safety sometimes. I broke the school's receiving record when I was a freshman." T.J. said, beaming.

"That's great. Tell us something else we don't know about you" Teek encouraged.

"I don't know, let's see…I love to sing, and I love girls" he laughed.

"No shit!" The girls laughed, all except Keisha anyway. She was sitting there stewing in her anger at Dre`'s comments. Keisha was the one who held on the most to the teasing and drama that Jackie and her friends had caused. She was extremely hurt by any remarks that would characterize her as anything other than who she truly was.

As a female athlete Keisha as well as her teammates would have to put up with people assuming that because they played sports or, because they were good at them, that they were all lesbians. Keisha started hearing comments like, butch, dyke or tomboy in junior high and she never learned how to just brush them off. She took everything to heart.

While the cousins were at their table having a good time, Kelly was sitting at his table fuming. He could not believe that Angel was having such a good time, and not even bothering to sneak a peek at him. His admirers however were getting bored with him ignoring them and pissed off that he kept staring at Angel. They all got up and left once they realized that he wasn't really interested.

Kelly eventually got so fed up with Angel not paying him any mind that he got up and went over to their table.

"Yo T, what's up? Let me holla at you for a minute." T.J. excused himself and followed Kelly back to the other table.

"What's up with you man? Why are you sitting over here like you don't know us?"

"Man, forget all that. You and Teek said that Angel was all sad and shit, but she up in here all happy and acting like she don't know me from Adam. What's up with that?" Kelly asked, openly pissed.

"I don't know man. All I can say is, those girls' moods change from one minute to the next. How you going to be mad when you were just sitting over here with a bunch of girls? Angel don't strike me as the type to play games and it's obvious that she knows how to bounce back from some shit. So, what are you going to do?"

"I'm not going to do anything. Shit, if that girl wants me, she's going to have to come to me."

"Well, I hate to break it to you, but it don't look like that's going to happen." T.J. directed Kelly's attention toward their table.

The table was now surrounded by boys, and Angel was deep in conversation with a guy who had been watching her since she'd walked in the door. Kelly was pissed even more then. Not only had Angel not given a damn about him sitting with other girls, she was smiling in some other guy's face.

"Who the fuck is that?

"I don't know him, but if you're this mad, maybe you should stop acting stupid and go talk to her damn it! To be honest, this dumb shit between you and my cousin is getting old. Get over yourself and do something about it nigga."

Kelly didn't say anything else. He got up and went over to the guy who was talking to Angel and said, "Yo nigga, you need to back up out of her face."

"What? Who the fuck are you?" The guy asked.

"I'm that nigga that's going to fuck you up if you don't back off now!" Kelly said through gritted teeth, ready to fight, skates and all. Angel stood up to put a stop to the nonsense. Everyone at the table was shocked into silence at Kelly's aggressive outburst for what appeared to be no reason at all. Angel grabbed his arm and dragged him away. She found a table in a corner at the other side of the rink.

"What's your problem?!" She yelled, more because the music seemed to be getting louder than because she was angry.

"You know what, don't even answer that. I'm going to get my shoes and I'll meet you out front." Kelly had to agree, and he too went to exchange his skates.

Once outside, Angel asked, "What the hell was that scene about?"

Kelly didn't really know how to answer that question. He too was a little surprised by his behavior. He could kick ass if he needed to, but he'd rather not be bothered. He had never been jealous before. He was usually the one walking away from a girl before she could even think about another guy. He searched his brain for an explanation to give Angel, but he drew a blank.

Noticing that an answer was not forthcoming, Angel got frustrated.

"Listen Kelly, whatever your deal is, I'm not interested. The bottom line is, you sent me on my way and no matter how I felt about that then, I'm over it now. If you're feeling some type of way, you need to speak on it, otherwise I got nothing for you. I won't be chasing you and I damn sure won't be wasting any more time stressing over you."

Kelly looked at her sideways. He didn't know what to make of that hard, soft girl. Her self- possession was something he had never seen in someone so young.

Teen girls could be silly and unsure in his experience. Angel totally threw him off his game with her little speech because, he had no doubt that she meant every word she'd said. He still couldn't speak because his thoughts were so jumbled at that point.

"OK well, if you don't have anything to say, I'm going back inside." Angel said, then turned to leave. Kelly became more agitated by the thought of her walking away from him.

"Angel, wait." He said as he took her hand. "I'm sorry. I got a little crazy in there because I couldn't stand to see you with another dude." Kelly finally confessed.

"Why Kelly? You've made it clear for the last week that you don't want to be bothered with me."

"That's not true Angel. Come sit over there on that bench with me." Kelly was prepared to go for broke. T.J.'s words played back in his mind. *"Grow some balls and talk to her."*

"Angel, I sent you away that night because, I felt like you had rejected me." *"Damn, where did that come from?"* He secretly questioned but pressed on. "That feeling is new for me, and I stayed away because I didn't know what to do with having real feelings for a girl." Kelly said sincerely, although he was mentally kicking himself for being so open with her. Angel sensed his uneasiness and said, "Kelly, I know how you guys hate to express your feelings. Hell, I know y'all probably hate to even have feelings" she smiled, "So I won't repeat what you say, but I can't deal with you trying to hide behind some ridiculous male bravado. With me, you have to say it and mean it, or keep it moving. All of that being hard and shutting off is not something that I'm going to give any of my energy to."

"What do you mean by that?"

"I mean, one of the reasons I liked you was because you seemed to be mature, but the way you've been acting is anything but. I have no idea who I'll be in the future, but I do know fifteen-year-old Angel very well, and this Angel won't be putting up with any drama of any kind.

I've already been through enough so, if you want to be my boyfriend or just my friend, learn how to step up and make it good for me. Now, while you think about that, I'm going back inside with my family." With that, Angel got up and left.

Kelly sat there shaking his head in disbelief. She can't be real, he thought. She damn sure can't be fifteen. Kelly didn't know what to do with her, but he vowed he would figure it out because, if nothing else, he was sure that he was not going to let that one go…ever.

Denise Coleman

CHAPTER 14

Kelly awoke with Angel on his mind. She had been his first thought when he woke up in the mornings and his last thought at night, every day since he'd met her.

She had him so stunned the night before, that he couldn't even go back into the skating rink. He went home and spent the rest of the night trying to figure out how to keep that girl in his life.

He had never been afraid of anything in his life before, but the thought of not having the opportunity to really get closer to Angel and to learn what made her tick, had him shook.

Kelly was more intrigued by her than ever after the previous night's confrontation. From the moment he'd met her, she set off things in him that he didn't know were there. His attraction to her was the most intense he'd ever experienced, and despite his behavior, the past week, he had a strong desire to protect her and keep her safe.

Kelly had enough sense to figure out that he had been tripping because all of those new feelings were messing up his head. He also had enough sense to figure out that whatever Angel wanted, he was going to do whatever it took to make her happy. He even admitted to himself that when he told her on the day, they'd met that he was going to marry her...he meant it.

After Sunday services and their phone calls home, the girls, except Troi who had disappeared right after they'd returned home, set about helping their aunt with dinner. Keisha was at the stove mashing potatoes when she said, "Auntie, I know you're feeding four extra mouths these days, but we haven't had to make this much food until now. What's up?"

"I know sweetie. We're having guests today."

"Oh?"

"Yes, every other Sunday, Kelly, Dre` and Rachel have dinner with us because their mother is at work all day so she can't cook for them."
Angel nearly dropped the pan of dinner rolls she was removing from the oven when she heard that news.

"Angel, are you alright?"

"Yes Ma'am. On second thought, may I speak to you for a minute?"

"Of course, you can. Let's go sit in the dining room" Karen suggested.
Once they were seated at the table, Karen asked Angel what was on her mind.

"Well, for about the last week, Kelly and I haven't been speaking."

"Oh, OK. I was wondering why he hadn't been hanging around here lately. What happened?"
Angel went on to explain everything that had transpired, including the events of the night before. Karen leaned forward and took Angel's hands into hers and said, "I have to tell you, I'm really impressed by you."

"Really, why?"

"Girl, it takes some women years to understand their worth and to not take any crap off of a man. Angel, at fifteen you already know what you want in a partner and not only that, you put it out there and refuse to settle for anything less from that boy. That takes a level of strength and courage that girls don't usually possess so early in life."

"I don't know anything about that Auntie. All I know is that I let that boy make me sad, and I decided that I won't be putting up with that. I didn't like it at all. I've been sad enough for the last few months and no matter how much I like Kelly; I refuse to allow another person to make me miserable." Angel stated emphatically.

"Good for you! Now tell me, what are you going to do when he gets here?"

"I'm going to enjoy Sunday dinner with my family, and if that boy has anything to say to me, I'll listen. He'd just better make sure he comes at me the right way."

"Well Angel, I think you're going to be just fine. You really didn't need my advice at all. It sounds like you have a handle on yourself *and* this situation. Now, let's go finish preparing dinner."

Karen remained seated for a minute after Angel got up. She was smiling to herself. She was flattered that Angel felt comfortable enough to want to share her experiences with a boy, with her. Karen was getting to know the girls individually. Their specific personalities were already beginning to shine through.

Keisha was sensitive and still unsure of who she was and would need guidance. Angel was the care giver and obviously a no-nonsense girl. Teek was the one that Karen was having a hard time getting to know. Teek, until that point was still running hot and cold and didn't share too much of herself with Karen. And Troi, although, down to earth and mature, was a piece of work who outwardly exhibited her animosity towards Karen.

Being the woman of the house, she refused to give up on trying to give Troi what she felt the girl needed. However, she wouldn't be trying for too long. If Troi kept up her bullshit, things were going to get real ugly between them.

Kelly and his siblings arrived around three, and although dinner was pleasant enough, Angel sensed that Kelly was uncomfortable being himself in her presence. Not that she was all that sure of who *"himself"* really was just yet. Nevertheless, after dinner he at least had the courage to ask her if he could speak to her alone. They went out and took their usual seat on the porch swing.

"Angel, I've thought a lot about what you said last night and all I can say is that I'm not sure of who you want me to be."

"I want you to be yourself. The thing is, if the depth of who you are is the silly boy who tried to make me jealous last night, or the boy who shuts me out over a misunderstanding, then I'm not interested."

"Why are you making this hard? I don't think I understand what you're getting at." Kelly said, clearly getting frustrated by Angel's unyielding stance.

"Alright Kelly, I'm going to tell you just like I told my Auntie earlier…

"Wait, you talked to Miss Karen about us" he interrupted.

"Yes, I did and could you not interrupt me" Angel asked. Kelly just smiled at that strange and different girl.

"Anyway, I told her that I didn't like the way I've been feeling about what's gone down between us, and that I won't allow you to make me feel that way again. I thought I'd made myself clear last night, but apparently, I didn't.

The only thing I can say to make you get it is…don't play games with me. If you feel a certain way about something, express it. If you're thinking it, say it. I can't read minds and I can't interpret feelings, so I just need you to tell me. Now, if that's too much for you then I understand."

"See, that's what I mean. You lay all that on me like you're interested, but at the same time, you tell me you can do without me. That kind of shit fucks with a dude's ego big time" Kelly snapped.

"Yes, so?"

"Yes, so? Is that all you have to say" he implored.

"Uh yeah, what else do you want me to say? I'm not responsible for your ego." Kelly looked at her like she was crazy for a few seconds then, he started laughing.

"Angel, I am sitting here getting completely frustrated by you, but you know what, I like it. You are so different from any girl I've ever known, and all I'm sure of is that I want to know you even more. But really, you need to lighten up girl."

Angel thought about what he'd said and in doing so, realized that she was giving him an unnecessarily hard time. Looking into his eyes, she had an epiphany. Angel realized that what had happened between them was not that big. The sadness she'd felt about their incident was more than likely intensified by everything else that had gone on in her life, than it was by Kelly himself. Not to mention, she didn't know anything about having a boyfriend or what to do with one.

"Kelly, I'm sorry. It just hit me that, I've been stuffing down my feelings about being here and I clung to you from the moment we met. You kept me from having to feel the pain and I guess when you sent me away, I no longer had a distraction from that, and this made things a million times worse." Angel said wisely.

"You're just now figuring all of that out?" Kelly asked with a little smile on his face.

"Boy, don't sit there looking like you had it figured out, because we both know you didn't." She smiled and plucked him on the arm.

"I know right." He laughed with her.

"So, angel, do you think we could start over and really get to know one another?"

"Sure, I think we should, but I meant what I said. You have to keep it real with me at all times."

"Well, I would say, you do the same but obviously, that's not a problem for you" he laughed.

"That's right and don't you forget it." Angel laughed along with him. Then she became serious for a moment. "So, Kelly, what do we do now?"

"I guess the only thing we can do is be a couple. I mean, we have to start there if you're going to marry me someday, which we both know you already agreed to."

"OK fool, we're a couple. Not that I know what that entails."

"Entails? Angel, please... could you just speak English?"

She laughed, "Boy, you'd better read a damn book and learn some non-hood English your damn self."
Kelly leaned in and kissed her cheek. "I really am going to marry you."

"I know" she smiled.

Denise Coleman

CHAPTER 15

The next year of the girls' lives turned out to be better than they could have anticipated. Not that they expected much at all. As it turned out, going to Woodrow Wilson was actually a far cry better than any experience they'd had back home.

Not only did the girls avoid having to deal with any drama, they actually made friends for the first time in their lives. In Camden they didn't have to deal with hateful, jealous girls. They were welcomed by their peers. Of course, a lot of that had to do with the fact that quite a few girls were being nice because they wanted an inside track to T.J.

Nevertheless, it was good for them. Some of those girls actually liked them for who they were once they'd taken the time to get to know them. All four girls jumped right back into the activities they liked and finally got to enjoy the high school experience.

The girls seemed to be blossoming despite their circumstances. Troi immersed herself in her part time job and her schoolwork. She was determined to go to Law School, and as a junior, it was important that she save every penny she could, as well as, keeping her grades as high as possible in her last two years.

She still wanted nothing to do with Karen and every chance she got, Troi gave the woman the cold shoulder. And, no matter what she had going on in her life, she still kept her mind on chasing Tim.

Shortly after school started, she made a move in his direction. The girls had gone to the mall with Karen and Troi begged off, knowing that only Tim would be home.

"Hey Tim." She said as she entered the living room.

"Hi Troi. Why didn't you go shopping with the rest of them?"

Troi turned on the sadness. She allowed tears to well up in her eyes just enough for Tim to notice. "I couldn't go shopping again. My mom already sent as much money as she could for my school clothes."

"Oh, so did you get everything you needed?" Bingo! That was the magic question. Troi wasted no time with that opening.

"As a matter of fact, I didn't. I got a couple of outfits, but I still don't have shoes and my book bag is falling apart."

"I'm sorry to hear that, Troi. Maybe you should think about getting more hours at your part time job." Tim's suggestion was not what she wanted to hear. She wanted him to foot the bill for her intended shopping spree. She changed tactics quickly. Troi plopped herself down on the arm of Tim's recliner and put her arm around his shoulder as if it were the most natural thing in the world.

"I think that's a good idea. I'll ask tomorrow." She said as she softly rubbed his shoulder.
Tim began to heat up instantly, but he didn't know if he actually wanted her to stop. He hadn't felt a woman's touch in so long that, he couldn't pull himself away from that one simple act.

"Tim, you feel tense. Let me just do your shoulders right quick." She said and jumped up and moved around to the back of his chair.
Before he could protest, Troi was working out the kinks in his neck and shoulders. As disturbed as he was, Tim still could not bring himself to end the moment.

"So, how does that feel?"

"It feels great." He said and rolled his neck to release the remaining tension.

"So Tim, if I promise to pay you back, do you think you could front me some money?" She said as she continued to massage him.

"Uh, I guess that would be OK. How much do you need?"

"About five hundred will do."

"What?! Five hundred dollars?! How are you going to pay that back?"

"It won't be a problem. I promise, as soon as I get those extra hours, I'll give you my whole check until it's paid off." Troi smiled, knowing damned well that she had no intention of paying Tim back. She leaned forward, placing her breasts on his shoulders as she hugged him from behind. Again, she said, "I promise, I'll pay you back."

"OK, I'll loan you my credit card."
Troi squealed with delight. "Thank you so much. She kissed Tim on the cheek, so close to his mouth that he felt her tongue brush the corner of his lips. His penis reacted.

Tim reached into his pocket and pulled out his wallet. He handed her the credit card quickly and said, "You're welcome."
Troi grabbed the card and ran out the front door before he changed his mind. She thought, if getting money out of Tim was that easy, she'd have him eating out of her hands in no time. She didn't plan to spend any of her own money on expenses. Every penny she earned would be saved for college.

******

During that year, Keisha lived and breathed basketball as usual, and quickly became one of the stars of the team, which made her very popular with the boys. However, her crush on Dre`, who didn't really pay her much attention, continued to grow, sometimes to the detriment of her happiness. Every time she saw him with a girl, it would send her into a funk that it sometimes took days for her to get out of.

Angel joined the dance team where she made a new friend, Whisper. The two had hit it off immediately. Upon meeting, Teek and Whisper were drawn to one another as well. The three would joke that they became friends because there weren't already enough females in the family, and they just had to have one more.

Angel and Whisper had to convince Teek to join the dance team with them because Angel was worried about her twin. Teek was still running hot and cold and other than her schoolwork, she didn't seem to be interested in anything. Angel often wondered if her sister would ever be happy. Teek would never discuss what was bothering her which in itself was odd, because she never kept anything from her twin.

By October of that year, Kelly and Angel were going strong and getting closer each day. They did everything together. It was rare that you'd see one without the other. When Angel had dance rehearsal, he was there. When Kelly had band or baseball practice, she was there.

They had become the most popular couple in school, mostly due to the fact that no matter which boy or girl tried to talk to either of them, they would let it be known that the one belonged to the other. Nothing could come between them.

T.J. and Dre` were busy with their sports and the attention they got from the girls. Neither of them was taking the girls too seriously, however. Dre`, because he was on a mission to do as many of them as he could, Troi especially by this time, and T.J. because he was a senior and couldn't wait to move out and move on to college women.

Although Dre` had a clue that Keisha was feeling him, his penis jumped every time he looked at Troi. In his mind, Keisha's crush was insignificant; something she would get over in no time. He honestly believed that their connection was nothing more than basketball and that Keisha valued their friendship more than her minor crush.

By the halfway point in the school year, Dre` and Troi 's attraction to one another had begun to intensify. So much so that, any thoughts of how Keisha or anyone else, would feel about the two of them hooking up, we're quickly dismissed.

Dre` approached Troi at her locker one day just before their lunch period. If nothing else, he was bold and would always go after what he wanted.

"What's up Troi." He asked with a smirk, believing full well that she knew what was on his mind.

"Nothing" she smiled. "I'm about to go to lunch. Why do you want to know?"

"I was just asking, damn."

"Oh, OK." She responded as she closed her locker door and spun the dial. Troi turned to face Dre` again as he nonchalantly leaned against the neighboring locker.

"So, Troi, what are you doing after school?"

"Nothing, just some homework, why?"

"Homework? It's Friday, you can save that for Sunday. You should be having fun."

"Really? What kind of fun?" She asked suspiciously.

"My kind of fun." Dre` said slyly.
Troi laughed, "I get the feeling that your kind of fun could be trouble for me."

"No, no, no. For real, I just want you to go to a movie with me" he smiled. Troi smiled in return, although she was thinking, *"A movie? That damn sure ain't what I had in mind."*

"Sure Dre`, I'll go to a movie with you." She said, knowingly. A movie was no more on his mind than it was on hers.

Later that evening, Troi slipped out of the house unnoticed. She was overly excited about the chance to finally spend time alone with Dre` without being under the watchful eyes of everyone else. She didn't want anyone questioning where she was going or who she was going with. She especially didn't want Keisha to know what was up. Troi was not in the mood for Keisha's pouting about her little schoolgirl crush.

Troi arrived at Dre`'s door just as he was coming out.

"Hey Troi, I was just about to come get you."

"Well now you don't have to."

"Right well, let's go." He said as he started walking up the street.

"Wait, where are you going?"

Dre` turned back to her. "To my boy's house so he can give us a ride."

Troi shook her head. "You were serious about that?"

"Yeah, I asked you about it earlier. What's up Troi?" He asked, just a little confused, although he secretly hoped that she would say out loud what he wasn't quite prepared to put out there himself. His ego wanted her to make the first move.

Troi didn't disappoint. She played right into his silliness.

"Look Dre`, stop trippin'. You know damn well I don't want to see some dumb ass movie."

"Oh no?"

"Don't play dumb. I see the way you look at me, and I know you see the way I look at you."

"So, what are you saying Troi?"

"Nigga! I'm saying, let's do this and forget the game playing that you're doing right now!"

"Damn, OK." Dre` said, practically jumping out of his skin. Troi was making this much easier than he'd anticipated. However, as far as he was concerned, this hook up was all her idea.

"Let's go!" He said as he took Troi's hand and led her into the house.

Kelly sat watching TV when he looked up and saw the two of them enter.

"Hey Troi." He said in a questioning tone.

"Hey Kelly." She said as if nothing was at all odd.

"So, Dre`, are you going to show me your room or what?"

Kelly nearly choked on the soda he was drinking. He sat his glass down and got up to go into the kitchen. He didn't want any part of whatever the hell was going on in that moment. He knew how Keisha felt about his brother and he knew that once this obvious liaison came out, all hell would break loose.

Denise Coleman

CHAPTER 16

Once in Dre`'s room, Troi wasted no time getting down to business. She considered herself experienced enough to take the lead. She had been dreaming and fantasizing about this moment. Troi quickly began to undress in front of Dre`, not the least bit embarrassed.

"Damn girl, you ain't fuckin' around. You're serious about this." Dre` said, grinning like a fool.

"Yeah, aren't you?"

"Uh yeah, I am. I just thought you might want to wait." He stumbled, slightly thrown off by her aggressiveness. Dre` was used to taking the lead and taking the moment a little slower. He thought that this was how all girls wanted it.

"Wait for what? Take your clothes off" she demanded.

Dre` hurriedly did as he was told. He was completely naked within seconds, his dick standing at attention. Troi stepped up to him without hesitation and kissed him deeply. She had laid low for months, waiting for this moment to happen. Every time she looked at him, her insides would quiver. In those moments, she could think of nothing other than feeling him inside of her.

She broke their connection long enough to look into his eyes. Sure, that he wouldn't back down, Troi slid down to her knees and took him into her mouth. Although she had no experience in *that* area, it didn't stop her from going for it.

For reasons she didn't know or understand, being near Dre` brought out things in her that she didn't know were there. The more he responded to her, the more she got into what she was doing.

Dre` was so overwhelmed with the pleasure she was giving him, he pulled himself away and laid her on the bed. He grabbed a condom from the nightstand and quickly slipped it on. He climbed on top of Troi quickly, and without any foreplay or working up to it, he entered her roughly and for one brief moment, Troi winced and held her breath. She relaxed, and regardless of his lack of romance and finesse, Troi was not disappointed.

There was something about the rough, aggressive way that Dre` moved in and out of her that turned her on even more. He had her worked up into a screaming frenzy in a matter of minutes. The more she screamed out her pleasure, the harder he went at her until they both exploded in unison.

Kelly was standing at the bottom of the stairs, shocked by what he was hearing.

"What the fuck is she doing up there with him" he whispered. Knowing that Keisha liked Dre` as much as she did, why would Troi do this to her cousin? He wondered. Kelly decided he wasn't going to wonder any longer. He picked up the phone and called Angel.

"Yo, you won't believe what's going on down here." He said as soon as she answered.

"What's going on?"

Kelly stepped outside onto the porch for privacy…not that Dre` or Troi would hear him considering what they were doing. Nevertheless, he whispered, "Troi is over here with my brother."

"OK, why are you whispering?"

"Oh, sorry. Anyway, what the fuck is up with your cousin?"

"What do you mean?"

"I said, she's upstairs with Dre`!"

"Doing what?" Angel asked in confusion.

"Some shit she ain't got no business doing, knowing how Keisha feels about him."

"Huh?" Angel said as she tried to process the information she was receiving. "Oh shit" realization dawned.

"Exactly!"

"What the hell?! Are you sure that's what's going on?"

"One hundred! And I ain't trying to judge your cousin, but for real Angel, that's some foul shit she's doing to Keisha."

"That's some foul shit they *both* doing to Keisha. Your brother isn't innocent" she corrected.

"Yeah, but Troi's her blood. Dre` don't owe her nothing and ain't never made no promises to her." Angel removed the phone from her ear and looked at it as if *it* were crazy.

"Whatever Kelly, I have to go." Angel hung up quickly, not wanting to argue with Kelly about Troi and Dre`, or who's more wrong in the situation.

"Damn, damn, damn, damn it!" Angel said as she stomped around in a circle; the impact of Troi's betrayal sinking in completely.

"What's wrong with you?" Teek asked as she entered the living room.

"Come up stairs with me!" Angel said and dragged Teek behind her.

"What is it?!" Teek asked, huffing and puffing as Angel closed and locked their bedroom door. She turned to face her twin. "Kelly just called me. Troi is at his house, having sex with Dre`!"

"What?" Teek squealed.

"Yup. She's down there right now in Dre`'s room."

"Are you sure that's what's up?" Teek asked in disbelief.

"Yessssss!"

"Oh my God! Keisha is going to lose it."

"I know. What are we going to do?"

"What do you mean, what are we going to do about it? We don't have anything to do with this mess." Teek said incredulously.

"Of course, we do."

"What?!"

"Teek, we don't keep secrets."

"This is not our secret to keep *or* tell, it's Troi's. If we tell Keisha, she's going to go all the way ham!"

"True, but she's going to be even more pissed if she finds out that we knew and didn't say anything" Angel reasoned.

Teek plopped down on the bed, not sure of what to do. "I am soooo not in the mood for this shit! What the hell is wrong with Troi?"

"I don't know, but I can say Troi hasn't been herself since we moved here. Oh, and by the way, I've noticed how she and Dre` have been looking at each other. I just didn't pay it any mind. I never thought that they would go this far."

"What? Looking at each other how?"

"With lust in their eyes." Angel stated flatly.

"Get the fuck out of here! Seriously?"

"Come on now Tiki, you never noticed it?"

"Hell no! Why didn't you say something to Troi when you saw it?"

"Like I said...I didn't think they would dismiss Keisha and go this far. I mean come on; would you ever believe that Troi would hurt any of us like this?"

"Awe damn. This is bad, and all over that silly ass Dre`! If we don't tell Keisha, we're betraying her, and if we do tell Keisha, we're betraying Troi."

"Yup" Angel nodded.

While the twins sat up in their room stewing over the situation, Keisha had come in and was downstairs calling Dre`'s phone. "Where the hell is this boy?" She questioned while she listened to his phone go straight to voicemail for the third time.

"Oh, forget this!" She said as she clicked the remote to turn off the TV.
As Keisha stepped out onto the porch, a strange feeling came over her. With every step she took closer to Dre`'s house, a sense of dread grew stronger. The more intense the feeling became, the faster she walked.

By the time she reached the house, she had worked up a sweat. Keisha stood at the front door trying to calm herself down. She had no idea why she was feeling the way she was, and it scared her to be experiencing such awful vibes for no apparent reason.

"Come on Keisha, pull yourself together." She told herself. She took several deep breaths and knocked.

Kelly's eyes nearly popped out of his head when he saw Keisha standing there.

"Damn, Angel didn't waste any time telling." He thought.

"Keisha!" He said a little too loudly.

"Hey Kelly, is Dre` here?" She asked tentatively.

"Uh, uh, I'm not sure." Kelly stuttered, not sure of how to handle the moment. Had it been anyone other than Angel's cousin in this messed up scenario, he would've simply said no and sent the girl away. This, however, was unfamiliar territory, which made him extremely uncomfortable.

Fortunately for him, he didn't have to say anything. At that very moment, Dre` and Troi came bouncing down the stairs like children. Their laughter caught Keisha's attention. She looked past Kelly to see who the sounds were coming from. For a brief second, Keisha was perplexed by the sight of her crush and her cousin together, but realization hit her quickly like a ton of bricks. Dre` didn't have a shirt on and Troi's always laid in place ponytail, sat crooked on her head. Her lipstick was smeared, and her clothes were disheveled.

Keisha began to hyperventilate. Kelly held her and pulled her into the house. Dre` and Troi stopped in their tracks when they say her. They had been so caught up in one another, they hadn't even noticed the door was sitting open, or Kelly and Keisha standing there watching them.

"Oh shit" Dre` whispered.

"Damn." Troi said with a slight smile on her face. Troi was more shocked by the split second of pleasure she'd felt over Keisha knowing what was up, than she was by seeing her cousin there at all. *"What the hell was that?"* She wondered to herself. Keisha was more than her cousin…she was as close to being her sister as anyone could get. There was no good reason for Troi to take any kind of pleasure in her cousin's pain, yet that's exactly how she felt for one fleeting moment.

Upon further reflection, Troi also realized that she didn't feel the least bit of regret for having sex with Dre` either. This too, had her head messed up. She knew she'd do it again every chance she got.

By the time the two of them reached the bottom of the stairs, Keisha had regained her breathing.

"How could you do this to me?! She yelled as she lunged for Troi. Before anyone could react, Keisha had Troi's crooked ponytail in a death grip and was repeatedly punching her in the face and head. Keisha had attacked her so swiftly and suddenly; Troi could not defend herself. The guys quickly grabbed Keisha and pulled her away.

"You slimy bitch" she screamed. "You know how I feel about him, and you go and fuck him behind my back?! I hate you!" Keisha snatched away from the boys and ran from the house before anyone could say a word.

She ran until she reached her bedroom where she found the twins settling down to watch a movie. As soon as they saw her tear-streaked face, they knew. Neither could utter a word for a minute. Angel finally asked, "What's wrong Keisha?" She fell into Angel's arms and spilled the entire incident through her tears and snot.

Neither twin could say anything. Certainly, there was nothing they could say in Troi's defense. They simply squeezed into the small bed with Keisha and held her until she'd cried herself to sleep.

Denise Coleman

CHAPTER 17

The next morning, Karen entered the girl's room to get them up to do their chores. Teek opened her eyes when she heard Karen open the door.

"Where's Troi?" Karen asked as she noticed the bed hadn't been slept in.

"I don't know. Maybe she's in the bathroom." Teek answered loud enough to rouse Angel and Keisha. She was not going to deal with Karen by herself.

"She's not in the bathroom. She's not in this house at all, now tell me where she is."
Keisha was alert by then and remembering the events of the previous night.

"That bitch is up the street having sex with Dre`."

"What?" Karen blinked rapidly and shook her head as if she was having trouble hearing. "She's what?" She asked again.

"You heard me Auntie…she's up the street having sex with Dre`." Keisha repeated with a tinge of venom in her tone.

"Oh my God!" Karen yelled as she ran out of the girl's room to go find Tim.

"Keisha, why'd you do that" Angel asked.

"Because I felt like it. I'm not covering for that ho."

"Ho? Damn girl, that's a little harsh don't you think" Teek said.

"Fuck no!" Keisha responded, trying to use anger to ward off the sadness that was quickly fighting through. Unfortunately, it didn't work. She broke down into tears immediately. "How could she do this to me? She's my cousin. Why would she want to hurt me? I haven't done anything to her to deserve this."

"Awe Keisha, we know that." Angel said, trying once again to calm Keisha's sobs.

The girls then heard Karen yelling like a lunatic.

"Troi's home." Teek remarked sarcastically.

"Good." Keisha said and jumped out of the bed at a dead run. The twins followed suit, knowing full well that Keisha was in attack mode again.

Karen was yelling at Troi while Tim was trying to calm her down. T.J. had come down as well, to see what the commotion was about. Keisha ran past T.J., Tim and Karen and punched Troi in the face.

This time Troi saw her coming and was prepared for the attack she knew was coming. She began throwing punches as well. They were in an all-out brawl right there in the middle of the living room. T.J. and Tim broke the two up before any real damage was done.

"You slimy ass whore" Keisha yelled.

"Fuck you!" Troi yelled in return. "That boy ain't thinking about you! I'm the one he wants, so get over it."

The others gasped at Troi's harshness and total disregard for Keisha's feelings.

"OK Troi, that's enough." Tim said as he held her in his grip.

"For real Troi, it's bad enough that you did Dre`, why do you have to be cruel on top of it" Teek asked.

"Shut up Teek!" Troi screamed and snatched away from Tim. She walked past the family with her head held high, displaying confidence and arrogance that she didn't really feel.

Once she was in her room, behind closed doors, Troi collapsed on her bed and began to cry. As attracted as she may have been to Dre`, deep down inside, she knew how Keisha felt about the guy.

What was even more upsetting was the fact that, although she loved her cousin, after only one night with Dre`, Troi was not willing to let him go.

Over the next few weeks, the tension in the family had become all consuming. Keisha refused to share a room with Troi and had taken to sleeping on the sofa. Tim had banned Dre` from the house and grounded

Troi, who for the first week had managed to sneak out of the house every night to go climb into Dre`'s bed.

Tim only figured out what was going on when he got up one night to get a drink. He was in the kitchen when he heard the front door creaking as it opened. He was standing in the dining room doorway, watching her, by the time she'd closed the door and locked it.

"Where the hell have you been?"
Troi nearly jumped out of her shoes when she heard Tim's voice.

"Uh, uh, uh", she stammered.

"Uh,uh,uh, my ass! You must think this is some kind of joke. Get your ass upstairs now!"

"But Tim, I hadn't done anything to be grounded for in the first place!"

"I can't have you running around here acting like the rules don't matter."

"Come on now, we both know the rules don't really matter to you Tim."

"What the hell are you talking about?"

"Listen, I've seen the way you look at me, and just to be clear…I know exactly what those looks mean." Tim stood perfectly still, not quite sure of how to respond to Troi's allegations. She slid a little closer to him and continued, "Let's make a deal. If you forget about this stupid grounding, I won't tell your wife how much you want me."
Tim chuckled nervously, "What do you mean, I want you? I'm sure you're mistaken about what you think you've seen."

"No, I'm not mistaken at all. Do you honestly think I haven't noticed how hard your dick gets every time I come near you? Something like it's doing right now." She said as she reached down a grabbed Tim's piece.

"Let me go." Tim said through gritted teeth.

"Why? We both know that you like it when I touch you, but if you let me be, I'll make a deal with you. Either I'll leave you alone as well, or I'll keep touching you as much as you want." Before Tim could formulate a response, Troi kissed him. Not the bullshit kisses on the cheek she'd been giving him, but a kiss so deep and penetrating, Tim couldn't resist. He grabbed her by the arms and roughly pulled her closer as he returned the same passion that she was giving. After a long moment, Troi broke their connection.

"So, what's it going to be Tim?"
He stood there staring at her with glazed eyes. Troi had set him completely on fire; something his wife hadn't done in years. Tim totally forgot himself *and* his reality. He grabbed Troi and kissed her more passionately than he had moments earlier.

There was no doubt in her mind that Tim was giving her an answer. Hell no, she wasn't grounded! Hell yes, he wanted her to keep touching him!
Again, Troi broke their connection. "Whatever you want Tim, but for now I'm tired, I have to go to bed."

Keisha remained perfectly still, under the covers, listening to the entire exchange. She refused to even breath…dumbfounded by what she'd just heard. Who the hell was *this* Troi, she wondered because, this version of her cousin was an out and out stranger.

Once the shock of Tim and Troi's exchange wore off, Keisha began contemplating how she could use the information to her advantage. She fully intended to rip Troi's world apart.

As she thought further, it hit her that her Uncle Tim was a slime. Keisha simply could not fathom what it was about Troi that a family man like Tim would jeopardize everything for her.

The one other thing that stuck out to Keisha was that, during the entire conversation, Troi never once said she'd stay away from Dre`.

It became clear to her that whatever was between Troi and Dre`, it wasn't going to end any time soon, and regardless of Troi's bizarre liaison with Tim, there wasn't anything she could do about that.

CHAPTER 18

For the first time in weeks, Keisha began to look at the situation with Dre` and her cousin differently. Initially, she'd spent all day and night feeling sorry for herself. However, she now needed answers, especially after hearing Troi and Tim. She was determined to get them.

On Saturday morning, she was up early, getting dressed for basketball practice. She knew that Dre` also had practice and she wasn't going to allow him to duck her, which is what he had done for the last two weeks.

Keisha slipped out of her own practice early and went to take her shower. By the time she was dressed, the boy's practice had ended. Keisha grabbed her things and planted herself outside the boy's locker room and waited. The second she saw Dre`, Keisha stepped up to him.

"What's up Dre`?" She asked with a shaky voice. Just the sight of him had her on the verge of tears.

"Um, hey Keisha, what's up?" He was shocked to see her there. Although he knew she'd been looking for him, he had begun to think, hope, that she had given up.

"Maybe you should tell me." She said with much less courage than she tried to exhibit.

"What do you mean?"

"You know exactly what I mean, asshole! Why the fuck would you do my cousin? You know how I feel about you."

Dre` hesitated before he spoke. He needed a moment to get his thoughts together.

"Look Keisha, it wasn't to hurt you. It's just that, I'm more attracted to Troi."

With that one sentence, her world fell apart again. As hard as she tried, she couldn't prevent the tears from falling.

"Oh Keisha, don't cry." Dre` said and pulled her close. "It's not that I don't think you're the shit yourself, it's just that, I look at you as a friend. Almost like one of the guys, maybe. I don't know. I just couldn't see you with me."

"Really, but you could see you with Troi" she sniffled.

"Well, yeah. I mean, Troi ain't looking for nothing I'm not willing to give."

"I don't get it."

"Keisha, you're a good girl. Troi is older and not so emotional about these things. You want a boyfriend. I'm not that dude and Troi don't give a damn about that kind of shit. She's just looking for a good time, no strings, just like I am."

Keisha stepped back and looked into Dre`'s eyes. "So basically, you're telling me that Troi is just some free pussy to you."

"Well, I wouldn't exactly put it like that." Dre` said, a little surprised by Keisha's bluntness.

"Oh please, there is no other way to put it. You want to smash with no obligation and my dumb ass cousin is letting you. Peace."

She might have felt a little sorry for Troi had she not been so angry with her. Keisha walked away from him with a smile on her face. She may not have gotten the answers she wanted, but she did get the truth. Dre` was a self-serving dog and there was nothing she could do to change that.

If only she had enough sense to realize sooner, that she had probably dodged a bullet by not getting involved him, she may have saved herself the heartache.

Keisha arrived home hoping to see Troi. She knew without a doubt, considering Troi's behavior, that she was interested in Dre` for more than just sex. Troi's actions and willingness to remain in the hot seat with Tim was proof that she had developed feelings for Dre`, and Keisha couldn't wait to throw in her face that he was just using her.

Troi was sitting on the sofa, not even bothering to pretend to be doing any chores when Keisha got into the house. Troi looked up, half expecting Keisha to hit her again, but when she noticed the smile on Keisha's face, she relaxed a little. However, after a moment's thought, to see Keisha smiling at all, especially at her, was extremely odd.

"Why are you grinning like that?"
Keisha placed her hands on her hips. "I just talked to Dre`."

"So." Troi said with disinterest, although she felt intense jealousy and anger. She was worried that Keisha may have any opportunity whatsoever to regain Dre`'s attention.

"So, I asked him why he chose you over me and he said, because you're an easy piece of ass that he doesn't have to take seriously" Keisha smirked. She didn't bother to wait for a response. The look of shock on Troi's face was satisfaction enough. Keisha laughed and walked off toward the kitchen.

Troi was stunned. Keisha was telling the truth and she knew it. Even if Dre` didn't want Keisha, he didn't really want her either. He'd said those words…otherwise Keisha wouldn't have taken so much pleasure in telling her. If she were lying, Troi would've known.

She began shaking uncontrollably. Troi had grown to care a great deal for Dre` in a very short time. Just the thought of him not really giving a damn about her, made Troi's stomach turn. *How could I have been so stupid?"* She wondered. "That son of a bitch!" She yelled and bolted to the front door. Troi took the steps two at a time and raced up the street.

Her vision was distorted by the tears streaming down her face. She didn't see Kelly, who was leaving his house, until she ran into him.

"Troi, what's wrong?" He asked when he took note of her obvious distress.

"Where's Dre`'s sorry ass?"
"He just went in the house. What's up?"

"None of your damn business!" She snatched away from Kelly and ran into the house. Dre` was just coming from the kitchen when she entered.

"You sorry ass sack of shit! So, you're just fucking me, huh? I'm an easy piece of ass? Really, that's what this is to you?!"

Dre` was stuck for a brief moment. Troi's words confused him until he'd absorbed what she was actually saying. Then it hit him…Keisha had apparently twisted his words to make them seem ugly in a way he hadn't intended.

"That's not what I said." He stated flatly.

"Oh really? Keisha was too happy to share that fucked up news. If it wasn't true, she wouldn't have bothered!"

"Are you sure about that?" Dre` asked and reached for her. She snatched away and sat down in the armchair. She held her head in her hands as she continued to cry. Dre` couldn't believe his eyes. He had no idea that Troi cared enough about him to be upset by anything Keisha said. He thought that she viewed the situation as casually as he did. This new revelation both confused and intrigued him. However, his dominant thought was *"I can't be bothered with this emotional shit."*

"Come on Troi don't cry. I can't deal with the tears."

Dre` was taken aback by Troi's behavior. He quickly became annoyed. As much as he liked her, he didn't have any desire for a serious relationship with Troi or anyone else.

"Alright Troi, we need to talk right quick. All I said to Keisha was that we aren't together. At least that's all I meant. I care for you as a friend, but I'm not looking for a girlfriend right now. I thought you could handle this for what it is, but if not, I'm done."

"What?" Troi looked at him bug-eyed.

"Don't play dumb Troi. You know this was just sex. I never made any promises to you. Like I said, I thought you were good with that, and if you're not, we have to end it."

Troi was pissed. Dre`'s cold and callous delivery of his truth was just another kick in the gut. Learning that he only wanted sex was the one thing she didn't want to hear when she'd stormed down there. Regardless of how or why it began, her desires had changed. For Dre` to tell her these things with no feeling, care or concern, enraged her.

"You fucked up son of a bitch!" Troi yelled as she jumped from her seat and lunged at him. She had her hands wrapped around his neck before he could stop her.

"Troi, stop it damn it!" Dre` seethed as he ripped Troi's hands away. She then dug her nails into his face. Again, he ripped her hands away removing tiny pieces of his skin in the process.

His cheeks felt inflamed. He touched his face and felt the warmth of blood oozing from him. When he looked down and saw his blood stained fingertips, he snapped. "You crazy bitch! Get the fuck out of my house!"

The timber and rage in his voice had Troi taking a step backwards. She stared at him in disbelief, tears streaming down her face rapidly.

"But I…" she stammered.

"But nothing! Get out!"

"You know what, go to hell Dre`! I'm fucking Tim anyway! I don't need you!"

Troi exited the house, shocked by the unexpected turn of events in her life. Just a few hours earlier, she was daydreaming about Dre` and their future, to her complete surprise. She had never thought of any guy in that way, and now it was over.

She stopped and sat on a random step and considered her options. Should she try to convince Dre` that she could remove all emotion from the equation, or should she just step up her game with Tim and see where that would take her? The bigger questions were, could she truly be unemotional, no strings, with Dre`, and would Tim go so far as to become her substitute lover? The hell if she knew the answers to any of it. For the moment, she just wanted to go home and be alone. As she walked, her tears began to fall again. This tripped her out. She was actually, really feeling Dre`.

Dre` was still standing in the spot Troi had left him in. "What the fuck did she just say? She's fucking Tim? Does that mean T.J. or, Mr. Tim? What the fuck?!" The only thing Dre` knew for sure was that he didn't give a damn which one she was talking about. As long as she left him alone without all that drama, he was cool.

Denise Coleman

CHAPTER 19

Troi returned home hoping to avoid her cousins, especially Keisha. However, she wasn't so lucky. The girls were sitting on the porch with T.J and Kelly, discussing what they were going to do with their Saturday, when she walked up. She tried to quickly wipe the tears from her face, but it was too late. Keisha had spotted her and noticed her distress.

"Look at this bitch" Keisha mumbled.

The others looked up to see Troi hesitantly approaching.

"What's wrong with you" Angel asked.

Troi couldn't bring herself to answer. She ran past the group and into the house as quickly as her legs would carry her.

Noting everyone's confusion, Keisha decided to fill them in on what she knew... part of it anyway. Kelly followed with her behavior towards him. Angel was pissed.

"Your brother ain't shit! I should go down there and kick his ass."

"Stop trippin' Angel. It's not that bad. My brother is who he is."

"And that makes it OK? You can't be serious."

"No, it's not OK, but I'm sure he didn't lie to her about where he was coming from."

"Go 'head with that bullshit dude. Your brother's a fuckin' dog and you know it" T.J. interjected.

"Maybe he is but, like I said, Troi had to know what she was getting into. That nigga's ways ain't no secret."

T.J. and the girls considered Kelly's words. They had all witnessed Dre`'s actions with other girls by then...not to mention the way he had chosen between the cousins.

"Alright, we get it. Dre` *ain't* shit when it comes to females, but what he did to Troi is still fucked up" T.J. asserted.

"Oh please, that bitch got what she deserved." Keisha said coldly.

"Wow Keisha, you could cut the girl a break. She's still your cousin and she's hurting right now." Angel stated, ever the empathetic cousin.

"Get out of here with that Angel. You can't possibly expect me to feel sorry for her after how she betrayed me. Where they do that dumb shit at, cause is sure as hell ain't happening here. Besides, sleeping with Dre` is not the only fucked up stuff she's doing." Not wanting to get into an argument with Keisha over Troi, Angel shut her mouth.

After Keisha's last statement, no one else had anything more to say on the subject. None of them knew what to do with the craziness that had gone on for the past several weeks anyway.

Angel decided that she would at least check on Troi regardless of the other's disinterest. She found Troi sitting out in the back yard, still in tears. She sat doubled over in a lawn chair shivering from the autumn breeze.

"Troi, maybe you should come in the house. It's getting cold out here."

"What's wrong with me?"

"What do you mean? There's nothing wrong with you." Angel rubbed her arm.

"Of course, there is." How could I be so stupid? I've never let anyone play me like that, and never thought I would. I'm always the one in control of these situations. I usually get what I want and keep it moving."

"What situations? How many boys have you been with?"

"Well, Dre` wasn't the first, but I mean in every situation period." Troi said with a humorless laugh. Angel was shocked and disturbed by this admission. She thought she knew all there was to know about her cousin, but, as she really thought about it, there would be times that Troi had disappeared in the past and not bothered to share what she was into.

Angel also had to admit to herself that, Troi had often exhibited small moments of being all about herself, but they'd all let them slide because it was Troi, their leader.

Troi laughed that laugh again when she saw the look of astonishment on Angel's face.

"Oh Angel, don't be so naïve. Let's just say, I wasn't an innocent before we came here. I simply chose to keep some of my business to myself. I don't have to tell y'all everything."

"Of course, you don't. I'm just surprised you were able to keep the big stuff to yourself, that's all. Anyway, what did you mean when you asked what's wrong with you?"
Troi sat up and rubbed the remaining tears from her eyes.

"Well first, I mean this shit with Dre`. Like I said, he wasn't the first, and I wasn't even attracted to him when we first got here. But somehow I go from not thinking anything about him, to wanting him so bad I couldn't help myself."

"Obviously."

"Can I finish?" Troi rolled her eyes. Angel nodded. "Anyway, after one night with that ass, he's all I can think about? That makes no sense to me. I actually want him to be mine. I mean the sex wasn't even that great. Trust, the others were better, yet he's all I can think about? Really? Then I continue even after learning how much Keisha really *does* like him."

"Wait, you mean you didn't already know that before she kicked your ass?"

"No, I didn't. It was just a crush that didn't mean anything in the grown-up world. To me a crush is child's play; something that fades in like five seconds. Besides, it was clear that Dre` wasn't checkin' for her. So, I just figured she'd move on to the next thing like she always does. You know how she can't stay focused on anything other than basketball for more than a minute."

"Wait, did you say others, as in several?"

"Let that go right now Angel" Troi warned.

"Alright, so what do you plan to do to fix this?"

"How can I fix this? He doesn't want me the way I want him. He was just screwing me."

"Damn Troi, I'm not talking about that simple ass Dre`! What are you going to do about Keisha...she's practically your *sister*? You two were as close as me and Teek."

"Please, I can't deal with Keisha's issues right now. I'm hurting here. I'm only concerned with my own shit at the moment."

Angel could not believe her ears. This self-absorbed Troi was not the cousin she knew, and she didn't know how to deal with that. There was nothing she could say, therefore, she got up and left Troi to herself.

Troi continued to sit out in the cold trying to figure out what to do next. Although it was uncharacteristic of her, she decided to do her best to let go of her feelings for Dre`. She also decided that for the next few weeks, she'd steer clear of Keisha as much as possible. She had to deal with her own heartache. Keisha's feelings didn't matter to her at the time being.

She felt a little better knowing that in just a few weeks they would be getting out of Camden for a few days.

******

During that year, the cousins got to go home for Thanksgiving, Christmas and Easter vacation. They also got to spend the first half of the summer there as well. Teek and Angel had finally adjusted to the changes and were happy to have both sides of their family in their lives. Troi and Keisha however, felt differently. Neither of them had really gotten over Dre` completely during their time away. They certainly hadn't resolved anything between them.

Troi couldn't bring herself to try and Keisha made it clear that she didn't want to hear anything from

Troi anyway. The biggest issue would be the four of them living in the same room again amidst the tension between the two, which had become palpable. The time spent apart hadn't helped to ease the resentment and anger between them.

Denise Coleman

CHAPTER 20

The cousins arrived back in Camden from their summer visit back home, two days after the twins' sixteenth birthday. Although Troi and Teek had to go through the emotional transition again, they were happy to be back. Teek was anyway. Troi's feelings about Karen and being away from her mom hadn't changed. Her only relief was that she'd get to see Dre` again, no matter how much it hurt, and she could hopefully use Tim to help ease the pain.

Keisha was looking forward to school starting again. She missed basketball. It was the only thing that kept her from being a complete emotional wreck during their first year.

Angel on the other hand, had missed Kelly so much that she was more thrilled than any of them to be back in Jersey.

As soon as they'd gotten to the house, Angel ran up to put her things away so she could go running up the street to see Kelly. However, by the time she got back downstairs, he was on the porch waiting for her. Keisha followed Angel out the door, still holding a little hope that Dre` might be with his brother and possibly see her differently. She'd secretly fantasized about him coming to his senses and declaring that he couldn't live without her.

She couldn't hide her disappointment that Dre` wasn't there as well. "Where's your brother" she asked.

"He and T went up to the park. You know it's Saturday and they live for that shit up there."

"Oh yeah, I wasn't even thinking about that. Thanks Kelly. I'm going to see if Teek wants to go up there with me." She told Angel and went back in to get her cousin.

Angel had stood there waiting patiently for Keisha to leave them. She smiled, "Hi Kelly."

"Hi Angel." He smiled in return, and in two seconds flat, they were in each other's arms. They were each holding on so tightly, you would've thought that they had been away from one another for years. After a few moments, Kelly released her just long enough to look at her face.

"What are you staring at" she asked.

"Nothing, I just wanted to see if you've changed at all."

"Kelly, how much could I have changed in six weeks?"

"I don't know but, you do look different to me."

"Really, how do I look different?"

"I don't know that either but trust me… there's something."

There was something alright. Keisha and the twins had gone through a physical transition that summer. Their bodies had started filling out in places that the guys loved and developing those womanly curves that Troi already had being eighteen.

"Whatever you say Kelly, come sit down with me." The two of them sat on what had become *their* porch swing in the last year. Even in the dead of winter, those two could be found huddled up together on that swing.

"Happy belated birthday." Kelly said and kissed her as soon as they were seated. Angel wanted to say thank you, but she couldn't. She was too caught up in the kisses she had been missing for that last six weeks.

Kelly had spent their time apart fantasizing about her. Before Angel, he had been getting sex on a regular basis. He never had to wait for it, and although he didn't pressure her or try to rush into anything, it was getting harder and harder for him to hold out.

What Kelly didn't know was that Angel had spent the majority of her time away thinking about taking their relationship future. Angel knew she loved him, and she also knew that without a doubt, that he loved her too.

She was the one person that Kelly would share everything with: his hopes and dreams and, his fears and worries. At seventeen, Kelly had a lot of responsibilities. He was taking care of home for his mom, as well as working part time to help her out. Kelly also tried to keep his grades up and keep his place on the baseball team.

He barely had a minute to breathe most days. Only Angel knew of the pressure he felt to hold things together. Only she knew of the nights his mother cried herself to sleep because she was lonely and constantly worried about her finances. He told Angel *everything*.

While most people believed that Kelly wanted to be a professional baseball player because he loved the game, Angel knew that he wanted to be an R&B singer. Kelly, T.J. and Dre` would enter every talent contest they could find in the past couple of years, and once they'd found out that the girls sang, they'd gotten them to enter a few as well. However, everyone thought Kelly did it just for fun like they did. Angel knew that singing meant more than anything to him.

"So Kelly, what have you been doing all summer?"

He sheepishly said, "I was thinking about you."

"Oh yeah, were they good thoughts?"

"Of course, they were. I don't think I could have a bad thought about you. Do you want to know what the best part of my summer was?"

"Sure."

"It was talking to you on the phone. Before I met you, I liked how my life was going, mostly, but since I've met you, I get bored when you're not around. Except for music, not much else excites me these days. Seriously, when you were away, part of me was gone too" Kelly confessed.

Angel looked at him with total understanding because she too had experienced those same feelings.

"Kelly, when I met you last summer, you were not the kind of guy who would say these things to a girl, but now, you just spill your guts at the drop of a hat" she laughed.

"I know right? For real, sometimes I get so pissed off at myself for that. I don't know, it's like you have some kind of mind control over me or something" he laughed.

"Boy, that's not it. I know exactly what makes you talk" she stated.

"Oh, really and what's that?"

"Let me enlighten you right quick. You tell me all the things guys really feel, which by the way, are the things girls really want to hear, because deep down inside you know you're safe with me." Angel stated seriously. Kelly sat for a minute with her words rolling around in his head.

"I think you're right. Do you remember that night at the skating rink when you told me that you would never repeat anything I say?" Angel nodded yes. "Well, for some reason, I believed you. I hardly knew you, but I trusted your word. Besides, it's kind of hard to be with someone as open as you are and be secretive and shut down about my own shit."

Angel didn't really have anything more to say. She just sat there staring into his eyes. She couldn't help it, but the more she opened herself to him, the more caught up in him she became. In just a matter of a year, Angel had gone from being a girl who never had more than a minor crush on a boy, to a young woman who was deeply in love with a man whom she couldn't imagine her life without.

"Oh, guess what" Angel asked.

"What?"

"We finally got cell phones the other day. She grinned and whipped it out to show him. "Now we can call home as much as we want, and I can talk to you at night as much as I want."

Kelly laughed, "Guess what? I broke down and got one too."

"Get out of here!" She slapped his arm.

"Yeah, I had to. It's ridiculous to be walking around, the only guy in the city without a phone. Shit, the plan is basic, and I can pay the bill myself and still help my mom out." They exchanged numbers and went back to chilling."

While Angel and Kelly were still sitting on the swing, boo loving, the girls came out, ready to go to the park.

"Are y'all coming to park with us" Teek asked.

"No, I'd rather just stay here. It's too hot to be sitting out in the sun" Angel replied.

"OK, suite yourself, we're out of here." Keisha said, but Teek gave her that *"You're following that stupid boy"* look.

Once the girls had started walking up the street, Angel asked, "What are you doing later Kelly?"

"Nothing, really. Rachel is spending the night at Tiffany's house, so I don't have to watch her. Why, what's up?"

"I just want to spend some time with you, just the two of us. Is that alright?" Angel asked feeling a little apprehensive about Kelly's response. It didn't occur to her that she shouldn't be nervous, and that only she knew what was on her mind. Kelly couldn't have a clue as to what was going on in her head.

"That sounds good to me. You can come with me to walk Rachel around to Tiff's" he smiled.

In that moment Angel's nerves began to get the better of her. She hadn't even broached the subject of sex with Kelly, but she was already feeling the nerves of anticipation.

"Kelly, I'm really tired. I've been up since four this morning. Do you mind if I go in and take a nap?"

"No, go ahead and I'll see you later." He kissed her cheek.

Angel waited until he had gone then she went running into the house like a damned fool.

"Are the police after you or what" Karen asked.

"I just want to get some rest before the rest of them come back from the park with all of their noise making, that's all."

There was no way she was going to tell Karen that she was overly nervous and excited about what lay ahead.

"Oh, OK. Enjoy your nap sweetie."

Angel raced up the stairs and into her room. She couldn't get away from her Auntie fast enough. She was afraid that if Karen looked at her hard enough, that she would be able to see what Angel had planned.

Angel knew that this night would change her life forever, but she had no way of knowing just how much.

Denise Coleman

CHAPTER 21

The family was out in the yard cooking while Angel was in her bedroom taking special care to prepare herself for Kelly. She picked out a new yellow strapless sundress (Kelly's favorite color on her) that her mom had purchased for her just before she'd left home. She also picked out a pair of yellow sandals with four-inch heels because Kelly said he loved the way her legs looked in high heels.

After her nap, Angel had spent an hour soaking in a scented bubble bath. She thought that the longer she sat there, the more the fragrance would stay on her skin. She didn't have a clue about how silly that thinking was. She also felt the need to shave every part of her body, although she didn't know why. Angel had no idea about a lot of things having to do with sex, but so far, she thought she was doing a pretty good job of guessing.

When she had spoken to her mother about Kelly, the only thing Leigh told her was not to let any boy pressure her into doing anything she didn't want to do. Angel wanted to *do* alright. Leigh would later blame herself for dropping the ball on that one. She had no idea that such a good girl like Angel would be considering sex at sixteen.

It wasn't that she thought sixteen was too young to be thinking about it. It was more about who Angel was as a person that had Leigh believing that she had more time. Even though Angel was extremely mature, she still possessed a certain level of innocence.

Having her daughters be away for nearly a year and then only having six weeks with them didn't give Leigh the proper time to see who they were becoming.

Teek didn't do more than stay in her room most of the time. She had withdrawn more, and Leigh couldn't get through to her. Teek would simply say she was fine and happy to be home. Or, that she was thinking about the up-coming school year. Anything to keep her mom from asking too many questions because, she didn't have the answers anyway.

Angel, however, was always on the phone with Kelly or Whisper, or having fun with the rest of her siblings and cousins. They were each changing in different ways, but the biggest change for Leigh to accept was their independence. They were learning how to live without her being a constant influence in their lives.

Angel put the final touches on her makeup and sprayed herself with perfume. She checked herself out from head to toe and concluded that Kelly would be pleased. In the last year Angel had gotten to know a lot about Kelly's likes and dislikes. She even knew the small things like how he liked his peanut butter and jelly sandwiches.

Angel went down and stuck her head out the back door and told her family that she was going to eat at Kelly's house. Fortunately, no one paid attention to her. Although her mother had brought the dress for her and didn't mind the way it fit her body, Angel did not want her aunt and uncle to see just how much of her cleavage it revealed. Uncle Tim was even more overprotective than her dad, therefore there was no way in hell she would have gotten out of the house if he'd seen her in that dress.

On what Angel wanted to be the most special day of her life, she looked the part of a sexy, sophisticated woman. Tim surely would not have been able to deal with this side of Angel.

The closer she got to Kelly's house; the more nervous Angel became. By the time she'd made it to the steps of his front porch, she was walking on wobbly legs. She could barely contain herself. *"What am I doing here? Am I really ready for this?"* Angel questioned in her mind. Luckily Kelly and Rachel came out before she could allow her thoughts to go further, otherwise she may have changed her mind. However, the look on his face immediately put her mind at ease. He looked at her as if he'd never seen her before. His eyes popped out and his mouth hung open, in awe of her beauty. In that moment Kelly had lost the gift of speech. Rachel spoke instead.

"Angel, you look so pretty! I love your dress!"

"Thank you" Angel smiled.

"I want to be as pretty as you when I grow up" Rachel continued. Angel bent down and pulled the child into a hug.

"You're already the prettiest girl in this neighborhood. If you get any prettier, the girls around here will be crying the blues all of the time" Angel teased.

Rachel blushed, "I'm so glad you're my brother's girlfriend."

I'm glad too, and do you want to know why?"

"Why?"

"Because if I wasn't, I might not have met you, and you're one of my most favorite people to know." Angel stated honestly. She had grown to love Kelly's little sister and she'd come to mean almost as much to Angel as her own little sister Kya did. For Rachel, Angel was the be all and end all of teenaged girls.

Having three older brothers and a mother who couldn't be around much, Angel was the first true female influence for Rachel. She loved her mom and her mom loved her; quality time was not in the cards for them. Angel's presence helped a great deal. She would genuinely show Rachel care and concern and was never too busy with Kelly to give Rachel the attention she wanted.

By now, Kelly had regained his senses. "Angel, you look beautiful" he whispered.

"Thank you."

"Why are you dressed like that just to sit out with me?"

"Well, I just wanted to look special for you." Angel whispered as well, with a wink in her eye. She was hoping Kelly would get the point without her having to say what was on her mind, especially in front of Rachel. But, as sure as she was standing there, Kelly was a guy, and taking a hint was not his forte`. He just stood there gawking at her, unable to comprehend how his sweet young Angel had transformed into the sexy young woman who stood before him. Kelly leaned in and whispered again, "Angel, do you have something specific on your mind?"

"Yes, I do. Now, can we go drop your sister off so we can come back and talk?"

"OK, let's go!" He said and they hurried off to get rid of Rachel. He may not have known initially what she wanted but he wasn't *that* slow. He'd had enough girls to be able to recognize when one was serving it up, and Angel was definitely putting it out there.

In less than ten minutes, they had dropped Rachel off and were back at the house. Kelly escorted Angel to the sofa and went in the kitchen to get her something to drink. Once he had given her the drink, he sat beside her and said, "It's obvious what's on your mind. Are you sure you're ready for this?"

"Yes Kelly, I'm very sure." Angel responded pointedly.

"I don't understand Angel. We've never really talked about this before. The only thing you've ever said about us being together is that you'd let me know when you're ready."

"Well basically, that's exactly what I just told you."

"I know but…Kelly just shook his head. He wasn't able to finish his sentence because he was blown away by Angel's approach to their first sexual encounter. It didn't matter that she'd told him that she would let him know when she was ready, he was surprised nevertheless, because he didn't see that day coming anytime soon.

Angel slid closer to him and took his hands in hers. "I know you're a little surprised by this, but I've been thinking about it for a while now. Every time you kiss me or touch me, things happen to me…wonderful things. I have these feelings that don't go away. Or… She was having a difficult time finding the words she needed to explain herself clearly. Sensing her struggle, he rubbed her arm to encourage her. "Take your time, I'm not going anywhere."

Angel took a deep breath and continued. "Well, it's this feeling that goes down the center of my body. It's a heated, tingly sensation that leaves me feeling um, unsatisfied, I guess is the word I'm looking for. I couldn't figure it out until I was away. The reason I was feeling empty or like there was more to that feeling was because there *is* more. That hot, tingly sensation is just the beginning of what two people are meant to share and I'm ready to experience the completion of those feelings." Angel signed heavily.

Once again, Kelly was blown away by the girl's insight. She may have struggled with the words, but she knew exactly where she was at that point in her life, and she knew exactly what she wanted.

"Babe, I don't even know how to be that hard ass dude with you. Let me tell you, in the past, if a girl would tell me no, I would dismiss her and move on to the next one. In this past year, because of you, I've learned how to show care and concern. Because of you, I now understand the importance of treating a girl with respect. Shit, your ass wouldn't settle for less than that anyway" he laughed. "Anyway, because of you, I'm learning more about who I am and the kind of man I want to become. Angel, I love you, I want you, and I'll never hurt you." Kelly said while looking deep into her eyes. He loved that girl so much that he was just as nervous as she was about what was about to happen between them.

Denise Coleman

CHAPTER 22

Kelly had gone to his room ahead of her to create a romantic atmosphere. He found some candles in the kitchen and lit them around the room. He put the slow jams station on the radio and made his bed. When he called Angel upstairs, his excitement kicked into overdrive, as did hers. She couldn't convince herself not to be nervous. She was actually afraid but not quite sure why. Angel knew that she trusted Kelly and that he would take care of her, but the closer she got to that moment, the more she began to tremble. She stood there in his room; her eyes glued to the bed.

"Angel, are you alright?"

"Uh, yeah, I'm fine." Angel said while rubbing her hands together in an attempt to quiet her nerves.

"You don't seem fine, come here." Kelly took her in his arms and said, "You can change your mind if you want to. I told you, I'm not going anywhere, and I won't be mad or anything like that."

"I haven't changed my mind. It's just that I just realized that I have no idea of what to do. My mom hasn't discussed sex with us, and I never asked. The girls never really talked about it and up until recently, we didn't even have girlfriends to talk with. Wow Kelly, I really have led a very sheltered life. By now, I should know more than just the basics" she expressed.

Kelly knew for sure that he had to take the lead. He certainly didn't have a problem with that. Angel's openness and honesty had been a huge turn on for him from the day they met. Add that to the fact that his girl was standing in the middle of his bedroom looking sexy as hell and his dick got harder by the second.

"Come sit down with me Angel." She followed him to the bed where they sat on the edge. Kelly didn't feel that more words were necessary. He placed his hand on her cheek and turned her face toward him. He looked into her eyes, willing her to see how much he loved her. She saw it all in that instant. Angel sighed heavily and closed her eyes for a brief moment. There would be no turning back for her. She wanted more than anything to express her love for her guy.

"Open your eyes Angel. I want you to look at me." She did. Kelly kneeled down to the floor and slowly slid his hands down her leg to her sandal. He removed one, then the other. Heat began to envelope her immediately. He stood and pulled Angel to her feet.

"Turn around."

She did so, and he slowly unzipped her dress. It fell to the floor. His fingers grazed her back. The sensation this act created had Angel wet instantly. Kelly turned her around to face him and was completely mesmerized by her naked body.

Angel stood there in her panties and nothing else, completely exposed and vulnerable.

"Oh my, oh my, you are so beautiful." He said on the verge of actually drooling.

"Thank you." Angel sighed while fighting the tears that were about to fall. She was totally overwhelmed by the depth of her feelings and her attraction to him.

He kissed her deeply and laid her on the bed without breaking their physical connection. Angel's passion built until she was consumed by anticipation.

"Kelly, Kelly please, are you going to take your clothes off?" Angel asked breathlessly.

"Oh yeah, sure. Are you OK?"

"Yes, I'm fine."

Kelly wasted no time relieving himself of his clothing. He stood before her butt ass naked in all his young, strong glory.

Angel had never seen a man's body before, but even she recognized that Kelly was well hung. Staring at his piece elicited a moment of fear in her which, she quickly shook. Passion and pure sexual arousal took over her. Angel had no idea she was a natural sexual being, but if her reaction to Kelly's bare body was any indication, he would never be disappointed with her.

Kelly climbed back onto the bed never breaking eye contact. He took his time removing her panties. He leaned in and kissed her stomach, then began rolling his tongue around her navel, causing a tickling sensation that drove her crazy. His teasing was getting the better of her. Angel's body began dripping like a faucet. Kelly nearly lost it when he used his fingers to test her readiness. However, he knew not to rush in, so he focused his attention on her breast to keep from moving too fast. He didn't want to hurt her, and he definitely wanted her to enjoy every minute of their encounter.

Little did he know, sweet, virginal Angel was ready for the real thing by then.

"Please don't make me wait any longer" she pleaded.

"Are you sure?"

"Yes Kelly, please."

"OK." Kelly used his knee to open Angel's legs. He laid on top of her and grabbed a hold of both her hands. As the tip of his dick made contact with her body, Angel winced.

"Are you OK?" He asked, concerned.

"Yes, I just...I don't know, please just go slow." Kelly tried to enter her tightness again. Angel winced again but said, "Don't stop, I'm not afraid. I want you." Kelly tried again. This time Angel braced herself for the inevitable pain but remained still. He kept pushing gently until finally he'd broken through. Angel squeezed his hands tight and let out a small scream that she tried desperately to muffle. Kelly stayed statue still until she caught her breath. He whispered in her ear. "Do you want me to stop?"

"No, I'm fine."

Kelly kissed the tears that had rolled down her face and began to move in and out of her slowly. He had never had sex without a condom before and the feel of Angel's tight, wetness made his head spin.

After the initial shock of the pain wore off, Angel got bold and began to meet Kelly thrust for thrust.

Her pussy contracted and relaxed around him and the more she moved with him, the hotter she got. Angel's natural sexuality started taking over and she began moving faster, wanting more of what he was giving her. He began thrusting into her harder and faster. Angel wrapped her legs around his back, and he lost it. "Damn girl, you feel so good" he stuttered. Kelly's praise turned her on even more. Angel raised her knees up to her shoulders, opening herself completely to him. Then she grabbed his ass and held on for dear life. He went at her even faster and harder and, Angel loved every bit of it.

The friction of their thrusting generated a tingle in her that started at the bottom of her feet and worked its way up to her chest. She was lost in all of the new feelings her body was experiencing. Heat continued to build until that tingle became a raging pulsation that she couldn't control. Sensing her pussy contracting more, he hunched up on his knees so he could see her ecstasy happening.

Angel being the boldest girl he'd ever known opened her eyes and looked directly into his, unashamed and unembarrassed with a passion and sensuality that Kelly had never known. He couldn't hold it any longer. He thrust deeper into her and screamed at the magnitude of an orgasm that rocked his entire body.

At the very moment of Kelly's juices coating her walls, Angel contracted and exploded all over him. Kelly had to pull out at the force of her own orgasm. He was shocked by the sight of Angel's body spraying his with her own juices.

Angel laid there completely drained, trying to catch her breath. Kelly was still on his knees staring at her with his mouth hanging open. *"Oh my God, she squirts!"* Kelly screamed in his head. He couldn't move, he couldn't speak, he was stuck with that thought repeating itself over and over again.

After a few moments Angel sensed the stillness in the room. She opened her eyes and saw Kelly looking dumbfounded.

"Kelly, are you alright?"

"Huh?"

"I said, are you alright?"

He blinked several times and tried to gather himself.

"Uh, uh…" he stammered.

"Kelly, look at me please." He looked into her eyes again, this time noticing tears were building. She didn't understand his silence. "Did I do something wrong" she asked.

"No, no, definitely not. You were amazing Angel. Don't cry." He said and laid down beside her. He began stroking her cheek and asked, "Did you know your body could do that?"

"Do what?" Angel looked at him with confusion. It was then that he realized that Angel couldn't possibly know what she was capable of. She was a virgin after all. As far as she knew, her body did what any other woman's would.

"Oh, nothing really. You just really blew me away with how you responded to me." Kelly tried to cover his amazement.

"Well, does that mean you liked it?"

"Girl are you kidding?! I loved every minute of you. You have no idea how much" he beamed.

Seeing his smile relaxed Angel entirely.

"In that case, I want to do it again." She stated this with a gleam in her eye and shyness in her voice. Kelly had to laugh at the different sides of herself that Angel displayed in those few moments. She spoke those words as if she feared he might actually say no. If she only knew that young man would never tell her no, about anything.

"Hell yeah we can do it again! Are you kidding" he laughed.

Angel laughed too. "Good, because I think I really, really like sex Kelly!" She giggled loudly.

"Angel, you're a nut!"

"Takes one to like one."

Kelly quickly got serious when the thought occurred to him that going again might hurt her body.

"Angel, how do you feel?"

"I feel happy and exhilarated!" She answered honestly.

"No, I mean how do you feel down there?" he said pointing between her legs.

"Ohhh. A little sore but mostly it feels, awake!"

"Awake" he laughed. Damn, I love the hell out of you, girl."

At that very moment, Keith Sweat's Make it last forever, came on the radio. Kelly continued stroking her face and began singing along. Angel smiled like she always did when she heard his voice and joined in with him. When the song ended, Angel said, "Now that we've gotten that romantic shit out of the way, can we get to it?"

Kelly laughed 'til his eyes watered.

"Awe shit, I've unleashed a fiend." He laughed and climbed on top of her.

Denise Coleman

CHAPTER 23

Back at the house the girls were getting ready to chill and watch a movie in their room.

"Where the hell is my sister?" Teek wondered aloud.

"I know you heard her say she was going to Kelly's" Troi answered.

"Of course, I did, but it's damn near ten o'clock. She should be home by now." Teek said with an edge in her voice. She was visibly agitated by Angel's absence.

"What the hell's wrong with you" Keisha asked.

"Nothing, just put the movie on." Teek told her.

"Fine, but whatever your problem is, you better stop snapping at me. Or better yet, stop hating on your sister." Keisha said with her hand on her hip, neck rolling.

"Ain't nobody hatin'. Where'd you get that from?" Teek was clearly offended by Keisha's assessment of her mood.

"Uh, maybe I got it from that stank ass attitude you spittin'."

"Would both of y'all shut up so we can watch the movie" Troi yelled. She was already fed up with her cousins' nonsense. She continued to speak. "Tiki, if you're so bothered by Angel not being here, either go up the street and get her or get over it."

Teek decided to take Troi's advice and she got up and stormed out of the room.

"What was that about?" Troi asked Keisha.

"Bitch, don't sit there talking to me like shit is cool between us."

"Whatever" Troi sighed.

"Go to hell Troi."

"See you there Keisha."

Karen knocked as she opened the girls' door. Troi walked past her, sucked her teeth and rolled her eyes as their paths crossed.

"That girl is a piece of work." Karen said as she sat across from Keisha. When she didn't respond, Karen looked closer and noticed the look of consternation on Keisha's face.

"What are you so worried about" she asked.

"I'm concerned about Teek. She hasn't been herself since we moved here, and her fuse is getting shorter. It's been a year. Don't you think that by now she would have adjusted?"

"I guess so. Maybe it's just harder for her than the rest of you."

"I don't think so. As much time as we spend on the phone calling home, it's almost like being there. And think about it, when we were living back home Teek spent all of her time with me, Troi or Angel anyway. That hasn't changed, but she sure has. I just know it's something else." Keisha said while still chewing on her lip. Then a thought occurred to her.

"Maybe she's trippin' over some boy" Keisha suggested.

"No child...that would be you" Karen laughed. "Anyway, that girl has never mentioned a boy. If that was all it was, she would've said so." Karen went on to say.

"Oh well, whatever it is, maybe I can get Angel to get it out of her. How does that sound?" Keisha asked.

"That sounds good except for the fact that Angel's world revolves around Kelly. You've been back less than a day and she's been gone every minute of that time" Karen stated.

"Oh well, whatever. I'm tired of talking about Teek and her issues. I'm going out front with the boys." Keisha announced and got up and slid her feet back into her flip flops.

Karen laughed, "Just like I said, tripping over a boy, that would be you."

"Very funny Auntie."

Keisha left Karen alone and went down to see what the boys were up to. She stepped out onto the porch to find T.J. and Dre` cracking up with laughter at a couple who were arguing across the street.

"What's going on" she asked.

"Those two nuts are over there arguing about who cheated on who first" Dre` laughed.

"Get the hell out of here. So, they're a hot mess together, huh?"

"Must be because, she just knocked the shit out of dude" T.J. said.

"Damn, did he hit her back?"

"Nope. He just went stumbling backwards into the street" Dre` answered.

Keisha sat down next to Dre` as they watched the couple stomp off down the street, still arguing.

Keisha wasted no time trying to get close to Dre`. She still harbored a crush on him, but he didn't seem to notice, or didn't want to notice.

"So, Dre` did you miss me while I was gone?"

"Uh, sure I did. I missed all of y'all crazy asses" he chuckled.

"Boy, I didn't ask you about all of us. I asked if you missed me!" She stated heatedly.

"I guess so. I didn't really think about it Keisha."

"You know what? You really are a big ass jerk Dre`!" Keisha got up and went back into the house, slamming the screen door behind her.

"What the fuck was that about?" Dre` asked as he turned towards T.J.

"Man, don't act like you don't know that that girl's still got it bad for you, *despite* that shit you did with Troi."

"Maybe" Dre` smirked.

"Ain't no maybe about it. This shit ain't news to you, and if you're still not feeling her then tell her that. And you definitely tell her *and* Troi that you've moved on."

Dre` sat there quietly for a moment, contemplating whether or not he could be honest with the girls about the fact that he was seeing someone. To his surprise, during the time the girls had been gone, Dre` was really getting close to a new girl named Rickale and was thinking about getting serious with her. At least what he considered serious.

"Alright T. Look man, when it's about basketball, it's all good. We get along great. The conversation goes smoothly, and we laugh a lot. She's my dog but that's it" Dre` admitted.

"Then you need to tell her that."

"What, you don't think she knows that after what happened with me and Troi?"

"Obviously not. Didn't she just ask you if you missed her?" T.J. asked, looking at Dre` like he was an idiot. "And what about Rickale" he continued.

"She's easier to deal with. We may not have as much in common, but there's something about her."

"Then you better figure out how to stay away from my cousin. Tell her you don't want her so she can get on with it. Stop running game on her."

"Man, can't nobody run game on Keisha or any of them. Your cousins are different than most girls. They speak their minds; they don't back down and they don't fall for the bullshit."

"Look nigga, for real yo, if you think you can't step up, choose her, and treat her right then stay away from her."

"Stay away? What, like all of the time?" Dre` asked incredulously.

"Yeah, damn it. Like I said that girl is really feeling you. She was more upset with Troi than she was with you, and for whatever reason, she still wants you. Simple friendship isn't going to cut it, so if you can't step up, then back the fuck off" T.J. demanded.

"Go 'head with that T. How am I supposed to just stop being her friend? She'll really hate me then."

"Better that than you stringing her along."

"How is me staying her friend stringing her

along?" Dre` asked, astonished that T.J. would think that he could just walk away from Keisha completely. Regardless of what he'd done, he selfishly still wanted Keisha's friendship.

"Dre`, she can't get over that crush on you if you're always in her face. It's not fair to her if you keep hanging around her when you know how she feels, and you're not willing to reciprocate."

"Damn T, I know she's your cousin and all, but you can't tell me how to handle this. And you for damned sure can't tell me who I can be friends with."

T.J. wanted to put up a fight, but he couldn't. Instinctively he wanted to protect his cousin's feelings, but realistically, he knew that he couldn't tell Dre` what to do, and Keisha wasn't going to just let it go anyway.

"You know what man, you're right. I'm just going to mind my own business and let y'all do whatever."

"That's good 'cause, I was about to slam you" Dre` laughed.

"Yeah, I bet you believe that shit too" T.J. chuckled.

Dre` and T.J. were still sitting on the porch a few minutes later when Teek came marching up the street as if she were headed to war.

"What's up with you Teek" T.J asked.

"Don't worry about it!" She yelled as she ran into the house.

"What is with that girl" Dre` questioned.

"Who knows? Sometimes I wonder if Teek is actually crazy.

Teek stormed into the girls' room and began pacing back and forth. She was chewing on her fingernail in concentration like she was trying to figure something out.

"What's up Tiki?" Troi asked as she walked in behind her.

154

"I just caught Angel in bed with Kelly" she exclaimed.

"What?!" Troi and Keisha said in unison. Keisha jumped off of her bed where she sat fuming over Dre` blowing her off.

"No, you didn't" she said.

"Yes, I did damn it!"

"Wait a minute Teek, what do you mean, you caught her? What was she doing?" Troi asked.

"What the hell do you think she was doing" Teek screamed.

"I don't know, that's why I'm asking. Now, what exactly was she doing" Troi demanded.

Teek flopped down on Angel's bed and said, "She was sleeping when I walked in there, but they were both naked. Now, what does it sound like they had been doing?"

Teek was beyond upset over the new phase her twins' life had taken. Certainly, Teek didn't expect her sister to remain a virgin forever, but Angel taking such a major step in her life, made Teek feel a monumental disconnect from her twin somehow.

"How could she do this" Teek whined.

"Damn Tiki, you act like she did you wrong in some way." Keisha chimed in. Teek looked at Keisha like she was speaking gibberish.

"Yeah, you really do" Troi added. "Let's say that you're right and Angel did have sex…what does any of that have to do with you" Troi questioned.

"I don't know! Just leave me the fuck alone!" Teek yelled and walked out.

"I swear that girl is coming unhinged" Troi surmised.

"Yup. I wonder where she ran off to."

"Don't worry about it. Before you know it, she'll be back here stomping, pouting and slamming shit like always."

"I know she better be quiet before she wakes up Uncle Tim." Keisha added, surprised by her somewhat normal exchange with Troi. For one brief moment she'd forgotten how angry she still was with her cousin. She was not willing to allow herself to fall victim to the love she once shared with Troi. Keisha quickly got up to leave the room. She took one step and walked right into Angel who was just rushing in.

"Where's Tiki" Angel asked.

"We don't know, Miss hot ass" Keisha laughed. Angel sucked her teeth at Keisha and directed her attention to Troi.

"Where's Teek?"

"I don't know. She came in here and told us about you and Kelly, then she left. She was pissed about it too." Troi informed Angel.

"I knew she was mad."

"Well, what happened down there?" Keisha asked and sat back down and made herself comfortable, wanting to hear every detail.

"Look at you Keisha, sitting there like you're about to hear some juicy gossip. Well, you're not. I'm not giving any details. Anyway, Teek came walking up in Kelly's room and woke us up, she screamed my name so loudly. Then she started yelling something about how I could be so stupid. Then she ran out before I could even get a word out" Angel explained.

"So, what if Tiki's mad. She's been mad for the last year. Are you going to tell us about the sex or not?" Keisha asked.

"Not! Now go wherever you were going when I came in here."

"Awe fuck you Angel. Oh wait, Kelly already did that, huh?" Keisha laughed as she left to go take a shower.

"That girl…" Angel said while shaking her head. "Anyway Troi, I don't understand why Tiki is so upset. It doesn't make any sense to me."

"I know it doesn't Angel, but she's the only one who can explain it so, when she gets back, you two can talk. In the meantime, I want to know about you and Mr. Taylor."

"Mr. Taylor? I never met him. He left years ago."

Troi shook her head. "What?! I'm talking about Kelly, you damn idiot."

"Oh." Angel giggled... her mind clearly on her twin and not the subject of sex.

"So, how do you feel? Is your body hurting?"

"Not as much as I thought it would actually. But really Troi, I feel wonderful, excited, happy and free! This may sound a little strange, but for some reason, I feel more like my true self than I ever have before."

"Huh, what does that mean?" Troi asked, confused by Angel's statement.

"I can't really explain it. All I know is that's how I feel. Anyway, I don't want to talk about this anymore right now. I only want to know where my sister is." Angel said, wringing her hands in concern for her twin's emotional state.

Denise Coleman

CHAPTER 24

Teek ignored T.J. and Dre` when she'd left the
house and started walking. She had no particular
destination in mind when she'd left. She only knew that
she needed to get away. Teek herself wasn't really sure
as to why she was so upset about Angel. After all, there
was nothing wrong in what she had done.

As Teek walked, she searched her spirit for the
true cause of her unhappiness. She knew that it was not
about having to live away from home. Teek loved her
Camden family as much as she did her Chicago family,
and although no one could really tell, she had adjusted to
the change. Teek's unrest went much deeper than her
living arrangements.

She walked and walked until she found herself
at the park. She took a seat on a bench and forced herself
to dig deep. She was so tired of the sadness that had
pervaded her being, that she was willing to face her own
truths about who she was. She had been keeping her
secret for long enough; living in denial out of fear. Fear
that her family would turn away from her, or that they
would be so ashamed of her that they wouldn't love her
anymore. Teek feared being an outcast because she was
different from her sisters in the most basic way.

Finding Angel in bed with Kelly had Teek
convinced of her differences more than ever. As much as
she needed her twin, Teek questioned whether or not
Angel would understand her, and most importantly, if
she would still love her. Teek needed the closeness she
shared with Angel if she was ever going to able to be
honest, but after what she had witnessed, she felt that
Angel had somehow moved away from her.

Teek had been sitting on that bench for at least
thirty minutes when she noticed a familiar figure
walking towards her. She was relieved to see that it was
T.J. coming to sit beside her.

"What are you doing here?"

"I came looking for you. Do you know how late it is? You're lucky my parents are knocked out and can sleep through anything" he laughed.

"I didn't mean to be out so late. I guess I lost track of time" Teek apologized.

"It's no big deal, Tiki. It's just that you shouldn't be out here by yourself, and Angel is at the house losing it because you're upset."

Hearing that Angel was worried about her gave Teek a little hope that her sister would still be the same supportive twin she'd always been.

"What's wrong cuz? You've been sad sense you moved here. You've never let anyone in and you're the only cousin who's still a stranger to me."

Teek heard the sincerity in T.J,'s voice and noted the same in his eyes. She desperately needed someone to confide in, and her cousin was trying in that very moment to be that person.

"T.J. there is something I've been struggling with for a very long time. I haven't been able to talk to anyone about it, and if I don't get this out of me, I'm afraid I'm going to lose my mind." Teek expressed through tears that she could no longer keep from falling.

"OK, I know I'm a guy, but I'm your blood. You can tell me anything and I promise, no matter what it is, I got your back."

Teek decided right then and there that she would just go for it. She took a deep breath, squeezed her eyes shut and said, "I'm gay. I've never been attracted to a boy, and ever since I met Whisper, she's all I can think about." She rambled off her confession quickly and exhaled deeply when she was done. Teek waited for T.J. to say something, anything that would give her an indication that it was alright. Or, that she wasn't a freak who would be disowned. She was so terrified of what he might say, she couldn't open her eyes.

T.J. sat there stunned by Teek's revelation, not sure of what to say or how to react. Teek couldn't stand another moment of his silence. She spoke, still without opening her eyes to look at him. Fear of seeing condemnation in his eyes gripped her soul.

"T.J., please say something" Teek implored.

"I don't know what to say." T.J. turned toward her and took her by the shoulders.

"Open your eyes Tiki. Just look at me." Teek did as she was asked, however reluctant.

"I guess the only question I have is… are you sure?"

Teek smiled a bashful smile. "Yes, I am sure. For a long time, I didn't understand it, but for the last six months, it's been becoming more and more obvious to me that I'm a messed-up freak!" she began to cry again.

"Awe cuz, don't cry, and don't call yourself a freak. There's nothing wrong with you."

"Oh no?" Teek laughed sarcastically. "What would you call it then?"

"I'm not sure. How about, you're different, no, special or, unique! How about that?"

Teek giggled a little at T.J.'s attempt at levity.

"Listen Tiki, I'm not going to pretend to understand what you're going through, but I will say, I love you regardless."

"You do?"

"Of course, I do. Now, explain all of this to me." Teek took a deep breath before she could speak.

"Well, while we were growing up, I never paid boys any mind. Actually, I didn't notice girls either. Anyway, there came a time when I got older that I began to realize that I wasn't attracted to *any* guy I'd ever met, and right before we moved here, I started having these feelings whenever I looked at other girls. But, we were going through so much at the time, I sort of dismissed it or ignored it. I refused to focus on it period."

"Hold up Tiki, what kind of feelings did you get?"

Teek lowered her head in embarrassment for a second. She took another deep breath and said, "I would feel heat that would travel from the center of my chest, down to my pussy and land in my panties."

"Whoa! Damn Tiki?"

"Well, you asked. Don't get all squeamish on me now."

"I'm sorry, damn. I just wasn't expecting all that."

"Obviously! Can I finish before you start acting like a little bitch again?" Teek laughed.

"Oh so, you got jokes huh? Go ahead smart ass."

"Anyway, once we got here, I started to notice that nothing had changed. I was still not attracted to boys, but I was looking at girls more and more. That was really fucking with my head T, because I kind of knew what it meant, but I damn sure didn't want to deal with it.

But then, when me and Angel met Whisper, something grabbed a hold of me and I couldn't shake it. I started looking at her and thinking about her in ways I should've been looking at and thinking about boys. I would watch Angel and Kelly and wish that that could be me and Whisper. So, all in all, I would say yes, I'm sure about who I am. I'm not so sure if I want to be this way, but the problem with that is, there's no way in hell I can change it. I at least know that I can't be happy if I don't accept this" Teek concluded.

T.J. put his arm around her and pulled her close. Teek laid her head on his shoulder, grateful for the comfort and support.

"Cousin, I wish I could make you feel better about this, or take away, oh I don't know, your struggle I guess."

"Yeah, it's a struggle alright. Some days I think this is fine. I am who I am and the world just better deal with it. Then there are those days when I'm questioning God and why did he choose to punish me in this way."

"I don't think being gay is a punishment Tiki. We're all different in many ways, that's what makes us special. Besides, I don't think God is in the business of punishing us. He's the one who created us as we are."

"Wow T that was very profound. Who knew you could have a deep thought?" Teek said sarcastically.

"Very funny." He pretended to pout.

"Awe, I'm sorry little baby." Teek said while squeezing his cheeks.

T.J. just laughed, "You are so stupid. Now, back to the business at hand, what's next?"

"I don't know really. I mean, I want to tell the family. Well, Angel anyway, but I'm not sure of how she'll take it. If Angel can't accept this... that would kill me."

"What makes you think she won't accept it? You're twins and I don't know two people closer than you two are."

"Well mainly because, she had sex with Kelly tonight and she didn't even tell me that she was thinking about going there, let alone actually doing it. How close does that really make us T.J.?"

"She did what with who" he yelled.

"You heard me. They had sex, but seriously T, this isn't about that right now."

T.J. just shook his head while waiting for Teek to continue. He would deal with his boy later.

"Anyway, if Angel can't accept this, how can I expect the rest of the family to? At this point, they are my only concern. I can't live this life without my family."

"So, it sounds like you *are* accepting this?"

"Yeah, I guess I am. I just want to be able to breathe again. After everything that's happened in the last eighteen months, all I want is to be at peace. Battling with my reality has worn me out! I feel sixty instead of sixteen.

If I could just be free and speak it out loud to everyone, maybe I can get back to being my happy carefree self."

It seems like that's exactly what you need. I mean… to say it out loud."

"Yeah, it is. You know what's been the strangest part of all of this? I haven't once worried about what the rest of the world would think or what kind of prejudices I might have to face. My only concern has been about our family's reaction."

"Well shit, in that case, you'll be fine. If nothing else, take comfort in knowing that this family of ours loves hard and unconditionally."

"You're right. I really have lost sight of a lot by keeping this secret. I haven't been able to see much of anything clearly because I've been so stuck in my whirlwind of turmoil.

"OK so, you're not stuck anymore. Can we please go home? I'm Tired!"

"You're tired? I'm exhausted! Yes, we can go home, but you have to promise me that you won't tell anybody about this. I have to do it in my own time, in my own way."

"I promise, now let's go." T.J. said as he stood. He pulled Teek up from the bench and embraced her.

"I love you cousin and I got your back." T.J. said sincerely.

"Thanks T, for everything."

"You're welcome, but there's one more thing." He said as they started walking.

"What's that?"

"Don't be going after any of my chicks" he laughed."

"Teek laughed and punched him in the arm. "You don't have to worry about that. I've seen the kind of girls you like and believe me, they're not my type." Teek continued to laugh, feeling as if a huge weight had been lifted from her spirit.

Denise Coleman

CHAPTER 25

Troi didn't know what to do with herself her first night back. Once the drama with Angel and Teek had subsided, and the reality that Keisha still didn't want to be bothered with her, she was alone.

Her only thought was to seek out Tim. Maybe he could help her loneliness to subside. Although he'd barely acknowledged her presence on the ride from the airport, she hoped that the time apart hadn't erased any progress she'd made with him.

Tim was relaxing in his recliner, as usual, when Troi entered the living room.

"Hi Tim, what's up?"

"Just watching a little television." Tim said, while trying not to make eye contact. Truth be told, he'd missed her menacing presence in his life. Things hadn't and wouldn't get better with Karen, and although Troi was a mere eighteen years old, her minor flirtations had actually come to be a pleasant distraction for him.

While she was gone, the decent part of him knew how wrong it was for him to respond to Troi, however, having her back in his home stirred up those familiar, unwanted, sometimes wanted, feeling. Troi jumped right in.

"So, did you miss me" she asked.

"Troi, please don't start this again."

"Start what? I just asked if you thought about me at all while I was gone."
Tim took a deep breath before he spoke. He clicked the remote and turned to face her dead on.

"Listen Troi, it's really flattering that you have a crush on me but, it's not something that I'll ever act on, so, you might as well give it up."
Troi snickered at that statement. "First of all, I don't have a crush on you…that's for children, and I'm far from being a child. Second of all, I don't give up on anything. You should know that by now."

"Really Troi, I've had enough of this." He said, completely dismissing her last statement.

"Oh please." Troi didn't want to hear that shit. She slid down onto the floor, in front of his chair. She rubbed her hands up and down the length of his thighs and laid her head in his lap.

Tim's first thought was to remove her from his space, but in truth, he really liked the way she felt as she rubbed her cheek on his expanding penis.

"Seriously Tim, I don't have a crush on you, but I can tell you that I really want to see what this is all about." She said as she squeezed his penis.

"Troi stop!" Tim said although he didn't really mean it. Troi's touch had aroused him completely.

"You don't mean that" she said. "I know damn well Karen's whack ass ain't giving you what you need."

"My marriage is none of your business." He stuttered as Troi continued to massage him. She ignored his weak protest and expertly unzipped his pants to expose his penis.

"Damn!" She whispered just before she lowered her mouth and took him in. Tim's eyes rolled back in his head and closed as the pleasure of her warm mouth engulfed him. He began to slowly move in and out, loving every second of what she was giving him.

In less than a minute, she abruptly stopped. Tim's eyes popped open, "Why'd you stop?" He asked, not believing his own words. He really wanted Troi above all else in that moment. He couldn't deny that right then, all he wanted was for Troi to continue blowing him.

"Someone might come in. Let's go to the basement...no one goes down there." She took his hand and led him to the basement rec room. Once there, Tim sat on the sofa, encouraging her to finish what she had started.

Troi willingly proceeded, excited by the thrill of being in control of an actual grown man, instead of the ridiculous boys she'd known.

Tim began to moan in pleasure. It had been so long since he'd felt a woman's touch, that he couldn't control himself. Within moments, he released his semen into Troi's mouth. She slowly allowed his juice to drip down her chin and onto his dick. This simple act excited him all over again.

Still trying to catch his breath, Tim changed positions with Troi. He laid her down, then slid her dress up to her waist. Her pink lace thong briefly reminded him of how young she was, but it certainly didn't stop him. He gently pulled them off, spread her legs and buried his face between her thighs.

Troi was a bit stunned when she felt Tim's tongue touch her. This was new to her, however, the more Tim licked and sucked gently on her lips, the more she got into it. Troi's young mind was reeling from the new and strange sensations her body was experiencing. He continued at a steady pace until her body began writhing and shuddering. "Oh my God!" She screamed as her own pleasure increased.

"Please don't stop." She huffed as she started moving her hips in a circular motion to receive more pressure from Tim's tongue.

The sight, feel and taste of her turned him on even more. Tim began lapping and sucking every drop of her as if her body was the last meal he'd ever have.

Troi opened her legs wider, moved her pussy faster and grabbed Tim's head. She pushed his tongue deeper into her just as her orgasm exploded from her.

Troi laid there trying to catch her breath while Tim sat on the floor with his back against the sofa. He was both stunned and exhilarated by what had just transpired between the two of them. The one thing that stuck in his mind was that he didn't feel the least bit guilty or ashamed of his actions.

Just like him, Troi didn't feel an ounce of remorse. As far as she was concerned, she was going to do whatever she wanted with Tim, especially considering the new things he had just introduced her to. Troi didn't care about anything more than Tim lining her pockets and sticking his face between her legs whenever she wanted.

Regardless of her unexplainable feelings for Dre`, Troi was real clear about her situation with Tim. He was a married man with a now grown son. He was not her future…but a great way to pass time, forget Dre,` *and* bank coin until she got to her future.

Neither said a word as they readjusted their clothing. They simply looked at one another with silent understanding. Troi snuck back upstairs, and Tim, out the back door.

Denise Coleman

CHAPTER 26

The next day, Troi and Keisha couldn't wait for church to end so that they could get home and give Angel and Teek the third degree. Angel because of the obvious; she'd had sex, and Teek because once she'd finally gone home the night before, she went in the house laughing and joking with T.J. like nothing had ever been wrong in the first place.

The twins avoided the questions as they prepared for church, but there was no way they would be getting out of the interrogation that afternoon. Angel was still on cloud nine from the night before to the point where she didn't even bother questioning Teek about her behavior. Teek still refused to talk until she was ready anyway.

When they returned home, the cousins were grateful that there was enough food from the night before that they didn't have to help prepare Sunday dinner and could go about their business. As soon as they could, they all ran up to change their clothes. Angel wanted to hurry down to Kelly's house to see him, but the others weren't having it. They were determined to get the scoop about her first sexual encounter.

"Alright Angel, we've had enough of you avoiding what happened last night. Now, we want to know how you got to the point of having sex" Troi said.

"Yeah, and don't leave anything out" Keisha said.

"So, you two are cool now?" Angel asked of the feuding cousins.

"Hell no" Keisha said. "I just want to know what's up with you. This bitch just happens to live in the same room so…"

"I'm not going to be too many more bitches, Keisha" Troi said.

"Alright y'all, please don't start" Angel said. Teek didn't say anything. She just sat beside Keisha, staring at her sister. She was not so much concerned about the sex as she was about how Angel's feelings about her may have changed because of it. Teek still harbored the fear that her and Angel's closeness was diminishing.

"OK, OK! I don't really know what you all want me to say. The only thing I can tell you is that I love Kelly and I really wanted to get closer to him."

"And sex was the only way you could think of to accomplish that" Troi asked.

"Yes. It's what I wanted, and before you even ask, no, he didn't pressure me. Honestly, I now know what horny means, and that's how I'd been feeling for a long time."

"Oh Angel, you're a big ole whore" Keisha laughed.

"Oh Keisha, you're a hater!" Angel laughed with her.

"Whatever. All I want to know is, did it hurt" Keisha asked.

"Just a little at first. Well actually, a lot at first, but then something changed, and it was the best feeling I've ever had. My body just seemed to respond like it had been deprived of oxygen or something for my entire life." Angel said while staring off into space like she was back there in that place.

"Let me ask you something. Did you use protection?" Troi asked.

"Protection, like what?"

"Uh like condoms maybe, after all, you're not on the pill." Troi looked at Angel sideways and thought, *"This girl is not stupid. She can't be sitting here looking like she doesn't have a clue."*

"Well, no we didn't, but don't worry, everything's fine." Angel tried to reassure Troi, although it was more herself, she needed to reassure, because until the moment Troi broached the subject, Angel hadn't once thought about the consequences of unprotected sex.

169

"How can you say don't worry when you didn't use anything? Angel, you'd better pray that nothing more than sex happened last night" Troi admonished.

Teek sat and listened to the exchange and got more worried by the second. She recognized the look on Angel's face and knew immediately that she hadn't thought far enough ahead about the path she had chosen. She saw the glint of worry in Angel's eyes when Troi posed the question of protection.

"Alright, that's enough with the twenty questions" Teek said. "If she said don't worry, then don't worry."

"OK, we won't worry about Angel. Let's get on the subject you, and your stank ass behavior last night" Keisha said. "What the hell is your problem Tiki?"

"Even though it's none of your business, I'm going to tell you what I've been going through, but not until I talk to my sister first."

Keisha was tempted to make a snide remark until she saw the pleading look in Teek's eyes. Troi and Angel also noticed Teek's expression. It was one of fear and neither of them knew where it was coming from. Troi was the only one to speak.

"Do you want me and Keisha to leave you two alone?"

"Yes please. I really want to get this over and done with."

That statement had all three girls worried about what was up with Teek. Her demeanor and her tone had set them a little on edge. They each knew that Teek had been unhappy, but never had they thought that it was anything truly serious.

"Sure Tiki, we'll go. Just holler if you need us." Troi said and quickly ushered Keisha out of the room. She knew that the sooner they left, the sooner their questions about Teek's mood swings might be answered.

While the girls were in their room, T.J. was in his room, changing as well. He was determined to get out of the house and up to Kelly's as quickly as possible. T.J. was pissed that Kelly had gone so far with his cousin. He was a little irrational in his thoughts about the situation, however.

It didn't matter to him that he knew full well how much Kelly loved Angel. Nor did it matter that he believed whole heartedly that his boy would never intentionally hurt her. All that T.J. could think about was who his boy used to be, and that fact alone had him itching for a fight. He was also at the point where he was tired of all the drama between his friends and his cousins.

T.J. had changed and made it to Kelly's house in record time. He was about to knock on the door when he saw Kelly coming around the corner.

"Hey, what's up T?" Kelly asked with a big goofy grin on his face. That grin pissed T.J. off even more, because he knew that it was his, *"I just got laid"* look. T.J. ran off the porch and rushed him. Before Kelly even realized what had happened, T.J. had him pinned up against the car that was parked in from of his house. He was choking the shit out of Kelly and saying, "What the fuck is wrong with you, touching my cousin?!" Kelly tried in vain to pry T.J.'s hands from around his neck, and when that didn't work, he kneed him in the groin. T.J. doubled over in pain. That move calmed his ass down real quick. Kelly pulled himself off of the car, trying to catch his breath.

"What the fuck is your problem" Kelly sputtered.

"You nigga! Why you fucking my cousin?" He said, gasping for air.
Kelly was stunned by T.J.'s question. Not because he had found out about what he and Angel had done, but because T.J. was so upset about it. Kelly leaned down and helped his boy stand upright and led him to the steps.

"Yo man, sit down" Kelly suggested.

"No nigga! What the hell were you thinking? Angel's a good girl. You just couldn't keep your dick in your pants, could you?! You had to treat my cousin just like you do these chicks around here."

"Yo T man, your ass is way off the mark with that one. You know damned well I don't think of your cousin like that." Kelly was thoroughly insulted by T.J.'s insinuation that he would use Angel.

"Oh no? It wouldn't be the first time you used some girl for pussy."

Kelly took a deep breath before he spoke again. T.J. was his best friend, and if they didn't squash their shit right then and there, there would be no coming back from it. He also knew why T.J. was so upset. Angel was his cousin, and for both guys, family was everything.

Kelly knew that T.J. would do anything to protect those girls, but he felt that by then, T.J. should've known that he would do the same for all of them, especially Angel.

"Look T, I understand that you're pissed at me, but bro, for real, I would never use or hurt Angel. You know how I feel about her. That girl means everything to me." Kelly expressed openly without fear of sounding like a whipped punk in front of his boy.

T.J. went and sat on the steps not saying anything for a long moment. He understood that he had overreacted to the situation. He also understood that Kelly was sincere, and that he had become a very different guy since he'd met Angel. Not once had he back slid into his old ways, and for that, T.J. had been grateful. It was just the thought of knowing that Angel would be changed forever bothered T.J.

"Damn Kelly, I hear you man. I know you mean what you say about Angel, but shit, I don't know how to deal with my boy doing my cousin. Shit, she's sixteen man."

"And I'm only seventeen, so what? T.J., Angel ain't no baby, and I didn't ask or talk her into this. She came at me like that. Matter of fact, I gave her several chances to change her mind, but she wouldn't. She said she was ready to take it there and we did" Kelly explained.

"Yeah, you're right. She's not a baby, and she's pretty strong willed. By now I've learned that Angel and the rest of them are going to do whatever they want, and most definitely won't do something they don't want to do" T.J. conceded.

Kelly nodded in agreement and asked, "So, are we cool…no more of you coming down here trying to kill me?"

"Yeah man, we're cool, my bad."

"Good. Wait a minute…why didn't you go off like this on my brother? What he did was much worse."

T.J. had to take a moment to think about that question. He'd just attacked his best friend oversleeping with one of his cousins, but had barely reacted when Dre` had played two others.

"Yeah, what Dre` did was fucked up, but it didn't seem like Troi needed or wanted any protection. She's not innocent and inexperienced like Angel is. That's obvious in the way she carries herself. Besides, she hasn't really warmed up to my family like the others have. She doesn't want to be here, and she's disrespectful to my mom. I haven't made any real connection with her."

"Oh, OK, I understand. Now help me put this oil in my mom's car so she can go to work."

Back at the house, Teek and Angel sat across from one another in silence. Angel waited patiently for her sister to begin speaking. Teek however, was finding it difficult to formulate the words she needed to express herself. Although she had promised herself that she wouldn't rush her confession, she now simply wanted to have it over and done with.

Teek's nerves were so wound up that she was gnawing on her fingernails.

"Tiki, if you don't stop that, you won't have a finger left at all."

Teek quickly dropped her hand to her lap, but still didn't say anything.

"No matter what it is you want to tell me…I promise you it won't change anything between us" Angel stated.

Teek felt a glimmer of hope from her twin's words. "Are you sure, because I can't take it if I don't have you" Teek confessed.

"Of course, Teek. You're my twin. How could *I* live without *you*? Don't be afraid Tiki…just spit it out fast. Maybe that way, it won't be so hard to say" Angel encouraged.

Teek took several deep breaths, and just like the night before with T.J., she closed her eyes. "Angel, I think I'm gay. No, correction, I know I'm gay. I'm only attracted to girls." Teek said and exhaled slowly.

"Is that all?!" Angel asked with relief pouring out of her. "Girl, I thought you had something seriously wrong with you all this time. I didn't know what the heck to make out of your craziness. For a minute there I thought you might have a brain tumor or something" Angel chuckled.

Teek sat there in shock, staring at Angel as if she'd lost her mind.

"Angel, that's all you have to say?" Teek asked with confusion etched all over her face.

"What else do you want me to say girl?"

"I don't know! Maybe that you can't believe it, or that I could be going through a phase or, something more than…is that all?"

"OK, let's see then. How about, I love you no matter who you like? Or, yes, I can believe it, and no, it's not a phase because, I've seen the way you look at Whisper, so I kind of had a clue. Is that better for you Twin?" Angel asked with another chuckle.

Teek laughed a relieved laugh and threw Keisha's pillow at Angel.

"Are you kidding me? You've had this figured out and you didn't say a word to me?" Teek asked in disbelief.

"Oh please, who knows you better than me? I've always noticed all of the little differences in you, and guess what? I think mommy figured it out too. Anyway, what I didn't know was that this was the reason you've been acting like a damn nut."

"I don't know why not. Did you think it would be easy for me to face something like this?"

"Well kind of. I just figured that because you've always been so outgoing and comfortable in your own skin, that you'd be cool with your own sexuality." Angel said sincerely.

"Yeah well, that makes sense, but I wasn't. Oh shit! Did you just say mommy knows?" Teek asked in a panic once Angel's revelation about their mom sank in.

"Yup. I heard her trying to tell daddy one night, but he wasn't getting it. I also heard her on the phone with Aunt Hillie one time."

Teek stood up and started pacing the floor and chewing on her fingernails again.

"Damn Angel, I can't believe you never said anything to me about any of this."

"You never said anything either. I just thought you'd talk about it when you were ready."

"That's not what I mean. Why didn't you tell me that you *and* mommy knew? And how did she seem anyway? Do you think she was upset about it?" Teek rattled off questions.

"Calm down. She didn't seem to care either way. It was more like an acknowledgement, I guess. When she was talking to auntie, she sounded like it was no more serious than, *"Oh by the way, Teek got her ears pierced."*

Teek was shocked by Angel's words. She just sat there shaking her head like she couldn't believe how easily her mom and sister accepted who she was.

"Damn Angel, one of the biggest struggles I've had with this was how this family would react-mainly you- and you're sitting there telling me that I could have saved myself a ton of worry?"

"I guess so. Anyway, even if no one else can deal with it, you at least know me and mommy can. Hey maybe daddy will be OK with it too since now he won't have worry about no boys getting in you." Angel fell out laughing.

"You're not nearly as funny as you think you are. I bet you won't be laughing when daddy finds out about your hot ass." Teek teased and Angel's laughter dissipated.

"That's not funny Teek, and you better not tell. Daddy would have a damn stroke if he knew I let a boy have me."

"He sure would. I can see it now…Daddy would fly down here, shot gun in hand, ready to kill that boy" Teek laughed.

"Darn, poor Kelly wouldn't stand a chance against daddy."

"Speaking of Kelly, why didn't you tell me that you had been seriously thinking about sex?"

"Honestly, I'm not sure. Actually, that's not really it. I think it was more because I thought you might try to talk me out of it, and I didn't want that. Me wanting to be with Kelly started before we went home to visit, and while we were gone, my desire intensified."

"I understand, and you're right, I probably would have tried to talk you out of it, which doesn't matter because you would have done it anyway."

"That's true. So OK twin, let's make a deal. No matter how big or how small something is, we won't keep secrets from each other ever again." Angel said and stuck out her hand.

"That's a deal." Teek agreed and they shook on it.

"Now, you know Troi and Keisha can't wait to get back in here to find out what's up with your psychotic, lesbian ass." Angel fell out laughing again.

"Alright bitch, one more time…you are not as funny as you think you are!" Teek said as she jumped on Angel and smashed her face into the mattress.

"OK, OK, I give up, damn!" Angel said while trying to stifle her laughter.

"Seriously though, are you ready to tell them?"

"What choice do I really have? They know I'm in here confessing something, and there's no way I can lie or avoid them any longer. Besides, I told T.J. last night, and even though he's a guy and he has my back, he can't hold water for too long."

"Yeah, these guys around here can be worse than girls sometimes. Anyway, do you want me to call them in?"

"Sure, it's now or never." Teek stated flatly. She was not nearly as nervous as she had been before telling Angel. With her sister's support she was a little more comfortable about sharing her news with Troi and Keisha.

When Angel finally called her cousins back into the room and Teek spilled her news, Troi and Keisha's reactions were polar opposites. Troi was stunned into silence. Keisha on the other hand was quite vocal.

"Wow Tiki, girls?! Wow! Alright, alright so, Ok, damn! I don't know what to say" Keisha stumbled.

"You don't really have to say anything. I just wanted y'all to know why I've been so messed up for the past year or so. Just trying to face the truth about myself wasn't easy for me."

"But, you're too girly to be gay" Keisha said.

"Are you stupid Keisha" Angel asked.
Troi and Teek laughed. That was the first sound Troi had made since she'd come back into the room.

"I'm not stupid and stop laughing. I'm serious, Teek is the one who won't even go down to breakfast without lipstick on, and now she's saying she's attracted to other chicks. I don't get it" Keisha stated.

"I still am who I am Keisha. My sexuality doesn't have all that much to do with my personality or the things I like. I'm still me regardless of which gender I'm attracted to."

"Alright, whatever. I'm getting a headache and I don't want to talk about this anymore. Just do me a favor and don't come sniffing around any of my teammates" Keisha teased.

"Girl please, I'm not all of a sudden going to be some womanizing whore, and no offense but, some of your teammates are under cover brothas for real. I said I like girls, not boys" Teek laughed.

Angel noticed that Troi had gotten quiet again and asked her, "Troi, are you alright? You haven't had anything to say about any of this."

"Yes, I'm fine with it. Teek, how are you going to handle the outside world? Or do you even plan to tell anyone outside the family?"

"I hadn't really thought about that to be honest. Besides, it's no one's business but mine, and I don't see how telling other people would serve a purpose. Like I said, I just felt that you all deserved to know."

"That's fine Tiki, and we won't tell anyone your business either, will we?" Troi asked Keisha and Angel.

"Of course not." They both agreed.

"All that matters is that you're happy with yourself. That's the one thing our parents worry about...our happiness." Troi reminded her cousins.

"That's true. It freaks them out to have us living here. Can y'all imagine what it must be like as a parent to not have day to day contact with your own kids" Angel asked.

"No. I guess that's why I feel like as the oldest, I'm responsible for you three" Troi admitted.

"Troi, you're not responsible for us or our happiness" Teek said.

"Maybe not, but that's how I feel. I don't want our parents to think that because we don't have them every day that we can't create good lives for ourselves. I don't want them to feel guilty about anything, and that's exactly how they'll feel if any of us fall."

"Oh please, if you really believed that bullshit, you wouldn't have screwed Dre`. Where was all of your concern about my happiness and wellbeing when you did that" Keisha asked.

For the first time since her involvement with Dre`, Troi felt a slight twinge of regret for hurting Keisha. Mostly, she missed the good times she could be having with her cousins. Although the twins hadn't taken sides, the bond between the four had weakened because of her actions. Instead of camaraderie and support, all she felt was lonely and isolated.

Troi had spent the first half of the summer glued to her mother's side as much as possible. She hardly saw her cousins and coming back to Camden hadn't re-established their closeness.

If anything, the events of the past two days had proven that they were all growing in different directions. She may have wanted to fall back into the role of leader or protector, but the others didn't seem to need or want that.

Denise Coleman

CHAPTER 27

Keisha made a decision of her own during that conversation. She'd had enough of Troi and having to share a space with her. She immediately went to find Tim and Karen and asked if it was OK for her to move into the basement alone.

A few years earlier it had been converted into a recreation room for T.J. and his friends, who had long since lost interest in it. Considering the contention between the cousins, Tim had no problem allowing Keisha to move down there. In the back of his mind, he wasn't all that concerned about where he'd spend time with Troi...they'd find a place somehow.

In less than an hour, Keisha had the basement set up like her very own apartment. She couldn't have been more thrilled. She sat in silence formulating a plan to get back at Troi. If she had been willing in the least to forgive her cousin, that thought went out the window the very moment that Troi made her little speech about looking out for the three of them. Bullshit!

The truth was... her anger grew stronger every time she had to look at Troi, and every moment that Dre` kept her at arm's length.

Several scenarios rolled around in her mind, some of which had Troi dying a slow, painful death. Of course, she dismissed such thoughts. After all, if Troi were dead, how could she spend the rest of her life suffering?

Dre` however, was a different story all together. Keisha was determined more now than ever that he would be hers, and if Troi got hurt in the process, then so be it. She decided that whether or not she was ready, she was going to make Dre` an offer he couldn't refuse. Hell, if Troi could do it, so could she.

With her determination in mind, she left the house in search of Dre`. She didn't have far to go. Within seconds of stepping out the front door, Dre` was in her face.

"What's up Keisha?" He asked with his typical smirk. Keisha gathered her nerves and powered by her anger at Troi stated, "Look, I don't care what happened between you and Troi…I want to have sex with you."

Dre` was shocked to the point of dizziness. He stared at her for several moments before he could speak. He laughed a little and shook his head. "No, you really don't."

"Oh yes I do. I know what I want, and I'm tired of playing these stupid games. Obviously, I should have told you this way back in the beginning, and we could have avoided all of this drama. So, are you down or not?"

Dre` smiled to himself. In that very second, it didn't matter to him that he valued Keisha's friendship (contrary to how it appeared), his only concern was that he could hit it. In many ways, he could be considered a predator. The one thing racing through his mind was, *"Damn, I can do anything I want, and she'll still want me. She's not going anywhere."*

"Really Keisha? Have you ever been with anyone before?" He asked with the smallest amount of concern.

"No, but what difference does that make? I'm standing here telling you that this is what I want. So, are we going to do this or not?"
True to form, Dre` responded with his penis. "Hell yeah, we can do this. When?"

"Later" she smiled. "When everyone is asleep. My uncle let me move down to the basement by myself. Just knock on that door after twelve."

"Cool. See you then." Dre` said with a huge, stupid grin on his face. That boy stayed horny and satisfying himself was all that mattered to him ninety percent of the time. His new girl, Rickale didn't cross his mind until he saw her name come up on his ringing cell. "Oh shit!" He said as he walked toward the corner store.

"Hey Ricky, what's up?" He asked, playing it cool.

"I was thinking about going to a party tonight. I wanted to know if you'd go with me."

Without skipping a beat, he said, "No, I can't. I have to watch my sister tonight."

"Oh, Ok. I'll just go with my girls. I'll call you when I get home."

"Cool, bye." Dre` disconnected the call and went into the store. He was out of condoms and never was he going to let any girl have him caught up with some baby bullshit.

Rickale, whom he thought be cared for, was a distant memory within seconds, and Keisha's virgin ass was at the forefront of his mind.

******

Keisha made sure to set a romantic scene for her evening with Dre`. Although her fears were kicking in, she refused to give in to them. She was determined to have her guy once and for all. It no longer mattered that she wasn't really ready.

When Dre` arrived, she had no idea what to do. The only thing she was sure about was that she wouldn't be backing down.

Dre` did notice her hesitation as soon as he entered her makeshift basement apartment. He understood that he was dealing with a very different personality than Troi's. Keisha was the most fragile of the four, but human concern was not on Dre`'s mind. Looking out for anyone other than himself was irrelevant. All that mattered to him was that she didn't change her mind.

"I know you must be nervous." He stated as he sat next to her on the sofa.

"A little, but not enough to back out." She stated firmly.

"OK" he said. Dre` began kissing her deeply and slowly, hoping to build her up to the moment. Keisha however, wanted him to hurry up and get to it. She removed herself from his kisses and quickly disrobed. Dre` began to fondle her breasts as he kissed her again. He laid her down on her back. Keisha spread her legs with little prompting and closed her eyes in anticipation of what was to come. She sensed Dre` leaning over her and opened her eyes. Keisha wanted to see exactly what was happening. The first thing she noticed was his penis and thought… *"Is that it?"* Although she didn't have a clue about what a good size would be, something about Dre`'s mid-sized piece, instinctively disappointed her. *"Shouldn't it be bigger?"* She thought. *"Oh well, maybe this is normal. How would I know?"* Her mind continued.

She braced herself for the pain that would surely come. However, when Dre` entered her body, she realized that the discomfort wasn't as intense as she'd thought it would be. In fact, the entire experience was nothing like she'd thought it would be. Dre` had done very little in the way of foreplay, to build her desire beforehand. Nor did the actual sex itself do much for her. Although it began to become somewhat enjoyable, Keisha couldn't help but feel that there should have been something more exciting before and during the act. She felt deprived which, was a complete turnoff.

Dre` was enjoying her like no other girl he had ever been with. "Damn girl, this pussy is so tight and wet." He whispered, completely engrossed by her virginal goodness. He then increased his pace; feeling sensations that were knew to even his doggish self. Dre` continued to move in and out of her, his desire growing with each stroke. Within seconds, he could no longer control himself. This experience with Keisha was overwhelming him both physically and emotionally, and he couldn't stop it even if he wanted to.

He was very aware of the immediate changes that were occurring in him. Dre` was completely consumed by all that she was naturally; her scent, her touch and the small sounds of ecstasy that escaped her mouth. He looked down at her and the sweet, angelic expression on her face touched him deeply. The emotional charge he felt, jolted him and pierced his heart with an intense affection that he had never experienced. He silently questioned why he'd chosen anyone else over her.

Just a few minutes later, he climaxed more powerfully than he ever had before. The sounds that escaped him were more like a roar that came from his gut. He lay on top of her, trying to catch his breath, grinning from ear to ear.

"Wow Keisha, that shit was so good" he panted.

"Really? I didn't really do anything."

"With a pussy that good, you didn't have to" he complimented.

Keisha laid there once again thinking, *"Is that it?"* The overall experience for her was pleasant enough, but she was expecting fireworks and all she got was a slight fizzle. She thought that because her attraction to him was so intense; the sex should have and would have been amazing.

"Well, thank you I guess."

"You're welcome." He smiled, still lying on top of her.

"So, when can we do this again" he asked.

"Um, I don't know." She said, feeling a bit uneasy. "Can you get up off me, I can't breathe." Dre' reluctantly rolled off of her. He didn't want to move until she'd given him an answer about when they could get together again.

He lay there looking at her expectantly while she searched for the words to explain that just like that, she was totally and thoroughly over her crush on his ass. She didn't know how to express to him that, although she'd been crazy about him from day one, and even without having any previous sexual experience, the lack of chemistry with him, and that fact that she was positive he couldn't give her the ever-mysterious orgasm, was a complete and total turnoff. She actually laid there questioning what she had ever seen in him in the first place.

Fifteen minutes earlier, she was the happiest girl in the world. Finally, she was going to get close to the one and only guy she'd ever wanted. No one could have convinced her that this one encounter would forever change her thoughts about, and feelings for Andre Taylor. Keisha's mind was reeling from this revelation when he asked, "So, are you going to answer me or what?"

Keisha stumbled for the right words to say in the most awkward moment of her life, but before she could utter a sound, she was interrupted by the sound of footsteps on the stairs.

"Oh shit!" Dre` said as they both scrambled to cover themselves. Before they could accomplish this, they were both being pummeled by a barrage of punches.

"Troi stop!" Dre` said as he tried to get a grip on her hands. Troi couldn't be contained; she continued swinging at them. Keisha, however, didn't do anything to defend herself. She curled up in a ball to protect her face and let Troi get the rage out of her system.

Although she didn't feel guilty about what she had done, Keisha was no longer interested in fighting for Dre`. She was over it.

Dre managed to finally get a firm hold on Troi's arms. She had quickly run out of steam.

"Why did you do this, you dumb ass nigga? Why are you down here doing my cousin?!"

"Awe come on now Troi, you knew what we were doing. Besides, it's been over for a long time now."

"That's not the point, you fuckin' idiot! You chose me, now you're down her with her!" She yelled, as she pushed him. "You ain't shit" she continued. "I can't believe I fell for your sorry ass at all. We may have been wrong, but you don't turn around and stick her too! It's not OK to fuck both of us no matter how much time has passed. You asshole, we're still family; same blood line...get it? Once you made a choice, the other was off limits!"

Keisha listened to the exchange unmoved by any of it. She only hoped that they'd hurry up and get the hell out so she could get some sleep.

Dre` was standing there staring at Troi, not knowing what to say. Her and Keisha's family ties didn't occur to him. Besides, just like she had done, Keisha offered it and, in his mind, only a fool would turn it down.

He didn't really need to say anything. Troi had had enough of it all. She looked from one to the other then, slowly walked away from the scene, which annoyed Keisha, because she didn't want to be left alone with Dre`, who expected an answer. She spoke before he could even remember what was previously on his mind.

"Look Dre`, I'm really tired, and after all that noise Troi was making, you should go just in case my aunt or uncle heard and comes down here."

"Oh shit, you're right! I'll just call you when I get home." He said and hurriedly dressed. Dre` was gone in a flash. Keisha was thrilled to see him go.

Denise Coleman

186

CHAPTER 28

While Dre` was on top of the world. Troi was now only interested in her liaison with Tim, and Keisha was perplexed by her sudden and complete disinterest in Dre`.

The only thing on her mind was how to extinguish his newfound interest in her. It didn't take long for her to come up with a plan of action. Within minutes, she'd decided that the best way to send Dre` a message that would sink in was to show him. She wasn't going to waste any time trying to explain something she didn't really understand herself.

Keisha got up, got dressed and headed out. She intended to turn the tides immediately. After the previous night's events, she could finally see clearly how unworthy and messy Dre` was, partly due to Troi's words. That guy truly was self-serving and nasty. Unfortunately, she'd had to open her legs to see that fact.

Latrell Baylock was her target, and Keisha had known for a minute that he was feeling her. Being so caught up in Dre`, she had all but ignored his advances. Now was the time to move on. Literally overnight, Keisha was looking forward to actually being involved with a guy who wanted her; someone she could have a good time with and experience what a relationship might possibly be.

Normally, Keisha would be nervous about approaching a guy other than Dre`, but not today. She felt free more so than she'd felt since moving to Camden.

She walked around the corner quickly and knocked on Latrell's door. He answered immediately like he had been standing behind that door waiting for her. It was then and for the first time, that she noticed how truly handsome Latrell was. It hit her hard just how appealing this young man was. He was tall, fair skinned with copper-colored eyes and when he smiled, his right cheek dimpled.

"Damn, I've been ignoring this" she questioned.

"What's up? What are you doing here?" he smiled.

"Well, to tell you the truth, I came to invite you to Sunday dinner at my house."

"What, really?" He didn't hesitate. "Uh, I'll come." He stammered, a little thrown by her invitation out of the blue.

"Good, I'll see you at three."

"No, wait. What's this really about? I've been trying to holler at you for a while and you never gave me the time of day. Now you invite me to dinner with your family, what's up for real?"

Keisha smiled, "Honestly, I woke up. Let's just say, I see things clearly now, and it's time to do me. So, from where I'm standing, I think getting to know you better is a great start."

Latrell didn't bother to argue the point. Keisha was who he wanted, and he'd take her on any terms she offered.

"Sounds good to me. Why don't you let me run and put some clothes on and we can take a walk?" he asked.

"I'd like that."

During their walk, Keisha learned that she and Latrell had a lot more in common than she would've thought. She also learned that she enjoyed talking to him. He was funny, smart and laid back in a more mature manner than guys his age. It also didn't hurt that he was the star running back on their school's football team. By the time their walk had ended, she was mentally kicking herself for wasting some much time, *and* her virginity on Dre`.

Back at the house, everyone else was getting ready for church. Troi however, refused.

188

"Troi, get up before Auntie comes back in here" Angel said.

"Leave me the fuck alone! I'm not going" she yelled.

"What the hell is wrong with you?"

"Don't worry about it, just back off!"

Angel left her alone. At that point, she didn't give a damn about what was bugging Troi. Between her and Keisha, Angel had had enough of the mood swings. Their time away from Jersey hadn't done anything to help either of them get beyond Dre`, or so she thought.

"We're back to this dumb shit again." Teek whispered to Angel.

"I guess so."

"First Keisha, now you're tripping over that silly ass boy. His dick must be made of gold." Teek said to Troi.

"I doubt that, but Keisha wouldn't know about that either way, so Troi, you tell us, what is it about that ridiculous Dre`, that has y'all both losing your damned minds over him" Angel asked.

Troi thought about her answer first. No way in hell would she tell them that Dre` was a thing of the past because she'd found a more appealing set up with their uncle.

"I don't know." She said to Angel. She then directed her attention to Teek. "Yes Keisha does know what the dick is like. She had him down there last night."

"Down where" Teek asked.

"In the basement, in her bed. She was fuckin' him."

"Wait, what?" Teek stumbled backwards. "Now Keisha's fuckin' Dre`?!"

"Yes" Troi stated.

"Whoa" Angel exclaimed.

"This is all so ridiculous! I can't believe how petty and nasty y'all are being over that fool. Again, what is it about him?" Teek wondered aloud.

Angel was silent as Teek spoke. She was pissed. For sure Dre` was an ass, but for her cousins to be so fucked up with each other's feelings was too much for her.

Karen came walking in just as Teek finished her minor ranting.

"Where is Keisha" she asked.

"What do you mean" Angel asked.

"She's not in her room."

"We don't know. She was down there last night" Angel answered.

"Don't cover for her." Troi spoke up. "Y'all know where that whore is."

"Troi" Karen yelled. "Watch your mouth!"

"No! Keisha was in the basement fucking Dre` last night. Maybe she went to his house to continue after I busted them. So, why don't you get out of our room and go deal with that?" She stated matter- of- factly. Troi didn't really intend to rat out Keisha…she just wanted Karen out of their room.

Karen stood there stunned for a moment before she could react. She ran from the room to call the Taylor house.

"Really Troi?" Angel shook her head.

"Yup."

Keisha was on the porch saying goodbye to Latrell. He kissed her gently with a promise to see her at dinner.

Karen had just made it downstairs at the same time Keisha entered the house.

"Where the hell have you been?" Karen screamed when she spotted Keisha.

"I got up early, so I went for a walk. What's the problem Auntie?"
Karen was momentarily thrown by the innocent expression on Keisha's face.

"Are you sure you left here this morning and not last night?"

"Last night? I promise you; I didn't go anywhere last night." Keisha said sincerely.

Although Karen wanted to believe her, she wasn't sure.

"So, was Dre` here with you last night?"

Keisha knew that Troi had ratted her out, but she wasn't about to get into trouble for this. As far as she was concerned, her night with Dre` was such a waste; no way in hell was she going to take a punishment over him. The way she saw it, that night never happened.

"Of course not. Why would you ask me that? After what he did with Troi, I don't want any parts of that boy." Keisha said as honestly as she could.

Considering she and Troi had no bond at all, and she would categorize their relationship as friction filled at best, Karen was inclined to believe Keisha's word over Troi's any day.

"Anyway Auntie, can I go get dressed for church?"

"Oh, yes, yes, go." Karen said, no longer focused on Keisha. She couldn't understand why Troi was always so hateful. Karen went right back up to the girls' room to speak to Troi. When she got to there, Troi was still lying in bed.

"Why aren't you dressed, and why did you lie to me about Keisha and Dre`?"

Troi sprung forward from her lying position. "I didn't lie about anything! They were down there having sex!"

"Well, Keisha says that isn't true, and I believe her! Now get your ass up and get ready for church!"

"Fuck you! I'm not going anywhere!"

Karen and the twins' heads snapped back as if they'd been struck. Completely fed up with Troi's disrespect, smart mouth and all-around funky attitude, Karen lunged at her and slapped Troi across the face. Troi slapped her back. Karen stood paralyzed in shock, while Troi waited to see what she would do next.

"You're a demon!" Karen yelled, already in tears.

"Whatever, get out."

Angel quickly took her aunt by the shoulders and escorted her to her room. If she hadn't made a move, Karen and Troi would have been banging in the tiny bedroom.

Tim noticed the red handprint on his wife's face as soon as Angel opened the door.

"What the hell happened?"

Angel decided to let her uncle in on what had transpired. Karen was obviously in no condition to speak.

"That's it! That girl has to go! She hit my wife?!" Tim was in a state of disbelief, as if he truly gave a damn. He ran across the hall to the girl's room.

"Start packing your shit! I want you out of my house!"

"Fine." Troi said as she got up and started removing her clothes from the drawers.

"But, Uncle Tim, where is she going to go" Teek asked.

Tim stopped in his tracks. He'd promised to keep the girls because there was nowhere else for them to go. Where exactly was he sending her, he thought.

"I don't know, but she can't stay here."

Thinking quickly, he said, "I'm calling your mother. Come with me Troi." She followed Tim downstairs to the kitchen.

"Listen, no matter what's going on between you and I, *or* me and my wife, attacking her is not some shit I'll stand for."

"Oh so, now you're feeling guilty about something Tim?"

He gave Troi a *'don't test me'* look.

"OK, it's done, it's over, what happens now? I clearly can't stay here anymore, and I can't go back home yet. Contrary to what people may think, I really intend to finish high school, college and law school, so the first step is staying here so I can graduate."

Tim really did want Troi out of the house (It would be better for him) but, he'd promised to look after her as well. He sat at the table and tried to come up with a solution. After a while she said, "How about this? We'll find a room for you to rent. I'll pay for it, but you have to keep your job…and pay for personal your expenses."

Troi considered Tim's proposal, and the more she thought about it, the more excited she got about having a space of her own.

"Well, as you know, my mom sends money for my expenses, but it would probably be cool to pay my own way." She said it, but she didn't mean it.

"Then that's it. While they're all at church, we'll go check you into a motel room and first thing tomorrow, you can start looking for a room in a house somewhere."

Neither of them spoke about what would happen now that Troi would have a place away from the family. Once they'd crossed that line, they each had enough sense to never speak about it in Karen's house.

Denise Coleman

CHAPTER 29

Troi went back up and started packing, knowing she had somewhere to actually go. She thought about calling her mom, but she didn't want to have to explain what had happened.

Teek sat watching her, not quite believing the scene she had just witnessed.

"Are you a fucking lunatic or what? Why did you hit her?"

"That bitch hit me first. What did you expect me to do?"

"I don't know, but damn Troi, you don't have anywhere else to go."

"Yes, I do."

"Oh really, and where is that?"

Troi lied. "My mom is going to wire me some money so I can get a room."

"Oh shit, you're really leaving."

"Yup."

Tim was back in his room trying to comfort Karen and explain that Troi would be leaving for good.

"As soon as Tess finds out about this, she's going to come down here and cause trouble" Karen whined.

Tim rolled his eyes and informed her that it didn't matter what Tess might do. The important thing was that Troi was out of the house.

Karen was relieved to know that Troi would be gone from her home for good. She got up and did her best to snap out of her misery and finished getting ready for church. Extra prayer was definitely a must.

Keisha was the first through the door after services. She wanted to change her clothes before Latrell arrived for dinner. As soon as she was done, she went up to the kitchen to help. She could hear Kelly, Dre` and Rachel as they entered the house.

No matter how hesitant he may have been about joining his siblings at Tim's house, he rarely went near there in the last year, Dre` was not going to pass up a chance to see Keisha. The night before had been the best experience he'd ever had, and he couldn't wait to get her alone again.

Keisha on the other hand, barely acknowledged his presence when they came to greet everyone. Tim also chose to ignore Dre`. He still struggled with knowing of Dre`'s involvement with Troi, and the trouble it had caused in his family. As much as he cared for all the Taylors, Dre` was not one of his favorite people anymore.

Within the hour, dinner was on the table, and everyone took their seats. Troi had returned that evening to retrieve the rest of her belongings and had the balls to park her ass at the table with everyone else. She hadn't eaten all day and didn't care what anyone had to say about her presence there, despite the drama she had created that morning.

Karen and Tim both sat staring daggers at her. Troi couldn't have cared less about their feelings at the moment. Before the day was over, she would be happily out of their house.

The twins didn't know what to do with the tension in the room, Kelly was oblivious to it all, and Keisha was in her own little world. She was enjoying her dinner, knowing that at any moment, Latrell would be there and Dre` would know without a doubt that she had chosen someone else, just like he had done.

Keisha jumped at the sound of the doorbell, "I'll get it." She said as she jumped up and ran to the door. There were curious glances from the others, but they continued with their meal in silence, not thinking much of it.

When Keisha returned with Latrell, hand in hand, everyone froze. Keisha had managed to shock the house. The last thing any of them expected was to see her with a guy, especially if he wasn't Dre`.

"Uncle Tim, this is my friend Latrell. I invited him to dinner if you don't mind" she smiled.

"Uh no, of course not." Tim smiled behind the glass of wine he had to his lips. It was clear by the look on Dre`'s face that his niece had turned the tables.

"I knew you were lying!" Karen shouted at Troi.

"Lying about what" Tim asked.

"She told me Keisha was in the basement with Dre` last night!"

"She *was* in the basement with him!" Troi snapped back.

"What" Tim yelled.

"Hell yeah she was with me!" Dre` spoke up. "And what the fuck are you doing with this nigga?"

Keisha stood there with a smirk on her face and Latrell's smile quickly vanished. He turned to Keisha and whispered, "What is he talking about?"

"I'll tell you later."

Tim jumped from his seat. "Get your slimy ass out of my ass!" He said to Dre`.

"Nah, fuck that Mr. Tim!"

"Yo man, you better pump your breaks" T.J. interjected.

"Nah T man, this girl ain't right! Last night she was in bed with me…now she walks up in here with this busted ass negro?!" Dre` was hot.

Kelly took that moment to intercede. "Let's go Rachel." He said as he grabbed his brother and forcefully ushered him out of the house.

"Have you all lost your fucking minds" Tim screamed.

"Me and Angel don't have anything to do with this mess" Teek stated.

"Just shut up Teek" Karen said.
Teek and Angel got up and left the table without a word. Neither of them wanted to be a part of the craziness which had taken over their family.

Karen turned to Keisha, "Why did you lie to me when I asked you if Dre` had been here?"

"One moment Auntie. Rell, maybe you should go. I'll come see you when I'm done here."
Latrell reluctantly agreed to leave. He wanted answers just like everybody else did. Once he'd departed, Keisha addressed Karen.

"Well, to be honest with you Auntie, the sex was bad, boring… horrible actually. I expected my first time to be amazing and wonderful. Instead, it was a waste of time. I wasn't trying to be grounded over that dud."

Tim and Karen looked at Keisha, dumbfounded by her bluntness, and Troi busted out laughing. "I'm out of here" she stated.

"Me too, I have to go talk to Latrell."
Tim, Karen and T.J had no words. They sat at the table, tripping. *"What the hell just happened"*, was the collective thought.

Troi left to go get settled at the motel and Keisha went to go and talk to Latrell.

Convincing him that Dre` and their night together didn't mean anything was easier than she thought it would be. Latrell never could stand Dre` anyway, so taking Keisha away from him without even having to make an effort was fine with him.

By the time Keisha returned home, her Uncle had padlocked the outside entrance to the basement…she didn't care.

Denise Coleman

CHAPTER 30

The atmosphere in the house changed dramatically after Troi moved out. She'd spent the week following that Sunday, in a motel until she found a suitable room in a boarding house.

Everyone except the twins, were relieved to have her gone. Finally, they thought, there would be peace in the house. This, however, was a premature belief.

Tess arrived in Camden full of rage for what she considered the unfair treatment of her always innocent daughter. Because it was just the two of them, Tess overcompensated, and because of that, in Tess' eyes, Troi could do no wrong.

First thing Saturday morning, she and Troi headed for Tim's house. The girl did not care how fucked up she was being. She hated Karen and every chance she could get, she intended to fuck with her.

Angel answered the door and squealed with delight at the sight of her aunt standing there. Keisha and Teek came running to see what was up. They too were excited to see their aunt standing in the front room.

"What are you doing here Aunt Tess" Teek asked. She and Angel had no idea that Troi had called her mom crying and told her that Karen had slapped her and kicked her out of the house.

"I came here to take care of my daughter. I couldn't just leave her in this city all alone. Now, where are your uncle and that wife of his?" Tess asked this with so much attitude, the girls couldn't ignore it.

"What's wrong" Angel asked.
Before Tess could answer, Karen came walking down the stairs. She had never met Tess before, but it only took seconds for her to assess the situation and figure it out. Karen plastered a fake smile on her face and continued her approach.

"You must be Tess." She said as she extended her hand.

"That's right." Tess ignored the gesture. "And you must be the bitch who put her hands on my daughter."

"Awe shit." The twins whispered simultaneously.

Karen gasped at Tess' aggressive manner.

"Listen Tess, your daughter has been nothing but trouble since she got here. I've tried so many times to connect with her" Karen stated.

"You're a liar" Troi said.

"Bullshit! I know damned well you treated this girl like shit from the beginning" Tess admonished.

"What? That's not true at all." Karen defended herself.

"Yes it is" Troi yelled.

"Shut up Troi" Teek demanded.

"Why are you doing this? You know Aunt Karen hasn't done anything to you" Angel added.

Hearing Angel's statement, Tess turned her attention to her niece. "What are you talking about Angel?"

"Aunt Karen has done her best to make us all comfortable here, but Troi never tried at all to get along."

"Don't listen to her mommy. Angel's always kissing Karen's ass."

"What? You've become such a hateful person Troi. What happened to you" Angel asked.

"Both of you shut up" Tess stated. "The bottom line is you had no business putting your hands on my daughter." She said to Karen as she approached her and swung at her. Tess landed a blow directly to Karen's jaw that knocked her sideways.

"Auntie!" Teek yelled as she and Angel took action and grabbed Tess.

"Please stop this" Angel begged.

Seeing that her cousins weren't going to allow Tess to continue kicking Karen's ass, pissed Troi off. She snatched Teek from behind.

"Get off me Troi!"

"Hell no! Get off my mom!"

"Tim, Tim!" Karen yelled for her husband. Tim came running down the stairs to see the girls and Tess tussling with one another, and his wife once again, holding her face in tears. He promptly pulled the twins away from Troi and Tess.

"What the hell is wrong with you people?! Tess, take you daughter and get the fuck out of my house! If you ever come back here again, I'll have both your asses arrested!"

"Fuck you and your sorry ass family!" Tess screamed as she guided Troi out the door.

The twins and Keisha were momentarily stuck, watching Tim comfort Karen yet again because of something *their* blood had done.

"I can't believe Aunt Tess came up in here with that ratchet shit." Angel whispered to Teek as they removed themselves from the living room. Neither could stand to see Karen and Tim so upset.

"This shit is crazy" Keisha commented.

"I know, right? When did Troi become such a self-absorbed liar? She's not the cousin we grew up with at all."

I don't know and I hate to say it but, I'm glad she's gone."

"And what the hell was up with Auntie? She came through the door in attack mode. I can't believe she fell for Troi's bullshit" Keisha said.

"Really? You know Tess has always believed every word that girl has ever told her. She would lie in a heartbeat to keep from being grounded, and Auntie would accept it even if it sounded ridiculous."

"Yeah but, that was child's play. It wasn't like she was doing anything serious back then anyway. This shit she's been pulling here is over the top. She's become a stranger to me." Angel said as they sat at the kitchen table.

"It doesn't matter. Tess always believes her no matter how out of pocket that girl is."

"I guess so."

Denise Coleman

CHAPTER 31

Dre` was at home fuming. It had been two weeks since he'd last seen Keisha. The Sunday dinner revelations had his pride twisted in knots.

Every attempt he had made at trying to speak to Keisha was met with resistance and silence. She refused to explain herself and her immediate involvement with Latrell.

Kelly and Angel entered the house to find Dre` sitting on the sofa, staring into space with a look of despair on his face.

"What's up man?" Kelly asked, full of concern for his brother. He could not believe how much Dre`'s personality had changed so quickly. He was completely turned out by Keisha after just one encounter. To say that the teens found this bizarre would be an understatement.

"Nothing" was Dre`'s only response.

"I know you're not sitting here trippin' over Keisha and Latrell."

Dre` got angry at the mention of her name. "Fuck that ho! How the fuck is she going to choose that corny ass nigga over me?! The next damn day at that! What kind of shit is that?! Straight up ho!"

"Boy, if you call my cousin out of her name one more time…" Angel stated, becoming more irritated by the second.

"Well shit, it's not like I'm lying."

"What?! You've got a lot of fucking nerve. You're the asshole who was smashing two cousins" Angel snapped.

"I sure was. I can do whatever the fuck I want!"

"You sure can, and so can Keisha. It sucks to be your black ass right now, don't it" Angel smirked.

"Alright y'all, stop" Kelly said. "Look man, you may not want to hear this, but Angel's right…Keisha don't owe you nothing. I hate to tell you this, but you brought this on yourself. What you did to her was fucked up."

"What? How is doing me fucked up? I wanted Troi, Keisha should have accepted that."
Kelly couldn't believe how openly selfish his brother was. Although he knew Dre` could be all about himself, this much selfishness was beyond him.

"OK man, in that case, Keisha just took a page from your book. She chose Latrell, now, you need to accept that."

"That's right. Keisha spent all that time wanting you and you knew it. It's cool if you didn't want her, that's life, but you go and mess with her cousin of all people, how do you think that made her feel? Now you have the nerve to sit here feeling sorry for yourself and pissed at her for moving on…boy please" Angel added.

"But it was the next fucking day" Dre` yelled.

"Next day, next hour, who gives a shit? You don't deserve her anyway." With that, Angel said goodbye to Kelly and went back home. She was more than done with Dre`, Keisha, Troi and all of the drama.

Dre` on the other hand, couldn't handle Angel's words. Regardless of his own actions, he was in the dark about why Keisha was with Latrell, and he needed answers. After all, she'd wanted him, and he knew it. Dre`'s ego wouldn't allow him to believe that Keisha was serious about Latrell. It didn't make any sense in his self-absorbed mind.

Not willing to go another minute without getting some answers, Dre` left the house on a mission. His blood began to boil the moment he approached the house and saw Keisha sitting on the porch with Latrell.

"I want to talk to you now!" He said to Keisha. However, before she could say anything, Latrell spoke up.

"She don't have shit to say to you."

"Fuck you nigga! I ain't talkin' to your bitch ass!"

"But I'm talking to you. Either step the fuck off or step up."

"Oh, so you talkin' shit?" Dre` said as he stepped up onto the porch.

Keisha sat there with a smirk on her face, hoping Latrell would kick Dre`'s ass just because. Not only had she gotten over him, she had quickly began to resent him. Once her crush had worn off, she began to see things clearly. Keisha finally understood that Dre` had truly played her dirty and was willing to take advantage of her feelings for as long as she would let him. Those days were over!

As soon as Dre` got close enough, Latrell stood up and punched him so hard that he fell backwards down the steps. Keisha began to giggle uncontrollably. Dre` jumped back up with the intent to rush Latrell and kick his ass. However, the sound of Keisha laughing stopped him in his tracks. He was so humiliated he could do no more than stand there shaking his head. How could she have turned on him so quickly? Dre` wondered.

This embarrassment only served to piss him off even more. Dre` directed his anger towards Keisha. "Fuck you bitch! I never wanted you in the first place!"

For a brief moment, Keisha was stunned into silence, but quickly recovered.

"That may have been true before, but it obviously isn't true now. Kick rocks, jerk" she laughed.

"You heard her nigga…bounce."

"This shit ain't over. I will see your ass again." Dre` told Latrell as he walked away.

Denise Coleman

CHAPTER 32

By the time he'd returned home, Dre` was even more furious than he was during his confrontation with Latrell. As far as he was concerned, he had been treated like a bitch and he wasn't having that. The embarrassment that Latrell had caused only served to fuel his anger.

Dre` paced back and forth in front of his house, trying to figure out how to get back at the both of them. He wanted to do more than just make a fool out to them; he wanted them both to suffer.

The conniving part of Dre` began to kick in and his plan of attack began to fall into place in his mind. Dre` ran into his house and out the back door, to the shed in the yard. Marcus' things had been stored in there shortly after his imprisonment.

Dre` knew exactly where to find what he was looking for; a nine-millimeter pistol that Marcus had kept hidden in a shoe box under his bed. Dre` checked to make sure it was still loaded and headed back down the street.

Keisha and Latrell were still sitting on the porch when Dre` returned full of hatred and vengeance. The two were so caught up in one another that neither noticed him standing at the foot of the steps.

Watching Keisha boo loving with another guy had Dre` seething. His embarrassment and anger had bubbled over into rage. Latrell was going to pay for first…stealing Keisha before he himself had a good chance with her and second, for throwing hands period.

"Yo muthafucka" Dre` yelled.
The two jumped at the sudden intrusion into their quiet moment. Until then, Dre` had been all but forgotten about.

Latrell noticed the gun first and immediately jumped in front of Keisha. He needn't have bothered. Dre` knew exactly who his target was. Even in his current state, physically harming Keisha was never a consideration.

"Yo man, you don't want to do this." Latrell stammered as Dre` started up the steps. There were no more words. Dre` quickly and accurately pumped three bullets into Latrell's right knee.

Knowing he was their school's star running back, Dre` meant to ruin his nemesis' often mentioned, "bright future".

Keisha began screaming and couldn't stop as Latrell fell backwards into her arms. She thought for sure that she would be Dre`'s next target.

Tim, Karen and Angel came running out of the house with terror in their hearts, upon hearing Keisha's blood curdling screams.

The realization of what he had done didn't faze Dre` in the least. He turned and walked back to his house as if nothing had happened.

Tim quickly called for an ambulance and the police. Karen on the other hand, was as hysterical as Keisha, who sat crying and rocking Latrell. Karen continued screaming like a lunatic.

Angel did her best to calm Karen's hysterics, to no avail. She quickly turned her attention to Keisha. She lifted her cousin and sat her on the swing. She then checked to make sure that Latrell was still breathing as he had passed out from the pain.

"Keisha, try to pull yourself together. The ambulance will be here soon." Tim stated as he kneeled down to check Latrell's wounds.

"Angel, please take you Aunt and cousin inside."

Within seconds, both the ambulance and the police arrived.

Tim explained to the police exactly what he had witnessed while the paramedics worked on getting Latrell out of there as quickly as possible.

Dre` was sitting on his front steps when the police arrived. He never intended to run. There was no place for him to go even if he'd wanted to. He really didn't care at that point as long as Latrell understood that he wasn't to be fucked with. Dre` was sure that he'd gotten the message.

Back at the Kyle's, Keisha had insisted on riding to the hospital with Latrell. Tim went with her.

Angel managed to get Karen to lie down. As soon as her aunt was settled, she called Kelly and told him that he and T.J should come to the house right away.

******

"I wonder what's so important." T.J. said as he and Kelly headed toward his house.

"Beats me, but it must be important if Angel called us back there. She doesn't exaggerate anything.

The boys walked as fast as they could. Each in thought, wondering what could possibly be going down.

What they heard when they'd reached Angel blew them both away. Neither expected to hear something so crazy.

"Dre` did what?" Kelly asked, dumbfounded. "I just left him in the house sulking, not more than an hour ago."

"Yes, I know. The cops went down your house a while ago. I tried to call the County after I called you, but I couldn't get any information. You need to call your mom."

Kelly was frantic. Although he'd heard what Angel said and tried to act, he couldn't even get his fingers to cooperate. Having to give his mom that kind of news without having any details to give her had him shook.

Somehow, he managed to tell his mother as much as he knew and agreed to meet her at the station.

When all was said and done, Dre`'s bail was fifty thousand dollars. There would be no way in hell that Sarah could even come up with the ten percent. Dre` would have to sit.

Angel did her best to comfort Kelly and his mother on the car ride home, but there was nothing she could say to make this situation better. Dre` had shot someone and he was not going to get out of that.

Keisha and Tim sat patiently in the hospital waiting room for news about Latrell's injuries. Although she had never met her, Keisha recognized Latrell's mom on sight. She was the female version of her son.

Keisha wanted desperately to say something to the woman but couldn't muster the courage to approach her. Tim went to speak to her instead. He explained the incident which only agitated Ms. Baylock even more.

Moments later the surgeon came out to inform them of Latrell's condition. The news wasn't good. It would be a miracle if he managed to walk without a limp for the rest of his life. His knee had to be replaced, therefore there would be no football career in his future.

Keisha and Latrell's family were all devastated by this. Everyone understood how much the game meant to him; they all knew that at seventeen, it would be that more difficult for him to accept such a harsh truth.

Tim had to remove Keisha from the situation. Latrell's mom was angry, and he didn't want her to turn her wrath towards his niece. He convinced her to go home with the promise that he'd bring her back in the morning.

Denise Coleman

CHAPTER 33

Keisha was up and ready to go to the hospital first thing the next morning. Tim drove her as promised, although he felt uneasy. He hoped that Latrell's mother wouldn't be there. Tim sensed that her anger would be directed towards Keisha, and he didn't want to the girl to have to deal with that.

Keisha hesitantly entered Latrell's room. She had no idea of what she would say. There was a tremendous amount of guilt she felt.

She slowly sat in the chair next to his bed and touched his arm. Latrell opened his eyes and turned to focus on Keisha. The sight of her sent a wave of anger through him.

"What are you doing here" he asked.
There was no mistaking in his tone that he was not happy to see her.
Keisha stuttered, "I just wanted to see you…to be here with you."

"I don't want you here." Latrell stated through gritted teeth.

"What, why not?" Keisha asked while trying to keep the tears from falling.

"You're the reason I'm laying up here with no future."

"Me?" Keisha pressed her hands against her chest. "How can you say that?"

"Damn right it's your fault! If you hadn't been fucking with that asshole and playin' me, I'd still have a future!"

"Playing you?"
"Yeah bitch, playin' me!"
Latrell's last statement was like a kick in the gut. However, Keisha wasn't the girl she had been before her night with Dre`. The last thing she was going to do was take complete responsibility for what had happened. Surely, she felt badly, but no way in hell was she going to let Latrell take his shit out on her.

"First of all, I'm nobody's bitch, and second, this shit isn't my fault! I don't control anyone else's actions! As a matter of fact, fuck you!"

Keisha got up and walked out, leaving Latrell's bullshit behind as well. If she should have been more understanding or sympathetic…all of that flew out the window, the minute he called her a bitch. Keisha was tired of being treated like she wasn't worth crap by the dumb ass guys she cared for.

"I'm ready to go Uncle Tim."

"Already" Tim asked. "What happened that fast?"

"He snapped at me, called me a bitch and blamed this whole thing on me. I'm done with him and Dre`'s dumb asses."

Tim stood for a moment and watched her stomp out of the hospital. There was nothing he could say or do, so he followed her out to the car and drove home.

Keisha was still so angry when they got out of the car that it took her a moment to realize that Tim had walked away from the house. For a second, she thought about calling out to him to ask where he was going, but instead she decided to follow him.

When she rounded the corner, she noticed him on his cell phone. This piqued her curiosity even more. Where the hell was he going on foot, she wondered… Tim never walked anywhere.

Three blocks later, Tim stopped at a house and turned up the alley to a side entrance. He was so engrossed in his conversation that he hadn't noticed Keisha peeking around the wall from the front of the house. He ended his call and entered, using a key he'd pulled from his pocket.

"What the fuck" Keisha whispered. She crept down the alley and tried to peek in the window. However, the blinds were shut, barring her attempted voyeurism. Keisha was stuck for what to do, but she refused to leave before she got to the bottom of what was going on with her uncle.

After fifteen minutes of standing under that window, Keisha was ready to give up and go home. However, before she could take a step, she heard a familiar voice.

"Troi! What the…" Then she remembered that long ago encounter she'd witnessed between her uncle and cousin.

She thought about banging on the door, but a better idea struck her. Keisha walked back to the front of the house and knocked on the door. A petit Latina woman answered.

"Hi, my name is Keisha. The girl renting the room in the back is my cousin Troi." Keisha said. The woman nodded that indeed she knew Troi.

"I left something important in there yesterday, and she told me that I could ask you to let me in so I can get it." Keisha smiled at the woman *and* the stupid lie she'd just told; not thinking for one second that the woman would believe her.

For a brief moment the woman was skeptical, but Keisha appeared to be so genuine that she felt that it wouldn't cause any harm to let the girl in as long as she accompanied her.

"OK dear, let me get the spare key."
Keisha could not believe that bullshit worked, or that anybody would actually let a stranger into a tenant's room. She certainly wasn't going to back out now, regardless. The important thing was to find out what the hell Tim was doing in Troi's room, especially since he'd kicked her out of his house.

Although she hadn't mentioned it to anyone, Keisha hadn't forgotten the conversation she'd heard between her cousin and uncle. She'd simply thought that whatever it was had ended long before Tim kicked Troi out, because she hadn't witnessed any more inappropriate behaviors.

The landlord, Mrs. Santiago, fumbled the key a little before she could get it into the lock. Keisha stood dancing in place with nerves as she tried to be patient with the woman.

Once the door was opened, Keisha nearly knocked the old woman down, trying to get past her. Mrs. Santiago screamed, "Aye Dios Mio!"

"Oh my God!" Keisha's eyes bugged out of her head. She vomited a little in her mouth when she focused on the scene before her.

Tim and Troi were both naked. He had Troi bent over the only chair in the room as he hit from behind. All Keisha noticed was her uncle's bare ass pumping in and out as he pounded away at her cousin.

By the time Tim and Troi realized they'd heard the landlady's screams, Keisha had vomited again, all over the entrance.

"What the fuck?!" Tim yelled when he turned to see who had interrupted. His heart dropped when he saw Keisha standing in the doorway, getting sick all over.

"Oh shit" he whispered. Tim quickly pulled up his pants and ran to Keisha.

Mrs. Santiago, full of embarrassment, walked away. As much as she wanted to say something, her tenant was an adult and could entertain whomever she wanted. Besides, these people were strangers…she had no idea what was really going on and she wanted no parts of it. She got her rent on time…that's all that mattered.

Troi slammed the door behind Tim and Keisha, not able to witness the conversation that would take place. She began walking in circles around the small room, ringing her hands and sweating profusely.

She had done some fucked up things in her short life, but as long as no one knew about this one, she could pretend that it wasn't so bad. Once she'd moved and her mom went back home, she and Tim immediately jumped into a full-on sexual affair. For her, it wasn't a stretch that they would eventually go there, but to have their involvement exposed so quickly and completely, shook her to her core.

Troi stood still in the middle of her room. She began to shake involuntarily. Her skin became cold...so cold that it felt like she was being pricked by pins and needles all over. Her sight became clouded as memories began to flood her mind's eye. Every little lie, indiscretion and deceitful deed played out before her.

Picture after picture of every man who had come and gone from her mother's life; every lie her mom had told to get what she wanted, and the influence that witnessing those actions had on her own choices.

The constant battle between wanting to be as good as the other girls and being the person, her mother raised, raged on in the moment.

Although she still couldn't fully see exactly how wrong she was – she wanted what she wanted- something about being busted, butt ass naked in the act, elicited a level of vulnerability that she was unfamiliar with.

Troi climbed onto her bed and curled up in the fetal position and didn't move. She had to remind herself to breathe every few seconds. She was simply, lost.

On the other side of the door, Tim was still trying to calm Keisha down. Unfortunately for him, she wasn't trying to hear it. With every explanation he tried to give, she simply shook her head no, as if to say "bullshit".

Tim was at a loss for how to keep this situation from exploding in his face even more than it already had.

"Keisha, please try and understand that I didn't intend for any of this to happen" he pleaded.

"Fuck that, Uncle Tim! You're cheating on your wife with my freaking eighteen-year-old cousin! There is no excuse for that!" Keisha jumped up, outraged by it all. "I'm telling!" she yelled and ran off towards home.

Denise Coleman

CHAPTER 34

Keisha ran all the way home. She busted in the door, hysterical. She could not erase the images of Tim and Troi having sex from her mind.

"What's wrong? Did something happen to Latrell?" Angel asked when she noticed the state that Keisha was in. Keisha looked at Angel with confusion. "Latrell? What are you talking about?" She cried, barely able to comprehend what was going on around her. She was shaking, hiccupping and gasping for air.

Karen ran to her and guided her to a chair.

"Keisha, what the heck happened? Is Latrell alright?"

"Why do you keep asking me about Latrell?" She continued to cry.

"Because you went to the hospital to see him and now, you're in here falling apart. What happened?"

"Latrell? Fuck him! I just saw Uncle Tim..." she stuttered.

"What about Tim?" Karen asked with fear in her heart.

"I, I, I don't know."

Karen and the twins all became fearful of what Keisha was trying to say. They had never seen her so upset, not even the day before when Dre` shot Latrell did she lose compete control. The hysterics they were witnessing then, scared them.

"Keisha, you have to tell us what happened. What has you this distraught" Karen asked.

Keisha wiped her eyes but continued to sob and hyperventilate. Karen rubbed her back in an attempt to soothe the girl and get a straight answer out of her.

"It's OK sweetie, just say whatever it is" Karen coaxed.

"Alright, OK, alright, OK" Keisha stumbled. "I just caught Uncle Tim and Troi having sex!" She finally blurted out. The twins screamed, "Whaaat!

"What did you say" Karen asked. Keisha looked at her apologetically but couldn't say another word.

Karen sat frozen, staring at Keisha. She knew that she'd heard her correctly, and she also knew with everything in her being that it was the truth. This wasn't some bullshit practical joke Keisha was playing. Her husband was fucking a teenager.

Karen's eyes rolled in the back of her head just before she fainted.

"Oh Lord, here we go again" Teek said. "Angel, help me get her up off the floor.

Angel didn't move. She sat on the other side of Keisha replaying what she'd just heard.

"Uncle Tim is fucking Troi?" She whispered over and over again. Keisha flopped backwards on the sofa and continued with her own dramatics.

Teek stood there surveying the room. Angel was mumbling like an idiot. Keisha was having a nervous breakdown, and Karen was stretched out on the floor where she'd landed.

"Really? These bitches need to pull it together." Teek slapped her sister on the arm. "Angel, snap out of it! Help me get Auntie up, then take this fool upstairs and splash some cold water on her face until she acts normal again. Angel did as she was told while Teek ran to get a cold rag for Karen.

Up in the bathroom, Angel asked, "How did this happen?"

"What?"

"How did you see Tim and Troi?"

"I followed him to her room."

"OK but, I'm sure they didn't just let you in so, how did you see them?"

Keisha composed herself enough to fill Angel in on the details, starting with the first conversation she'd heard between them. By the time she was done, Angel was sitting on the edge of the tub with her mouth hanging open.

Moments later, they heard Karen screaming bloody murder.

Tim had raced home behind Keisha, prepared to face his firing squad. He hadn't had time to make a decision about what he should do or say, now that his dirt had been kicked up.

For as bad as his marriage was, Troi wasn't a viable option for him. She was a momentary distraction. Certainly, they didn't have a future together. The biggest issue for Tim was that he really didn't want to be with Karen anymore. His involvement with Troi had opened his eyes to that truth.

To so easily walk into an affair with a young girl was a clear indication to him, that his marriage wasn't worth shit.

"Oh shit! Uncle Tim's home…Let's go!" Angel said as she grabbed Keisha and dragged her out of the bathroom. They ran downstairs in time to see Teek trying to pry Karen's fingers from Tim's neck. Angel and Keisha helped Teek. By the time they'd dragged Karen away from Tim…she was exhausted.

Tim wasn't really affected by Karen's attack. At least not in a way she would have preferred. She wanted him to be remorseful and beg for her forgiveness.

Although Tim wasn't proud of his actions, he certainly wouldn't be begging for anything. However, when taking notice of his nieces' faces, Tim was reminded of the promise he'd made to his brothers, not to mention his own son. Although T.J would be graduating and leaving home in a few months, Keisha and the twins still had another year to go.

"Oh shit, T.J!" For the first time, it hit Tim just how far his betrayal would reach. His son was his life and knowing how much T.J. would be hurt by this, floored him. Tim took a seat in his recliner and broke down. At that moment, his foolishness became one hundred percent clear. "What the fuck have I done?" He said to himself.

The girls stood, staring at him, not knowing what to say, while Karen laid sprawled out on the sofa. Angel spoke first. "Uncle Tim, what were you thinking?" This news about her uncle was overwhelming. Angel had never felt so uneasy about anything in her life. Her confusion and disbelief were etched all over her face. Every time she thought their lives might become somewhat normal, something drastic would happen to blow her world up.

The last two days had been more than any of them were capable of handling. Tim didn't bother to try to answer Angel's question. There were no words. Nothing could justify his behavior.

Keisha decided to answer for him. "He's a fucking dog just like the rest of them."

"Stop right there Keisha" Tim said. "I may have fucked up in a huge way, but I will not have you being disrespectful. You'd better watch your mouth."

"Fuck you, nigga." Keisha said calmly and walked out of the room. That's how much respect she had for her uncle at the moment.

"Uncle, you have to say something. Please, help us understand this craziness" Teek pleaded.

"Not now Teek. I have to talk to your aunt. Give us a few minutes" he said.

Teek pulled Angel out the front door with her. Tim sat for a few more minutes, trying to calm his mind enough to explain himself to his wife.

Karen still laid sprawled on the sofa, sniffling, barely conscious of her surroundings. Tim approached her cautiously. He sat on the edge of the sofa and took her hand in his.

"Karen, can you hear me?" As depressing as his life with her had been, Tim hated the thought that he had caused her such devastating pain. She was after all, the mother of his son and the woman who had his back regardless.

"Karen, listen to me."

She focused on him as best as she could and found some strength. "You're sleeping with that demon child, there's nothing to explain. Get your shit and get your sorry ass out of my house." With a heavy heart, Karen dragged herself up off the sofa and up the stairs. Her truth: Despite her feelings about Troi, her marriage was nothing worth fighting for. She wasn't so weak that she couldn't face the fact that she and Tim had stayed together more for the sake of T.J. than any true, lasting love.

Their marriage had long since been on its last leg. Had it not been for Gary and Mercer's request for them to take care of the girls, they probably wouldn't still be together anyway.

Angel and Teek sat on the porch swing, dumbfounded. Neither could speak as they each tried to absorb the new level of insanity their family had reached.

T.J. walked up, dead tired from football practice. "What's up y'all?" When his cousins didn't respond, he stopped and really looked at them. "Awe damn, what the hell done happened now?" He asked once he saw their tear-stained faces.

"You should probably go talk to your parents" Angel said.

T.J. sighed and shook his head, wondering what could possibly be going on this time. He walked in the house to see his dad coming down the stairs with some of his luggage.

"Yo Pop, where you going?"

Tim dropped his head. The last thing he wanted to do was to have that conversation with T.J. right then.

Whatever it was, T.J. knew it was bad. The look on his father's face told him so.

"Just tell me man." T.J. said in a defeated, I'm so tired of drama, tone.

Tim didn't really know what to say. The truth was surely going to ruin the relationship he'd had with his son. How do you tell the one person in the world, who looked up to you the most, that you've behaved so selfishly? T.J. stood in the middle of the room, staring his dad down, waiting not so patiently for an answer.

"Uh, well son. I Uh, Well, your mom and I have decided to separate for a while." Tim finally spit out.

"What? Why?" T. J. was completely blindsided by that statement. Although he had lived in the same house with them, he had no idea what his parent's life together was really about. They'd always made it a point to hide their dissention from him, and they'd done a good job of it because, T. J. was shocked.

"Pop, say something. This doesn't make any sense. What happened?"

"Look son, it's just one of those things. Your mom and I haven't gotten along in a while now, and we felt it would be best if we spent some time apart. Who knows, a break might just bring us closer together." Tim said, not believing one word out of his own mouth.

"Huh? That doesn't make any sense either. You're blowing smoke man. I'm going to go ask mom what's really going on. Don't leave." T.J. dropped his cleats and went up to see Karen.

Tim took that opportunity to slip out. The guilt he felt would not allow him the courage to stand and face the rage he would certainly get from his son once Karen clued him in about the real reason he was leaving. He walked past the twins without a word.

Moments later, T.J. came rushing out to the porch. "Is what my mom said true? My dad is smashing Troi?" He asked in disbelief. The twins nodded. "T.J. I'm so sorry about this" Teek apologized.

"Why are you sorry?"

"Because she's *our* cousin, I guess. She came into this house with us. We brought the drama."

"This shit is my dad's fault and nobody else's. What the fuck is wrong with him" T.J. yelled. "I could kill both their asses!" He smashed his fist through the screen door.

Angel screamed out in surprise.

"T.J. please, try and calm down" she begged.

"Calm down? Are you crazy?! My dad is cheating on my mom with a fucking whore like Troi, and I'm supposed to calm down?! Fuck that!" T.J. stormed off towards Kelly's house.

"This shit is just going to get worse" Teek stated.

Denise Coleman

CHAPTER 35

The next few months were weird for the teens. Dre` was gone, Tim was gone, and of course Troi certainly never came around. Their seven had become five in what felt like a blink of an eye. Even when they ran into Troi at school, she had very little to say to any of her cousins. She could barely even look any of them in the eye.

Whenever Tim did come around to see his son, T.J. refused to hear him out. His anger and disappointment in his father continued to deepen with every day that passed. His mom had pretty much checked out of his life because she was too busy feeling sorry for herself instead of stepping up like a woman should.

T.J. blamed Tim for all the darkness in their home, and his mom's heart. He vowed he would never forgive Tim.

Those who were still there, hardly spent any time together as a group. Their laughter had all but left them, and none of them could figure out how to be their normal selves.

The drama and the changes in their lives had caused a shift in their personalities. No longer were they carefree, innocents who believed life could get better.

The only bright spot for the girls was that the holidays were approaching, and their parents would be coming to Camden to visit with them for the first time. However, their joy wouldn't be long lasting.

By the time the holidays rolled around, the girls were becoming more excited every day. They couldn't wait to share whatever good things they managed to create in their lives since moving there.

Just after Thanksgiving, Angel started to feel weird, as she called it. She was losing energy and kept a headache. Most days she couldn't keep anything down and suffered from dizzy spells. After a few weeks of being sick, her aunt insisted that she needed to see a doctor.

"Awe Auntie, I hate going to the doctor. Can't we just go to the drug store and get something?"

"No, we can't do that. We don't even know what's wrong with you."
Angel didn't want to hear that, but Karen wouldn't budge.

"Well can I at least ask Tiki to go with us?"

"Sure, just hurry up and get dressed so we can go."
Angel went back to her room to do as she was told. Keisha was sitting on her bed studying when Angel entered.

"Where are you going" she asked.

"Karen is making me go to the doctor's office." Angel stated with attitude. "I hate going to the damn doctor."

"Yeah, I know but, so what? You don't have a choice. You have to find out what's wrong with you."

"It's not that big a deal. I probably just have the flu or something."

"Or you're probably just pregnant or something." Keisha said sarcastically.
Angel's mouth fell open. "Why would you say that? I'm not pregnant."

"How the hell would you know? You've been walking around here for the last few months like you don't have a clue about anything. You've gotten so caught up in that damned Kelly that *you're* disappearing. You don't spend any time with the two of us, and everything you think and talk about is that damn guy."

Angel considered Keisha's words for a moment. She knew that something had changed in her, but she couldn't see what was wrong in that. She was in love and as far as she was concerned, all girls dreamed of having what she and Kelly had. Besides, ever since Dre` had been arrested, Kelly needed her even more.

"It doesn't matter Keisha. He loves me and he'll always take care of me."

"Oh really? How long do you think he'll hang around if there's a baby to take care of? He's already trying to maintain for his mom and taking care of Dre`'s dumb ass while he's sitting up in juvy. Do you think adding another person to that equation will make him happy?"

"I don't know why you're hating on me but you're wrong. Kelly would never leave me hanging. Besides, I'm not pregnant so there's nothing to worry about."

"You really don't believe that shit, do you?"

"I sure do."

"So let me ask you this, have you been using any birth control at all? And don't lie. Oh, and by the way, don't forget, I know your shit as well as I know my own therefore, I know you haven't had a period since October."

"OK well, it's only November, so now what?" Keisha just shook her head. "It's the middle of December girl. What the fuck is wrong with you?!"

Keisha was thoroughly exasperated with her cousin. She could not believe how foolish Angel had become as of late. She was quickly becoming a stranger too.

"Whatever, I'm not pregnant and when I get back from the doctor, I'll have proof that it's only the flu."

Angel finished dressing and went to find Teek so she could ride with her. The care ride there was a hell of a lot more pleasant than the car ride home. Although Angel didn't believe for moment that she could be pregnant, a simple blood test proved otherwise.

Her Aunt was so upset that she cried the entire way, wondering how she was going to explain to Angel's parents how she had dropped the ball on caring for their daughter. She had taken on the responsibility of parenting the girls after Tim left, and as far as Karen was concerned, she'd failed miserably.

"How could you do this Angel? Do you realize the mess you've made of your life?" Karen questioned. However, in her mind, she blamed Tim. Everything that was wrong was his fault.

Angel was too shocked to answer. Although she hadn't thought that she was pregnant, she wasn't concerned when she found out the truth. That girl knew with everything in her that Kelly would be there for her. She didn't have a problem starting a family with him. Nor did it matter that she was only sixteen.

"Angel, you hear me talking to you, girl. What were you thinking, having sex with that boy without using birth control? And you, Tiki, how could you let her do this?"

Teek looked at Karen like she was crazy. "Are you serious Auntie? What was I supposed to do about it?"

"You were supposed to talk her out of having sex."

"No Auntie, I wasn't. Angel can make her own choices. Not to mention, she didn't discuss her decision with me before she did it. Please don't try to blame this on me."

"I really wish you two would stop talking about me like I'm not here. And please, stop talking like I'm slow or something and need my sister's constant guidance."

"Angel, do you have any idea how upset your parents are going to be? This is the worst thing that could've happened."

"They'll get over it", was Angel's thought, but even *she* didn't have the balls to say that out loud.

The moment they pulled up to the house, Angel jumped out of the car and ran up to Kelly's house. She ignored her aunt yelling behind her to get her ass back here. She banged on the door, out of breath, she had run so fast.

"Babe, what's wrong?" Kelly asked when he answered the door to Angel huffing and puffing.

"We need to talk, right now."

"OK but, you still didn't answer the question. And why are you in a panic?"

"Kelly, will you just let me in before one of my people comes and snatches me away." She demanded as she pushed him aside.

"What the hell? Come on in here. Let's go in the kitchen."

Angel followed him into the kitchen and took a seat.

"Alright Angel, what's up with you?"

"Well, my Auntie just brought me back from the doctor and I'd better talk fast. My uncle's car was out there, and in a minute, he's going to be down here knocking down the door."

Kelly looked at her with confusion written all over his face.

"Why would Mr. Tim be coming down here?"

"Because right about now, my aunt is probably telling him that I'm pregnant."

"What?!" Kelly jumped from his chair so quickly that it toppled over.

"Calm down Kelly. Why are you freaking out?"

"Did you really just ask me that?! You come in here and announce that you're pregnant like it's no big deal, and you don't expect me to react?!"

Angel was a little confused by his reaction. Part of her hoped that he would be happy about her news.

"Come on now Kelly, we've never used any kind of birth control. You had to know that this could happen so, why are you acting so surprised?"

She had a point. There wasn't much he could say to that. The fear that they were being careless was always in the back of his mind, but in the heat of the moment, those fears were easy for him to dismiss. Although he was responsible by nature, with Angel he'd lose his good sense every time she touched him.

He sat back down slowly and held his head in his hands. "Oh my God, what are we going to do?" Before Angel could even fix her mouth to speak, they heard loud banging on the front door.

"Oh shit! I knew it, here they come" Angel announced.

"OK, OK, don't worry. We'll deal with this together." Kelly hadn't had a moment to think about the magnitude of Angel's revelation, but he was fully prepared to defend the two of them against whoever was on the other side of that front door.

"Open this door!" Tim yelled seconds later.

"Told you." Angel stated flatly.

Rachel heard the commotion and had gone down to answer the door before Angel and Kelly could get out of the kitchen. Just as they entered the living room, Tim came rushing through the door, eyes ablaze.

"You little bastard!" He yelled and rushed Kelly. In a flash, he was choking the shit out of Kelly.

"Uncle Tim, don't!"

"What's going on?" Rachel screamed and began crying.

"Uncle Tim, please stop!" Angel grabbed Tim and pulled him off Kelly. While she tried to hold Tim back, Kelly found his way to his feet.

"How dare you touch my niece you little fucker!"

"Uncle Timmy, stop it! Kelly didn't make me do anything I didn't want to do and you coming down here acting like a maniac won't change any of this!"

"Shut up and get your ass home!" Angel didn't move. "Right now, damn it!"

Again, she refused to move. Instead, she turned and walked over to check that Kelly was alright.

"Are you OK Kelly?"

"Yeah, but I sure am tired of the men in your family choking the shit out of me."

Angel giggled, "Good, you still have a sense of humor. You're going to need it before this is all over."

"Oh so, you two think this shit is funny? I swear Angel, if you don't get your ass over here now… you're going to be very sorry!"

"OK, I'm coning." Before she could make her next move, Tim said, "Don't even think about kissing that boy!"

"Just go Angel before he kills us all up in here." Angel went and stood next to her uncle and refused to leave without him. She knew full well that Tim might try to attack Kelly again. He seemed to have no regard for the scene he was creating in front of Rachel.

"Please, let's go home Uncle. You're scaring Rachel."
Only then did Tim even notice the girl in the room. He apologized to the child before saying to Kelly, "I will be calling your mom first thing in the morning. You won't be walking away from this girl or this situation you've created." With that said, Tim grabbed Angel and dragged her home.

Karen continued to cry over Angel's predicament while Teek tried to comfort her.

"What's the matter with her?" Keisha asked when she came in and saw how distraught Karen was.

"She's upset about Angel."

"Why, what's wrong with her?"

"Li ansent."

"Kisa?! Ansent?! I knew it! Your dad is going to kill her!"

"Yup. Can you go get Auntie a glass of water please?"
Keisha was on her way into the kitchen when she heard Tim and Angel coming through the front door, Tim yelling the entire time.

"I can't believe you could be so foolish Angel!"

"You've made that clear Uncle. Can you just please stop yelling at me?"

"You're worried about me yelling at you? Do you have any idea of what you're facing?"

"Actually, I do. No disrespect Uncle, but to be honest, this is something I should be fighting about with my parents. I see how you feel, but I really need time to let this sink in myself without you screaming at me." Tim just looked at her with disbelief at how calm she was behaving. To Tim, Angel acted as if the doctor hadn't told her anything more serious than, she has a cold.

He had to admit that this niece was the one he'd had the hardest time trying to figure out in the last year and a half. Angel had this way about her that threw him. She was always respectful and well behaved, but she did exactly what she wanted to do, whenever she felt like it.

Also, when confronted about her actions, she would accept whatever punishment or lecture due her as if she weren't phased, and still she continued to live her life how she saw fit. She never concerned herself with other's opinions of her. What could they do, Tim always wondered. She got excellent grades, did her chores without complaint and was always in the house in time for curfew. Except for her odd independence, she hadn't really been any trouble until now.

"Wow Angel, you really messed up girl. You're in big trouble with this" Keisha stated. There was no need for her to say, "I told you so."

"Keisha and Tiki, you two go up to your room" Tim said.

Before leaving, Teek pulled her twin into an embrace. "I got your back no matter what you decide to do."

"Sit down Angel. I have to call your mom and dad" Tim directed.

Angel sat while Karen tried to pull herself together. She was still flopped in the chair sobbing like the world was coming to an end. Angel just looked at her and shook her head. "Auntie, fix your wig will you, it's a little crooked." She laughed to herself, *"What a drama queen!"*

Teek and Keisha rushed into their bedroom. "Damn Keisha, Tim is about to call our parents. They're going to lose it."

"I know that's right. What is that girl going to do with a baby? Whoa, I wonder if she told Kelly yet!"

"Keisha for real, would you bring it down please?"

"Oh, sorry Teek, but seriously, I wonder what Kelly is going to say."

"Well, she went running down there as soon as she got out of the car, and she didn't seem to be upset when she came in. Actually, she didn't seem upset when she found out either."

"Evidently she doesn't care about being pregnant at sixteen. She believes that Kelly is going to take care of her and that her life will be wonderful no matter what."

"That's impossible. My sister isn't an idiot. She knows this is bad."

"You can keep thinking that if you want to, but I'm telling you, Angel is not worried at all. I swear that girl acts like she has a plan."

"What do you mean a plan? What, like she tried to trap that boy or something? Kelly ain't got shit" Teek stated.

"No, she's not trying to trap him. She's not that kind of insecure girl but you know how Angel is. She decides what she wants or how she wants things to be and she just does whatever. She's always been that way."

"That's true but, think about it...even if we don't get it or don't agree with it, she always seems to know what she's doing" Teek added.

"Oh yeah, remember that time in the seventh grade when she saved her money so she could get her hair cut short? Aunt Leigh told her she couldn't do it and Angel said, *"Mommy, it's my hair and I'm going to get it cut, but thanks for your input."* And she went out and did it anyway" Keisha laughed.

"Yeah, yeah, she waited two days until mommy felt like she had let it go. Damn, I know mommy wanted to wring her neck."

"To tell the truth though, it was a sharp ass hair cut for a seventh grader" Keisha laughed. "Your mom grounded her for two weeks."

"Yup, and Angel didn't give a damn. She loved that haircut."

"Yeah but, what Angel's done this time is way more serious. If she chooses to go through with this pregnancy, she'll be a teen mother" Keisha stated, bringing them back to the present issue with stubborn Angel.

"First of all, there is no "if" about it. She's going to have that baby...shit, its Kelly's."

"You're right and, since that's the case, what are we going to do" Keisha asked.

"Help her. Support her and just be there for her. This shit isn't going to go over well with our parents. Hell, you see how those two downstairs are reacting to it. She's going to need us" Teek said.

"Alright, we've been through everything together, and we promised each other that none of us would ever be alone in anything we go through, so I guess we're going to be that baby's momma too. Anyway, I'm going to sneak downstairs and see if I can hear what's going on."

Keisha was at the top of the landing, straining to hear the conversation between her aunts and Uncles and Angel. She wished they would turn that damn speakerphone up.
Leigh was saying, "I don't think it's a good idea for you to have this baby Angel."

"I know that mommy but, I am."

"I'm so disappointed in you." Her father said. This broke Angel's heart to hear. She never wanted to disappoint her dad, but her stubborn mind was made up.

"I'm sure you are daddy, but I have to do what I think is right for me."

"How in the hell is having a baby at sixteen good for you?!"

"Actually, I'll be seventeen and will have one more year of school left when the baby is born."

"You say that dumb shit like it's easy to do."

"I know better than that, but Kelly will be finished school this year and he can work during the day, and I can go to school at night."

"Oh so, you think you've got it all figured out, don't you? Well guess what. It's not that simple. And since you mentioned him, where the hell is that boy now? What does he have to say about this" Gary asked.

"Well, I don't know what he thinks or has to say since Uncle Tim came and attacked him and then drug me away!" Angel said sarcastically.

"Oh my God, who are you?! This is not the daughter I raised" Leigh yelled.

"Oh mommy please, don't be so dramatic. I'm exactly who you raised. I just think that maybe you didn't really see me."

That statement took everyone by surprise. They all had to stop and think for a moment...who is Angel? She was relatively quiet and unassuming, well behaved and respectful. And because of this, the grown-ups didn't pay much attention. They hadn't figured out what made her tick and never delved too deeply into what she was thinking or feeling about anything. They assumed that all was well with her. Maybe it was.

Her parents knew she was stubborn and free thinking, but still they thought she *was* a thinker. With this new development, they weren't so sure anymore.

"Angel, you're being ridiculous about this. You don't have a clue what you're in for. We'll be there in a few days, and we will be resolving this situation then." Her father stated.

"But daddy..."

231

"But daddy nothing, there's nothing else to talk about right now." Gary disconnected the call.

Denise Coleman

CHAPTER 36

During the three days that Angel and the others waited for their parents' arrival, Angel was not allowed to see or speak to Kelly. Karen watched her like a hawk. Kelly was not allowed in the house, and he wasn't allowed to call. Tim had confiscated all three of the girls' cell phones before he left. Teek and Keisha were livid considering they had nothing to do with any of it. Angel was dying inside. Although she knew he wouldn't leave her hanging, she hadn't had a chance to see where Kelly's mind was.

True to his word, the day after finding out about Angel's condition, her uncle went over to talk to Kelly's mom. Sarah Taylor cried and screamed at him about the state of their financial life and how in the hell was he going to support a baby with no college education and a part time job?

Kelly had been up half the night asking himself those same questions. He didn't have a plan and not having an opportunity to speak with Angel didn't help. He spent the next three days in turmoil. He knew Angel well enough to know that she would want to keep the baby. Sometimes, he could read her better than her twin could.

He also knew that he would give that girl anything she wanted so, no matter what the future held, he was in it with her.

Karen was still so upset by this turn of events that she watched every other teen in the house as hard as she watched Angel. No one was allowed to see or speak to Kelly. She knew for sure that the others would be trying to find a way to get the couple together. She kept them all apart for two reasons. One, Karen wanted Angel to see just what it would feel like to be alone in her predicament if Kelly decided to turn tail and run out on her. Second, she wanted the discussion about how to proceed to be done with Angel, Kelly and their parents in attendance.

For the first time since Tim's departure from her life, Karen felt like a human being again. Angel's issue gave her some sense of parenting purpose again. Because of her lack of involvement, T.J. had all but given up on her as well.

Two days before Christmas, the girl's parents arrived in Camden. Although they were happy about the visit, the girls knew that this wasn't going to be a happy holiday. There would be plenty of crying and fighting going on.

After the greetings, hugs and tears were all dispensed of, Leigh and Gary asked the others to find something to do outside the house and had Tim call and request the presence of Sarah and Kelly to the house. His brothers and sisters-in-law didn't know that he no longer lived in the house, or why.

Teek and T.J were allowed to stay. They insisted.

"She's my twin, I'm not leaving" was Teek's argument.

"He's my best friend and even if I don't agree with it, I got his back" was T.J.'s.

Although the parents were pleased to know that these kids would support one another through thick and thin, just as they were raised to do, this particular problem was not what they'd had in mind.

Tim made the introductions, and everyone took a seat. Angel and Kelly couldn't keep their eyes off of one another. Angel had major attitude with her aunt for keeping them apart. Kelly simply wanted to protect her from the tirade that would surely come. However, Leigh had convinced her husband that going off on them would only make matters worse. The look in Angel's eyes proved her right. That girl was ready for war and Leigh was shocked to see that side of her daughter.

Gary addressed Kelly first. "So young man, tell me, what exactly are you prepared to do about this mess you two have created?"

Kelly looked at Angel before he spoke. "I intend to do whatever I have to do to take care of Angel and our baby." His mom gasped openly because this was the last thing she expected to hear. She felt for sure that the two would decide not to have the baby at all.

"How can you possibly consider having this child when neither of you have anything" Sarah posed.

"Ma, I know you don't agree with this, but I'm going to marry her, and I *will* take care of my family. I'll be finished school in a few months. My boss will make me full time, which he has offered if I choose not to go to college right away."

"Oh really, and what about my daughter's education." Gary asked indignantly.

"I was thinking that she could take classes in the evening while I take care of the baby."

"So, you think you've got it all figured out, don't you?"

"No sir I don't, but I do know that your daughter means everything to me, and there's no way I would ever let her go through anything in this life alone."

"Where will you live" Leigh asked.

"Well, I was thinking that Angel could move in with us. I can't leave my mom hanging, and with my additional hours and pay increase we'll continue to maintain, together."

"But son, you have no idea how expensive a baby can be." Sarah expressed to him.

"Yes Ma, I kind of do. I've been there every step of the way with you and Rachel. I've been a part of your struggle so, I get it. Look, it's not all on me anyway. Just like I'll be in it with her, Angel's in it with me."

"Us too." Teek and T.J spoke up for the first time.

"Oh really, and what the hell can your broke asses do" Gary asked.

"Come on daddy. We're getting older, and believe it or not, we're capable of more than you all think we are."

"Tiki's right daddy. I applied for a part time job two weeks ago and I got a call yesterday. I can start after the holidays. This way if you and mommy will continue to provide for our expenses like you've been doing, I can save every dime of that money just to get a head start with the things we'll need for the baby." Angel believed with all of herself that this could work... especially after she'd heard what Kelly had to say. They were of one mind in their thinking.

"Listen to me little girl. You two talk like you have it all worked out but get this. A major part of your plans are dependent on us. You expect your mother and I to continue to support you, and you Kelly, expect your mother to allow you to move a girl and a baby into her home. It sounds to me like you're still sticking us with the responsibility of your child."

Listening to her father talk, and make sense, she knew not to try and change her sister's mind, but Teek wondered just how much the rest of them could actually help. They had plans to of their own, and for Teek, it didn't involve living close to home.

Nevertheless, she saw the sadness and determination battling in her sister's eyes, and until the day she chose to leave, she would help in any way possible.

"Look, I can get a job too. I'll help out whenever they need me too" Teek announced.

"I will too. Rowan University is only twenty minutes away, and if there's anything y'all need that I can provide, I will" T.J. promised.

"I really appreciate that man." Kelly stood to shake his hand. "But I think we can handle it" he continued.

"Have you all lost your damn minds" Leigh yelled. "My daughter is not old enough to be someone's mother, and she certainly isn't going to give up her future for it! You are not having this baby and that's that!" Damn, everyone looked at Leigh. She hadn't said too much 'til then, and she certainly hadn't said it that loudly.

Angel had had enough of the entire conversation and seeing her mother's outburst was more than enough for her. She stood to speak.

"Listen everyone, I understand how upset you are, and for that, I'm sorry. I also understand that having a baby was not in your plans for me mommy, but this is my reality right now. I have to tell you all that, I will not by any means have an abortion. I am having this baby, and whether you want to help in this or not, is up to you. However, the bottom line is, we've decided what we're going to do, and we're good with whatever you decide to do, or not do for that matter."

The adults just stared at her. Beyond anything else, it clicked for all of them that no matter how much bitching, moaning or crying they did, this girl was going to have that baby and anything short of tying her up and dragging her to a clinic, they couldn't stop her.

"Me and Kelly are going to wait in the kitchen while y'all talk about us." The teens left their parents to discuss whether or not they would support their children in this foolishness.

"Gary, what are we going to do with that girl? She can't have a baby; her life will be over" Leigh expressed.

"I hate to tell you this honey but, realistically there isn't anything we can do."

"We can take her home. Maybe if she's away from that boy, she'll be able to see this clearly."

"I really don't think snatching her away will solve the problem. If anything, taking her away from Kelly will only make matters worse."

"Both their minds are made up" Sarah added.

"This is true, so what do we do about it? Do we help them, or do we let them try it on their own?" Gary questioned.

Tim took this moment to speak up. "I know this is a horrible situation and I feel responsible for it. And, as angry as I am with both of them, I'm willing to help them as much as possible."

"This is not your fault. In case you hadn't noticed, my daughter is extremely stubborn and determined." Gary said to his brother.

"Yes, she is." Tim chuckled a little. It's a shame she didn't choose to put those qualities to use in building her future."

"Well, she didn't, so how do we plan to help them out? I don't want either of those kids to think that we're the slightest bit OK with this" Leigh stated.

Karen, who had remained quiet throughout the discussion, pulled herself together enough to participate.

"Just like Tim, I feel responsible for this. We thought we were keeping a good eye on the two of them. I really couldn't see that they had gone so far. Nor did I know that I needed to be discussing sex and protection with her." Karen wanted to say so much more, especially about Tim not being there, but she was too embarrassed to tell it.

"Let me stop you right there. Discussing those things was my job as her mother and I dropped the ball on that. Please, stop blaming yourself."

"Really, there's enough blame to go around if we want to take it there. Anyway, Sarah, you haven't said much. How do you feel about all of this?" Gary implored.

"Honestly, I'm very disappointed in those two but, I know my son and, he will move heaven and earth to take care of your daughter and their child. That's who my son is. And, since it looks like we're going to be grandparents regardless of our feelings, Angel and the baby can move in with us."

No one said anything for a long time after that. They each sat with their own thoughts until they could bring themselves around to accepting what would be. Tim spoke first.

"Sarah, I know how hard you work and having another person in the house might make things more difficult. Angel and the baby can stay here."

"You already have three girls in one room, where would you possibly put a baby? No, Angel can come to my house once the baby is born. Besides, you're practically a father to my children. It's the least I can do."

"As much as I hate the thought of my daughter playing house, Sarah's right. And as much as this breaks my heart to say, they should be in the same space so they can both see, together, how hard it's going to be. I'm her mother, but Angel made this choice, and she needs to deal with the consequences of that choice."

"I agree with my wife. Just don't let her get off lightly though. Sure, we'll send money but, as far as taking care of the baby, that's all on the two of them. They'll learn soon enough how hard it is to raise a child" Gary declared.

With that said, Angel and Kelly were called back in, and they were told of the minimal support they would get, but that the major care taking, and support would fall squarely on their shoulders.

Kelly was relieved to hear that his mother would allow him to have his new family with him. Aside from his fears of being a father, he believed that he and Angel could handle anything, together. Maybe.

Denise Coleman

CHAPTER 37

Keisha was enjoying the visit with her parents a great deal more than the twins were with theirs'. Angel felt bad that she had disappointed her parents. Teek was aggravated that because they were so upset with Angel that they couldn't have a good time with her either. She understood their feelings but, she didn't care. Teek needed some parental support.

She had been debating whether or not she should share the truth about her sexuality with them. Unfortunately, she didn't get the chance to make that decision one way or the other.

The family had just finished dinner when Keisha asked if she could be excused from doing the dishes because she wanted to go see the new guy, she had met a few weeks earlier. If she had known she could have had such an active dating life, she would have tried harder to get over Dre` a long time ago.

Considering Angel's situation, Mercer and Hillie became alarmed at Keisha's mention of a boy.

"Who is this boy?"

"He's about to be my new boyfriend daddy."

"Boyfriend? You're only sixteen. What do you need with a boyfriend?"

"Awe come on daddy, I'm not a baby. I'm a junior and almost seventeen now. Anyway, why shouldn't I have a boyfriend?"

"Have you taken a look at Angel? That's why." Her mother stated.

"But mom, I am not Angel and I'm not thinking of going there any time soon with this guy."

"Oh but, you are thinking about it at some point, huh" Mercer questioned.

"Dag dad, that's not what I said." Keisha quickly became frustrated by her parents' tag team tactics.

"You better not even so much as kiss that boy!" Hillie said a little too forcefully. Keisha could not believe her ears. She hadn't even considered having sex with this guy yet.

"Oh my God! I can't believe y'all are trippin' on me because Angel went stupid! I'm not her" Keisha yelled.

"We know you're not her, but you girls have not been making wise decisions in the last couple of years" Hillie said.

Keisha became outraged and began yelling at the top of her lungs.

"Are you kidding mom?! What I have I really done wrong in my life, other than defend myself against Jackie?! You and dad are sitting here expecting the worse out of me for no food reason...comparing me to everybody else! So, what if Angel got pregnant? That's her, not me. And so what if Teek is a lesbian? That's her, not me! And by the way, Troi is the one you should be worried about. She's been screwing Uncle Tim! He doesn't even live here anymore!"

"Teek's a what?!" Gary yelled. Keisha's hands flew up to her mouth and she turned to Teek the very second she realized what she had just done. Her tears instantly welled up in her eyes.

"Oh Tiki, I'm so sorry. I didn't mean to say that" she cried.

Teek and everyone else in the dining room were stunned by Keisha's outburst. Leigh and her sister were not surprised. After all, she'd suspected this about her daughter for quite some time and had discussed her thoughts with Hillie. Then another thought hit them all at once. "Troi did what?!" Leigh and Hillie both yelled.

"Teek, is this true?" Gary asked with a *"You'd better say no"* expression on his face. He barely registered what Keisha had said about Troi. His only concern was what she'd said about *his* daughter.

Teek was so shocked that she didn't know what to say. It wasn't that she was ashamed or even afraid. It was that her father was her hero and the look on his face, led her to believe that he would not accept her truth.

Teek hesitated, however before she could respond, Angel spoke up.

"What difference does it make daddy? Would you love her any less if she just so happens to be attracted to females?" Angel posed her question in that manner because just like Teek, she sensed his disapproval. By questioning their father's love, she knew that this may make him think twice about how he handled the news. Angel was aware that Gary could be old school in his thinking about certain things however, she was also wise enough to know that in that very moment, he held the fate of Teek's well-being in his hands. Not having her father's support and understanding would devastate her.

Whether Gary understood Angel's meaning or not…he blew it big time.

"What the hell has gotten into the two of you? First this one foolishly gets herself pregnant and thinks she knows how to be an adult. Then you sit there telling me that you're a lesbian! Have you twins lost your fucking minds?!" Gary yelled so loudly; the walls seemed to shake. Leigh grabbed him by the arms and shook a little.

"Gary please, you have to calm down. This is not the way to handle this."

"Are you serious?! We sent these girls down here to continue their education, not to be fuckin' around like some bitches in heat!"

Leigh and the entire room gasped. The twins both looked at their dad as if he'd lost his mind. Neither could believe the words they'd just heard. Was this how their father viewed them…as bitches? Teek began sobbing and Angel exploded.

"How dare you call us bitches! I get that we haven't lived up to whatever standards you have for us, which by the way, we don't even know what those standards are, but we are not bitches in heat or anything like that. We're your daughters and you're supposed to love us unconditionally!"

"I will never accept a daughter of mine being a pussy loving dyke!" Gary yelled this statement so loudly that the dining room table reverberated with the force and harshness of his declaration. Teek could not believe her ears. She certainly hadn't expected that her parents would be OK with her sexuality, but for her father to be so completely nasty towards her, was something she couldn't comprehend.

Angel stepped up in defense of her sister once again. "Daddy! I can't believe you could say such a thing! Just because she's attracted to females doesn't give you a reason to treat her like crap!"

Gary grabbed his head with both hands, as if squeezing it would somehow release all of the disappointing thoughts that were racing through his mind. What had he done so wrong as a parent that his daughters would turn out this way?

"Please Gary, you have to calm down" Leigh stated. She understood full well that if her husband went much further with the bashing of his daughters, he could conceivably lose them forever. A divide of that nature was unacceptable to Leigh, and she knew that she needed to do something to fix the situation quickly.

She grabbed her husband, who was still holding his head, by the elbows and guided him to the sofa. "Gary" she whispered. "You absolutely have to bring it down. No matter how you feel about what's going on with the twins, they're your daughters and they deserve your patience and understanding. If you keep this up, you could lose them" she expressed.

"I don't care" he screamed. "What am I supposed to do, sit here and pretend like everything's just fine? That I'm OK with one daughter being a little whore and the other running around with girls?! Are you serious Leigh?!"

"Gary, please!"

"Please my ass!" Gary got up from his seat. "What I do know is that you both are a huge disappointment! I did not raise either of you to be this fucked up!"

Angel had heard enough, "Are you *serious*?! I'm not a whore and Teek isn't running around chasing girls. She's still a virgin if you want to know the truth. And I've never been with anyone but Kelly. How could you turn on us just because I got pregnant and Teek is attracted to girls?! You're the one who's fucked up!" The house collectively gasped again. By this time, Angel and Teek were both in tears, silently praying that their father would somehow change his tune. That he would take back his ugly words and hold them in his arms with promises of continuing to love them as he always had.

While the two stood there pleading with their eyes, Gary's eyes spit fire. Whatever apologies the twins were hoping for would not be forthcoming. Gary's next statement made that absolutely clear. He pointed at Angel and said, "How dare you talk to me that way! Since your ass is so grown and you know so much; you can take care of that bastard baby without any help from me or your mom!" To Teek he turned and said, "You just need a good guy in your life. Some dick will make you forget all about this lesbian bullshit."

Forget the collective gasp… the entire room was stunned into silence by Gary's remarks. You could've heard a pin drop. No one recognized this, Gary. Within moments he had gone from trying to be supportive and accepting with Angel, to practically disowning them both.

Teek stood in shock, shaking uncontrollably with tears streaming down her face. She was a daddy's girl and his rejection nearly destroyed her. Angel, however, was pissed. When it came to their parents, she was always the more forceful and stronger of the two.

"What a mean and hurtful thing to say to your own daughter! Well, guess what, we don't need you! We can take care of ourselves!"

Teek took strength in Angel's defense of them both and spoke up for herself.

"No matter what you think of either of us daddy, we haven't done anything wrong. Angel made a mistake and she's willing to do her best with it. Yes, I'm gay and no, I didn't choose this for myself but, it is what it is, and regardless of what you think of us, we're good girls. We always have been and that hasn't changed.

Daddy, I would love it if you could accept us as we are, but if you can't, that's too bad for you. You're the one who'll be missing out."

With that said, Teek took Angel by her hand, they grabbed their coats and left.

"Where are we going?" Angel asked as soon as they'd stepped off the porch.

"I don't know. I just couldn't stay in there another minute with daddy acting like that."

"I know. Can you believe he called us bitches like he was talking about any random chicks on the street? That was beyond over the top mean" Angel acknowledged.

"Yeah, it was. I swear twin, I just want to punch Keisha in her big ass mouth." Teek said, wiping her tears.

"She didn't mean to put you on blast like that."

"I don't give a damn what she meant. She needs to learn how to think before she runs her mouth! Now let's go."

"Wait, where are we going? It's cold out here, and you ain't dragging me all over town 'cause you're trying to get away from daddy."

"Angel, do me a favor right quick."

"What's that?"

"Shut the fuck up. You're starting to get on my nerves."

Angel was stuck for a split second before she busted out laughing. She laughed so hard, Teek had to join her.

"That was a good one, wasn't it? I bet to didn't see that coming."

"No, I didn't. You got me. Now where the hell are we going?"

"To your baby daddy's house."

"No Tiki, that's the first place they'll come looking for us."

"Does it really matter if they come looking for us?"

"It does if we don't want to be found."

"I don't care about being found; I just need to get away from here right now. I swear Angel… I'm never speaking to that man again! I can't believe he treated us like that. We deserve better." Teek began sobbing all over again. It would be a long time before she got beyond the pain Gary had caused.

The twins made their way down to the Taylor house and spent the rest of the evening there. Fortunately, no one came looking for them and the twins refused to come back until their parents had gone.

Denise Coleman

CHAPTER 38

"Gary, I can't believe you treated our daughter like that." Leigh said displaying her disappointment clearly.

"Uh excuse me! Did you three miss the part where Tim is sleeping with Troi!" Hillie yelled as loudly as she could.

"*Was* sleeping with Troi. At least that's what he says," Keisha stated dryly.

"Was, is, what difference does it make? Have you lost your fucking mind?" Mercer stated. "Is this shit true?"

"Yes it is." Karen spoke up for the first time since Keisha's initial outburst.
Tim's brothers and their wives openly stared at him like he had two heads.
Karen was so embarrassed that she couldn't look at any of them. However, she wanted to hear what Tim would say just as much as anyone because, over the last few months, she'd never gotten an answer to the question "why". Just like her son, she didn't want to be bothered.

Every time Tim showed his face, his family became more annoyed by his presence. They definitely weren't trying to hear anything he had to say.

"I guess you're all waiting for me to say something" Tim said. Everyone nodded.

"Of course, we are asshole. My niece, really" Hillie asked.

"Well, first of all, she was eighteen by the time we went that far." Tim said indignantly, like what he'd done wasn't completely out of pocket.

"Wait, hold up. Exactly how long was this going on, and what the hell was going on before you fucked her?!" Karen interjected at that spot.

"Yo man, you say that shit like what you did was OK" Mercer stated.

Everyone else chimed in at that point. They were coming down on Tim at once, prohibiting him from getting a word in.

"Hey!" He yelled to shut them up.

"Can I finish?"

"Sure, explain this dumb shit." Leigh said with her hands on her hips in a sista girl stance, ready to pounce on him.

Tim took a beat before he spoke again. Now was the time to come one hundred percent clean, but he knew that his truth would be harsh on Karen. Nevertheless, he forged ahead.

"OK. I have to start at the beginning for this to make any sense at all. So, just bear with me."

"Stop beating around the bush muthafucka" Leigh stated.

"Leigh, please give him a chance" Gary said. Leigh shot daggers at her husband. After the way he'd treated their daughters, she didn't give a damn about what he wanted.

"You mean like you did Teek and Angel?" Gary rolled his eyes at her but didn't respond. Tim continued after the minor interruptions. "Well, I guess I should start by saying I got married for the wrong reasons."

Karen winced audibly.

"Don't get me wrong...I loved Karen very early and easily back then, but I wasn't ready to be anybody's husband when she got pregnant with T.J. Nevertheless, I decided to do what I thought was the right thing.

Anyway, after a few years, I started to see things in you that I didn't like." Tim said in the direction of Karen. She just stared at him with hatred in her eyes.

"By the time our son was born, it had become obvious that I was alone in this situation. There was nothing I could go to her about." He continued as he directed his attention to the rest of the family. "I had to not only make the money...I had to actually write the checks and pay the bills myself. I didn't need or want to have complete control over everything, but she wouldn't do anything more than dote on the baby.

I thought that once he got older, this would change. It didn't. Anyway, as the years went by, she seemed to become weaker, emotionally. It felt like having *two* children in the house. I couldn't get any kind of support from my freakin' wife!"

All of Tim's resentment came rushing out of him the more he spoke.

"Every time I tried to have a conversation about any of our grown-up problems or issues like finances, the house, T.J.'s grades or behavior, or even our own lack of closeness, she would start crying and saying it was all too much for her. Shit, I couldn't even get pussy most of the time! What the hell was I supposed to do with that? Oh, and by the way…even through all of that, I never cheated before."

"That's all well and good but get to the part where you felt it was OK to fuck my eighteen- year-old niece" Leigh stated.

Tim rolled his eyes and continued. "OK so, by the time the girls arrived, we were absolutely on the last minutes of this marriage, but I decided that I had to stay for them. I gave my word. However, from the very beginning, Troi hated being here much more than the others, and she took it all out on Karen. The first week she was here, she cut up some of Karen's clothes. I think at some point, she was stealing from her and the worse thing…she started coming on to me. Now, at first, I thought I was mistaking some of her actions, but there came a time when she put her intentions out there.

It's not like I thought it was alright to respond to her, but she wore me down. Most of the time all I could think about was the fact that my own damn wife hadn't let me touch her in a fuckin' year!" There goes that resentment again.

"In Troi's presence, I became weaker and weaker and no matter how much I tried to reject her, I couldn't. Maybe I didn't want to, I don't know.

Something about her reminded of a time when love and desire for a woman was new and good and exciting. I want to say that that's what I was responding to."

"That's the biggest pile of shit I've ever heard" Leigh said.

"Who gives a damn about how messed up your marriage was, you laid down with my teenaged niece!" Hillie chimed in.

"Exactly! I'm calling Tess about this shit" Leigh stated.

"Now wait a minute, Leigh. How will calling Tess help? It's not as if Troi didn't learn this behavior from her in the first place." Mercer stated matter-of-factly.

"What the fuck? I know you better watch your step." Hillie said to her husband.

"Oh, I see where this is going. You two are going to sit here and condone your brother's sick behavior. Well, guess what, that shit ain't going down today. I'm calling my sister and if she says call the fucking cops and press charges, that's exactly what we'll do." Leigh informed the whole house.

"Really wife?"

"Hell yes, husband!"

"Alright now, everybody calm down" Karen spoke. "As much as I hate Tim for what he did, and as wrong as it was…Troi wasn't an innocent victim in this. You have to remember; she was living here for more than a year and the things I saw in her weren't those of a sheltered young girl. No offense ladies, but your niece is a piece of work."

Leigh and Hillie were clearly offended by Karen's words, but before either could respond, Keisha spoke up.

"She's right aunties. Troi has been nothing but trouble for the longest time. Uncle Tim didn't start that situation with Troi…she did. I overheard her one night and believe me, she was the aggressor." The adults in the room had all but forgotten that Keisha hadn't left the house. She had been sitting quietly in the dining room, listening to everything.

"The truth is… Troi is a self-serving, self-absorbed narcissist who only cares about what she wants. She even stabbed me in the back, and I always looked at her as a big sister." Keisha stated sadly.

"What did she do to you?" Hillie wanted to know.

"Well, I had a crush on Kelly's brother Dre`. Actually, I thought I was in love with him. Anyway, Troi knew this, yet she slept with him anyway. Not only that, but she also felt no remorse for doing it, no matter how I felt. And she didn't stop when I found out about it either. She's nobody's victim."
Hillie tried to hug her daughter, but Keisha didn't need it. She shrugged away and left the house.

The adults didn't know what to do or say. They simply sat quietly trying to digest all that had been uncovered in less than an hour.

"What the hell had happened to the sweet young girls they had sent to Camden?" *"How could they all have changed so much? Who were these messed up people they'd sent them to?"* These were their collective thoughts. They didn't need to voice them. It would not have mattered anyway…They certainly didn't have any answers regardless.

Denise Coleman

CHAPTER 39

The twins were getting a little antsy sitting at Kelly's house. Angel was not in the mood to be answering any questions from his mom that night, and neither her or Teek wanted to talk about their father's ugliness towards them. Teek whispered to her twin, "Let's get out of here. I can't sit still anymore."

"Where are we going this time? I'm not going back to that house right now."

"I know. Let's just go see if Troi's home" Teek suggested.

"Do you think she'll let us in? She hardly talks to us anymore."

"Of course, she will. She's just embarrassed about her ratchet ass shit, but who cares. We need to be out...let's go."

Angel told Kelly they needed to go out and would be back. He didn't like the idea of them walking the streets at night, but he also knew that he couldn't stop them either.

"OK, don't be out there too long." He said and kissed Angel's cheek.

"I won't."

She and Teek walked the four blocks to Troi's room as quickly as they could.

"I can't believe I let you get me back out in this cold" Angel laughed.

"Stop complaining, we'll be there in a few." They took a few mores steps and Angel stopped in her tracks.

"What's wrong" Teek asked.

"I don't know. I just got this weird feeling in my stomach."

"Is it the baby?"

"I don't think so. It's really hard to describe. It feels something like butterflies but, not."

"What?"

"I don't know, let's just go."

Within moments, they were standing on Troi's step.

"There's no bell, just knock" Teek said.

Angel knocked several times but didn't get an answer.

"I wonder where she could be" Angel stated.

"Maybe she's in the shower or something. Just knock harder. I can hear the television."

Angel knocked harder but still no response so, she tried the doorknob. It wasn't locked.

"Oh, it's open." She and Teek walked in hoping that Troi wouldn't give them a hard time about showing up un-announced.

"Oh my God" Angel screamed. Troi was lying in the middle of the floor.

"Oh shit! What done happened now?" Teek wondered aloud.

They rushed to Troi's aid and bent down to help her up.

"Troi!" Angel said as she shook her cousin, thinking that she may have fainted.

Troi didn't respond. When Teek tried to lift her head, she felt a sticky substance on her hand. That's when she saw the blood. "Oh, dear God" she whispered.

Angel noticed the blood on Teek's hand immediately. She began to cry, "Teek, check her pulse. Is she dead?"

Teek couldn't reply.

Prologue

Angel stood in the middle of her living room with tears streaming down her face and a gun in her hand. Only once before had she used that gun against another person. A year earlier, Angel had to put two bullets in the head of a man who had broken into her house and threatened to cut her unborn child from her body.

On this particular day however, her assailant was someone much closer to her personally. The enemy Angel had her piece trained on was her husband, Kelly. She stood there shaking her head in disbelief at the dramatic and devastating turn her life had taken in less than twenty- four hours. Just the day before, Angel was on top of the world. She had worked through her issues with her marriage and was ready for a fresh start. There was nothing – or so she thought – that could bring her down.

"Kelly, how could you do this to me, to our family?" She asked in shock. "In one night, you've destroyed everything" she said.

Her husband, not sure of what to do or to say, tried in vain to ease the sadness he had brought to his wife.

"Angel baby, please listen to me. I didn't mean for this to happen. Don't you understand that I would never intentionally hurt you?" He asked with his hands outstretched, as if begging for forgiveness...which of course he was. Angel on the other hand, wasn't hearing anything. She continued to stand there with the gun pointed at Kelly, waiting for him to say something that would make the pain go away. She waited for anything that would wake her from what had become a nightmare.

While Angel stood murmuring, "How could you do this?" ...Kelly took a step toward her.

"Don't!" She screamed at his sudden movement. "If you so much as think about touching me, so help me God, I'll put a bullet in your fucking head." Angel stated this with a coldness that he had never seen coming from his wife before. But, like a dumbass, knowing that Angel had done just that once before, he reached for her anyway. Her sister Teek screamed, "Angel, don't!" And without hesitation, Angel pulled the trigger.

Coming Soon
Shattered Innocence 2

Also, don't miss the conclusion of the
Shattered Trilogy

Shattered Innocence 3: Keisha's Betrayal

******

Discussion Questions

1. Do you think the girls' parents did all they could to keep them at home?
2. Should their parents have done more to remain a constant in the girls' upbringing?
3. If their parents had remained involved ... would the girls have changed as drastically as they did?
4. Did Angel really over Kelly or, can we consider that he remained a distraction that kept her true pain at bay?
5. Considering the bond that the two shared, why was Keisha the one cousin that Troi chose to betray?
6. How could someone like Dre` elicit such strong actions from Troi?
7. Once he was approached by Troi, did Tim do enough to dissuade her behavior? Or, did he really not want to?
8. Given Troi's upbringing and her desire to be like the others, why did she continually lose that battle?
9. Give your own in-depth interpretation of how and why being sent away from hoe changed the girls so dramatically.

Made in the USA
Middletown, DE
01 March 2023

25949202R00154